REVENGE OF JOE WILD

AN AMERICAN TALE OF MURDER, ESCAPE, AND ADVENTURE

BY ANDREW KOMARNYCKYJ

SANTA
MONICA
PRESS
TEEN

Published by: Santa Monica Press LLC
P.O. Box 850
Solana Beach, CA 92075
1-800-784-9553
www.santamonicapress.com
books@santamonicapress.com

Printed in the United States

Santa Monica Press books are available at special quantity discounts when purchased in bulk by corporations, organizations, or groups. Please call our Special Sales department at 1-800-784-9553.

ISBN-13 978-1-59580-111-1

Publisher's Cataloging-in-Publication data

Names: Komarnyckyj, Andrew, author.
Title: The revenge of Joe Wild : an American tale of murder , escape , and adventure / by Andrew Komarnyckyj.
Description: Includes footnotes. | Solana Beach, CA: Santa Monica Press, 2022.
Identifiers: ISBN: 978-1-59580-111-1 (paperback) | 978-1-59580-778-6 (ebook)
Subjects: LCSH Runaways--Fiction. | Runaway children--Fiction. | Illinois--History--19th century--Fiction. | United States--History--Civil War, 1861-1865--Fiction. | Murder--Fiction. | BISAC YOUNG ADULT FICTION / Historical / United States / 19th Century | YOUNG ADULT FICTION / Historical / United States / Civil War Period (1850-1877) | YOUNG ADULT FICTION / War & Military | YOUNG ADULT FICTION / Social Themes / Runaways
Classification: LCC PZ7.1.K67569 Rev 2022 | DDC 813.6--dc23

Cover and interior design and production by Future Studio

For Sadie and Mica

CONTENTS

1.

CALL ME JOE

THE SCHOOLHOUSE WAS THE WORST HOUSE IN the world 'cept our house. It had a bell on the roof that went right through you like a stone through a window when it rang. If you warn't inside when that bell rang woe betide you, you was in for a leatherin'. I knows better'n most about leatherin'. Miss Larsen reckoned the only way to make me learn was by using the cane on me. She tanned my hide every excuse she got. I'm not saying I didn't deserve it sometimes, but hand on heart, I got more'n my fair share of that cane. Hand on heart, it didn't make me no cleverer. It sure made me sneakier though.

You would have thought I would've whooped for joy every day when school finished, but I never did because I got no cause to. My ma was worse'n the schoolmarm. She tanned me with Pa's old belt whenever she got it into her head I was being ornery, which was more often than not.

Home was a two-room log cabin Pa built before he got useless. It had one room Ma and Pa slept in and another they called their front room. The front room had a couple of windows that was just square holes in the wall. When Pa thought to keep the wind out he nailed sheets over them and when the wind was bad he nailed wool blankets over them. I got used to knowing what time of year it was by those windows.

In summer we kept them as holes. In spring and autumn we had sheets over them. In winter Pa covered them with blankets.

I take nothing away from Pa. If there was a short cut to doing a job he'd find it. Mainly it was by not doing the job at all. Oftentimes it was by getting me to do it. If he really had to stir hisself he'd do a half-job, like the one with the sheets and blankets.

Finally we come to my room, the one I slept in and spent my time in, such time as I had to myself. My room was a wooden shed out back. It could have done with a lick of paint and some attention in the nailing department but it warn't bad as sheds go. It kept out the rain and snow although the wind always found a way of getting through. When it did the clapboards on the roof made a noise like a pit fulla rattlesnakes. That rattling kept me awake at night during the storms we got in our neck of the woods.

Guess it's time I introduced myself. I'm Joseph Wild, but you can call me Joe. Most folks do 'cept the ones who have names for me I can't repeat here.

My best year as a boy was 1861. It was also the worst. Five things made it special, and one thing made it bad. I'm not counting the beatings as bad, because they was a regular part of my life. The bad thing was something else, a tragedy among all the happiness. But I'm getting ahead of myself.

2.

CATHERINE BATS HER EYES

FIRST THING MADE 1861 SPECIAL WAS CATHERINE Purdy. To this day I don't know what I saw in her or she in me. Especially she in me. I was small for a twelve-year-old and skinnier than most, and God knows we was all skinny in our town. Plus, I was dirtier than most. The dirt alone woulda been enough to put most girls off. Not that I didn't wash, I did. But being a country boy I spent most of my time outdoors and a lotta time rolling in dirt creeping after animals and such. Ain't no way you can keep clean for long doing that sort of thing. But I always turned up at school clean. Miss Larsen saw to that. She caned me once for showing up dirty. I knowed not to let that happen twice. Miss Larsen found other excuses for caning me of course but at least she didn't get me on hygiene again.

In 1861 the world was a magical place when I warn't hungry or getting beaten. Life was good for a young feller in those parts. Full of nature, and I loved nature. The smell of flowers in spring, shadows on the forest floor in summer, the brown leaves of fall, the swollen river in winter. I felt the magic of life more powerfully in 1861 than ever before, and I ain't felt it so keenly since.

My body went out of kilter, that's why. Scary things got scarier, bright things brighter, attractive things more attractive, and girls didn't look the same.

They'd always been boys in dresses till then, but less interesting. Suddenly they became something else, and no matter how much figuring I did I couldn't work out what it was they'd become. It was like they had mysteries inside them I didn't know about, secrets makin' me dizzy with not knowin'.

I got right clumsy that year. Up until the age of twelve I could damn near do near anything I wanted. Climb trees, hop across a slippery log bridge on one leg, walk on my hands. Then it was like my body belonged to someone else, and I could barely cross the main street without I fell and hurt myself.

That main street in our town was a murderous dirt track, mind. When the weather was dry it baked hard, and everyone could cross it safely. Even the town drunk could cross it safely when he was brim full of liquor. But when it rained, crossing it was like walking on a river of eels. No wonder I fell over so. Wouldn't have done in my younger days. Age ten I could slide down the mud bank at the edge of the crick and dive in without once losing my footing. Hell, I could skip over a mudflat if I had to. Age twelve I spent as much time on my back and belly getting to the crick as I did on my feet. Catching rabbits got harder, too. Rocks didn't seem to go where I threw them. Threw them a lot harder, mind. I was killing more rabbits outright when I hit them aged twelve than ever before. Just not hitting as many as before.

My eyes must have changed. That's why I was missing so many rabbits, it's why the world got more colorful, and its why Catherine Purdy and the other girls looked different. I never took much notice of them before I was twelve, 'cept when we played hide and seek and such. They didn't register with me the

way the boys did. All of a sudden they was register-
in' more than the boys ever did. Other boys felt it,
too, some of them, at least. I knowed that because
sometimes I'd see one of them looking at a girl the
same way I was looking at her, then me and the boy
would exchange glances and we'd both grin. Made
a mistake once and did that with Sam O'Hara during
one of Miss Larsen's classes, Bible, I think. No need
to tell you what Miss Larsen did next. That was one
mistake me and Sam O'Hara never made again.

The girls in my town warn't all pretty but nearly all of them got something I wanted, I didn't know
what, and I had not the first clue what to do about it.
I spent much of the day most days wondering about
girls in general and Catherine Purdy in particular. The
schoolhouse didn't help. It had but one room with windows so high up a body couldn't see out of them even
when standing on tiptoe. What was the point of that?
All you could look at all day was Miss Larsen or your
books or the other children. You warn't gonna look
at Miss Larsen longer than you had to because she
was dried up like a prune, and she never once smiled.
Sorry, Miss Larsen, but you told me there warn't no
point writing this book unless'n I told the truth. You
warn't gonna look at your books longer than you had
to because they had nothing interesting in them, so
whenever Miss Larsen's head was turned the other
way you had no choice but to look at the other kids.
And at a certain age that meant mainly the girls if you
was a boy and mainly the boys if you was a girl. You
did it sneakily, mind. Didn't just stare. Sorta pretended to be busy doing your schoolwork then raised your
head a little and looked sideways on at them, rolling
your eyeballs this way or that.

My eyeballs always drifted to Catherine Purdy like she was magnetic no matter how hard I tried to stop them. Catherine had that look which told you she knowed things you didn't, and although Miss Larsen thought the proverbial butter wouldn't melt in Catherine's mouth, I knowed butter would melt quicker there than if it was lobbed into a red-hot frying pan on top of a blazing fire. Her lips told me so, not by saying anything as such. The curl at the corners of her mouth spoke to me. Made her look like she was always thinking about something funny and naughty at the same time. And she knowed how to bat her eyelashes. She did it to poke fun at the simpering women who had the glad eye for her brother Max. It was right funny, but it made me want to be with her, too.

About the time I got to know Ervan Foster I caught Cath looking at me in class. She looked away, but not before she'd stared into my eyes. It was one of those deep stares that tells you something, don't ask me what. I didn't know then, and I still don't know now. It's a hunger you get in your soul is the best way I can describe it. Well, I was hungering for Catherine all right, and that look we shared made me think she might be hungering for me but I dared not believe she was. I'd had no truck with girls up to that point. Not much, anyways. And all of a sudden girls got overwhelming, especially Catherine Purdy.

Catherine came from a good family, so-called. I didn't. It was widely known that my family warn't a good one. By the age of twelve even I'd figured that much out. Pa was trash and Ma warn't much better. I had my doubts about Cath (I'll call her Cath from now on because that's what I always called her) because she seemed too good for me. We Wilds warn't good enough for anyone. Townsfolk looked down on us, I knowed that right enough. Pa was the main reason, though Ma did her bit, and so did I without meaning to. Being dressed in rags gave a bad impression, and the way we Wilds spoke warn't all polite the way the better townsfolk did. Don't get me wrong, we had manners. But not in the well-spoken way, if you know what I mean.

When school finished each day I got to always watching longingly as Cath disappeared with her Ma to her home, which was one of the clapboard houses clustered around the edges of our small town. The cabin me and Ma and Pa lived in was on its own like the farms and homesteads scattered about the countryside. But it was different from those. It was surrounded by trees not by fields, and we didn't grow much. Pa always said the land was his larder, and he didn't need to do anything to it 'cept find where his dinner was every day. Sometimes I wished he was better at finding dinner. We all went hungry enough in our house to wish that much. The point is we Wilds was different from the other folks, and that was gonna make it hard for me to get to know Cath.

One morning when Miss Larsen's back was turned Martha Nash reached across the gap between her stool and mine and wriggled her hand with her fingers closed around something. Realizing she wanted me to have that mysterious something, I reached out my own hand, and she pressed it into my palm. It was a scrap of paper that felt damp from being in her hand. At that moment Miss Larsen wheeled round, and I pretended I was reading my bible like I was meant to. Even though I had my head down I could tell Miss Larsen was glaring at me. That glare of hers made my neck prickle but I kept my head lowered, and eventually she found someone else to glare at.

What was on the scrap of paper? Frankly, I didn't have the balls to find out with Miss Larsen around, so I kept it scrunched up in my fist while turning the pages of my bible. We was reading Leviticus that day. It was all about Moses. I couldn't see the point of it myself. Moses was long since dead and there was no bringing him back. I ain't never had any truck with dead people, 'cept my brother and one or two others I've known personally who've died.

After school I forgot about Leviticus and I forgot about the note, too, because as usual I wanted to watch Cath disappearing down the street with her Ma. As she did she turned her head and gave me that sly smile of hers over her shoulder. It sent a shiver right through me. When I got over her smile, which took about ten minutes, I looked at the note. Near as I can remember it said:

Joe
Meet me by the stables at 3 this afternoon.
Cath x

Those words made my heart flutter—especially the kiss at the end. Cath's ma and pa owned the town's stables, and I was to meet her there. What did she want? It didn't matter. All that mattered was it was me she wanted to meet. But there was a problem gnawing at me as I made my way home. I had chores to do. I'd have to do them right quick to be back to town in time to see Cath by the stables, or not do them and pay the price. Another problem was, I had no way of telling what time it was. I measured time by sunrise and sunset and when I was hungry and when I was tired and that was it. I knowed how to tell the time because Miss Larsen had taught me, but I was damned if I knowed where to find a clock. I'd just have to get to the stables good and early and hang around until Cath got there.

When I got home Pa warn't anywhere to be seen. I expect he was getting drunk or working to get the money to get drunk with. It's the only reason he worked. Ma filled my belly with cornbread then she sent me out to catch fish, which suited me. It meant that right away I could hightail it to the stables to see Cath, then I could go home and tell Ma the fish warn't biting. Soon as my belly was full of cornbread I left the house in the direction of the river then took a turn the other way to get on the trail back to town.

Finally I reached the stables. I must've got there just in time because Cath was waiting for me in front of them with a big grin on her face. It made me feel odd. Scared in a way but the muscles on my cheeks got tight, and I knowed I was grinning, too. The way my cheeks felt it must have been the biggest grin in history.

Just as I got close to Cath her pa came out of the stables. Neither of them told me who he was, but right away I knowed, and I got properly affrighted 'specially when he looked me up and down like he was sizing me up for something. Made me wonder if he was fixing on cowhiding me for bothering his daughter, or just for being a no-good Wild. He was the hardest man in town, a big man who looked like he could strap a body hard with a length of cowhide if he took it into his head to, and the frown on his face didn't bode well.

When he'd done sizing me up he turned to Cath.

"Is this the young man you told me 'bout?"

"Yes, Pa."

Turning to me he said, "I hear you're called Joe."

"Yessir," I said, doing my best to be all polite, grateful he warn't looking down on me like most folks did.

"Can you work, Joe?"

That threw me. "Work?"

"That's what I said: work."

"Yes, I can, sir. I do an awful lot of work at home for my folks."

That seemed to please him. "Wait here," he said, disappearing into the stables. He came out with a bucket, a brush, and a pitchfork. "I want you to muck out the stables, Joe. Cath here will show you what to do. There's ten cents in it for each for you."

My heart fell. Cath wanted me with her to do a job, not because she wanted me as her friend. Even so, I set-to on the work. Ten cents is ten cents after all. Put it bluntly, the work was cleaning out horseshit and re-placing it with hay. There was a lot of shit to clear, and it was a hot day, so I was soon sweating. Cath gave me a drink of water when we was half-done with the job and another when we was fully done. I say *we*. Cath didn't do much beyond tell me what to do.

I hadn't ever cleaned out a stable before, but I must've done it right because when Cath's pa came back he looked the place over and nodded at me, man-to-man. That nod said, "You've done all right, son." Then he gave us both ten cents, good as his word. "Don't be long, your Ma wants you inside," he told Cath.

"I won't," she said, then her pa disappeared again.

She looked at me with her mischievous smile. "We ought to go back into the stables, Joe, just to make sure we done it right."

My belly got a funny feeling in it. "You're right," I said, and we went in, and she closed the door and took my hand and led me to a pile of hay down at the end. We both fell on it and lay down together looking up at the roof still holding hands. We talked for a while. I don't know what about. It seemed important at the time, though. Then she rolled on top of me and kissed me with her salty lips. That took me by surprise, but even so I kissed her right back.

"I have to go now," she told me and got up.

I was happier than I'd ever been, but also disappointed our time in the hay had come to an end so quickly.

When we left the stables her brother Max was just arriving on his horse. His eyes was on us as we came out. Throwing his leg back over the side of the horse Max got off it slow and easy. He did everything slow and easy. I wished I could do things that way. He led his horse to the stable door without saying hello. Just put his hand to the broad brim of the hat he was wearing and dropped his hand away smiling while he was doing it. It was like he knowed what we'd been up to and didn't mind. Just found it funny. That made me like him more'n I already did. Funny thing was, I liked him without even knowing him. Max had that effect on me.

While he was in the stable I managed to blurt out to Cath, "It was nice seeing you."

She smiled. "I'm glad you enjoyed it," and she went indoors with me watching her every step of the way.

As the door shut behind her I heard Max's voice. "You taken a shine to my sister, Joe?"

Felt my face getting hot and hoped it warn't turning red, but it surely was. I said, "I think your sister's right nice, Max."

Max was leaning against the stable door, one leg crossed over the other, looking as easy as could be. How did he look so easy all the time? I wanted to know so I could look that way myself. He pushed his hat to the back of his head. "All the young boys like my sister. She's a pretty little thing. Strong-minded, too. Hope you know what you're letting yourself in for, Joe Wild."

"Don't know if I do, Max."

"I reckon you'll manage. You're a bright young fella with a heap of courage, I can see that. Good looking, too. You'll be a real lady killer one day."

"Thank you, Max, that means a lot to me."

He laughed like he knowed everything about me. "Think nothing of it, Joe."

"Well, I'll be getting along now, Max."

"All right, Joe, I'll see you around."

I ain't never heard anyone say that before. It sounded good so I decided I'd say it myself one day.

Soon as I walked through the door Ma asked me where the fish was.

"Not biting today, Ma."

"You're lying. You warn't down at the bend in the river fishin'. I checked."

"When they warn't biting I thought I'd try higher up, Ma, near the river island. It's meant to be good there."

"I checked there, too, you no-good little liar." By this time she had Pa's old belt in her hand, the one that was too wore out for wearin' round his pants, and she did her best to wear out what was left of it on my backside. Didn't take her long to turn my butt black and blue. It was worth it, though. Didn't sleep a wink that night for thinking about Cath.

The time I got together with Cath was all stolen time so to speak. I had to steal it outta the time I had for doing chores. I thought I was hard done by, but the truth is I didn't know I was born. For all the work I had to do, the beatings I got, and the hunger I felt most the time, I was living through my golden years. Soon they would turn to lead. But that all lay in the future.

Cath's pa was called Corman G. Purdy. Never did get to know what the G stood for. It could have been something Spanish. He'd let it be known he had Spanish roots. He was a big man in every sense. Tall and broad like a blacksmith with a booming voice and a big man around town, too. One of the rich folks. But he seemed to tolerate me more than most, more even than my own pa did it sometimes seemed. I was sure Mr. Purdy was gonna stop me seeing his daughter, but he never did.

Looking back on things I wonder if Cath knew any of the secrets that came to light when it was too late to stop things going the way they went.

"You know Ervan Foster, that friend of yours who helped you bring a log up from the river?" she said to me one day. "Pa says I can go with you to visit him if I want to." That was almost unheard of. A boy my age escorting his girlfriend out and about with the blessing of her pa.

"Your pa sure is a fine person, Cath," I said. "I wish my own pa was like him." First chance I got I took Cath to meet Ervan. By then Ervan was like the pa I wanted. I already had a pa of course but I didn't always feel like I wanted him.

So now I have to tell you about Ervan Foster.

3.

A BUNCH OF SECRETS

SECOND THING MADE 1861 SPECIAL FOR ME WAS getting to know Ervan Foster. He was the same age as my pa or near enough but unlike Pa he was big and kinda handsome. Ervan lived on one of the homesteads outside town. I passed it every day on my way to and from school. Only company Ervan kept so far as I knowed was his animals and the animal he spent most of his time with was his dog, a huge mongrel that looked more like a wolf than a dog. Could have had some wolf in it for all I knowed. It went by the name of Arthur which struck everybody as odd. Arthur's a man's name not a dog's name. I always steered well clear of Ervan's property on account of that dog. He let it run around loose, and it growled at you even if you was a good distance away. That was the point of it I suppose. No one was gonna rob Ervan without thinking twice about it. That dog's growl was enough to give anybody second thoughts about going anywhere near Ervan's property. Plus, Ervan had been in the militia when he was young and had never lost the habit of carrying a gun. Rumor had it he was pretty handy with his gun, so it was quite a gauntlet you'd be running if you wanted to take anything from Ervan without first getting his permission.

School finished at midday. All us schoolkids went home for food at midday. With me it was more the hope of food than the guarantee, as such. One afternoon

I was passing by Ervan's homestead with my belly rumbling when I saw a rooster scratching about on his land. It was land he hadn't tended because he'd gotten too much land for one man to keep on top of, and the patch the rooster was on was all overgrown with scrub. The rooster didn't belong to Ervan or anyone else come to that. I could tell by the look of it that it was wild. It might've belonged to somebody once, but it'd claimed its freedom and taken to the wild life same as the pigs we got in the valley bottom. Soon as I saw it I dropped into a crouch and stalked that old rooster, my mouth watering at the thought of what it'd taste like after I'd plucked it and roasted it over a fire.

I'd hunted all manner of animals, so I knowed how to stalk a wild rooster and sure enough I soon got right up close to it. I didn't have a rock in my hand to stun it with but I thought I'd find one lying around. I didn't want to risk my bare hands on that rooster without stunning it. A rooster can give you an awful scratching if you grab it without first knocking it senseless. I got close enough to touch that bird and it had no idea I was there. If there had been a rock at my feet, I coulda picked it up real slow and brained the rooster with it and been on my way before Ervan or Arthur was any the wiser.

But there was no rock. So by and by I made up my mind to grab the rooster. Hunger makes you take risks like that. Anyways I knowed what to do. I'd wringed chicken necks in my time so I was well-practiced in the art of killing big birds, and I knowed with a bird like this one you have to get hold of the neck and twist it right quick before it gets the chance to use its claws on you. The sun was up real high, and the sky hadn't so much as a single cloud in it. Away in the distance was Ervan Foster's house. He surely wouldn't miss one rooster that warn't even his.

The rooster scratched in the dirt between a couple of bushes. I waited for it to put its head down. When it did I'd pounce with my arms out. It'd hear me and stick its head up and my hands would go tight around it. I'd twist one hand one way and the other t'other way and have my dinner all ready to take home. It'd be using the land as my larder just like Pa said you should.

Before I could pounce I heard a low growl that sent shivers down my spine. In my eagerness to get dinner I'd forgotten about another risk, the biggest risk of all. Ervan Foster's wolf-dog. It'd taken against me. The rooster flew off but I warn't minded to go after it. I had other things on my plate. When I looked where the growl had come from, I saw the dog from hell headed my way with its mouth wide open, all too keen to use its teeth on me.

The dog had never behaved that way before. It'd always been content to just threaten me from afar. But that day it was after blood. I damn near wet my pants when I saw it coming. Bearing in mind I was half-starved most of the time, that dog weighed comfortably more than I did and on its hind legs stood a sight taller. One of my arms in its jaws might've been a good fit. Hell, one of my legs in its jaws might've been a good fit. That dog seemed minded to find out anyhow.

I wanted to hightail it, but I had visions of the dog sinking its teeth into my backside and tearing a piece off before bringing me down like a wolf brings down a baby deer. At the same time I knowed doing nothing would get me kilt just as certainly as doing something would. I looked around for a rock to throw at it but all I saw on the ground was dust and more dust. In the end I stood stiller than a tree not knowing what to do while it growled fit to chew off my head. It was going at a good lick and it covered the gap between us in a couple of seconds, it seemed.

Then it leaped up at me, and I shut my eyes and waited for the end, fully expectin' my throat to be ripped from my neck.

"Arthur, down, boy!" That was Ervan shouting.

Next thing I knowed I was lying on the ground. Arthur had crashed into me and knocked me over. With my eyes tight shut I waited for the dog to sink his teeth into me. I felt his tongue on my face licking it. Was he getting a taste to decide how big a bite to take outta me? After a minute or two of wondering how long it would be before Arthur kilt me I decided to take a look what he was up to. First I opened one eye, then the other, and I saw Arthur standing over me.

"Don't worry, he's well trained, and he won't bite. He knows not to now I've told him. Trained him myself from being a pup," said Ervan. He was standing next to Arthur reckoning to make me feel safe, but he failed in that endeavor.

I was too affrighted to move a muscle or even think about moving one. Arthur meanwhile got bored of licking my face and took to sniffing me all over particularly around the crotch area of my pants. I had a gaping hole there and he stuck his snout right in it. Felt cold and wet again my privates. I might have said a prayer at that point.

"Git up now," said Ervan waving the muzzle of his musket at me in a way that told me I had to do as he said or get my head blown off. Arthur removed his nose from inside my pants at that point, thank God, and I got up very carefully. When I was on my feet I beat the dust from my clothes. Ervan narrowed his eyes and his face got more lined. He was holding his musket like he was fixing on giving me a real warm welcome.

"What you doing on my land, boy?" he said, and I took the opportunity to look at him from close quarters so to speak. He had iron-gray hair, a strong, good-looking face, broad shoulders, calloused hands, and a six-gun pushed into his belt. A frontier man through-and-through.

"Nothing, sir."

He put the stock of his firearm to his shoulder and pointed the weapon right at me sighting along it. I was desperate to get out of the way, but knowed if I moved so much as a muscle my number was up. "You must've been doing something," he said. "Was you stealing my livestock?"

Shaking my head with my eyes lowered all humble I said, "No, sir," in the most quiet, respectful voice I could muster.

"Be truthful with me now. I hate liars. They make my trigger finger get all itchy. You wouldn't want it to get itchy with you in the firing line, would you?"

"No, sir, I wouldn't want that."

"Was you here to steal my livestock?"

"No, sir. I saw a rooster on your land and figured it was a wild one and you wouldn't mind me going after it."

"Anything on my land belongs to me, you got that, boy?"

"Yes I have got it, Mr. Foster, sir, now you've

explained it so well. I have well and truly got it. I wouldn't have had any truck with that rooster 'cept I was hungrier than a prairie wolf when it caught my eye." Then I told a lie. "I ain't eaten for three days, Mr. Foster, sir, that's why I was so hungry."

Lowering his musket he looked me up and down and said, "You're skinny enough to be telling the truth. Does that no-good father of yours never bring any food into your house?"

"Not often, sir."

He nodded. "Too busy drinking, I suppose." Turned his head and narrowed his eyes again looking at the rooster which had settled down now the fuss was over and found a new patch of dirt to scratch in, about fifty yards from where we was stood. Ervan put his gun to his shoulder, squeezed the trigger, and the bird fell dead.

"Arthur," he said, pointing. The dog ran and got the rooster in its mouth then brought it over to us. Foster took the rooster from it and smiled.

"Arthur's friendly ain't he?" *Friendly* ain't the word I would've used, but I kept my trap shut on that one and nodded.

Ervan's eyeballs moved down to my feet then back to my head. "You look like you need feeding up. If you pluck the rooster and cook it I'll share it with you."

By this time Arthur was smelling my hand so I knowed he warn't no threat anymore, and I said, "That sounds right good, Mr. Foster."

"You can call me Ervan."

"Alright, Ervan, thank you."

He nodded sideways, "Follow me," and we walked at a steady pace to his homestead.

First thing I noticed was his door warn't like you'd expect the door of a cabin to be out in the country. It didn't have a wood latch with a buckskin string on it like ours or even an iron latch. It had a brass knob on it like the rich folks in town had. Ervan turned the knob and let me in. Soon I was in a room he called his parlor. It looked like all he did in that room was sit around in it. There warn't a bed in it anyhow or anything you could cook on 'cept maybe the fire, but the fireplace in it looked like it'd never been used for fires never mind cooking. It was brick on the bottom, and Ervan had scrubbed the bricks clean. I'd never seen the inside of anybody's house before other than Ma and Pa's so I didn't know what to expect. It came as a shock to see that Ervan's house was clean everywhere and full of stuff. Our place was grubby everywhere and had almost nothing in it. In that parlor alone Ervan had a polished wood sideboard with pictures of people on it who looked real but for having no color in them other than brown, a fancy wood box of cigars, a fine polished table, more'n two chairs to set on and comfy chairs at that, a hatstand with a railroad cap hanging from it, and a top hat, too. He had a clock taller than me with the sun and moon on the face of it, and a load of pictures hanging on the wall. More stuff than I'd ever seen in one go in my life, including real whiskey in bottles. Not the rough shine Pa kept in his half-gallon jug in our cabin.

When Ervan had showed me round his house he took a watch from the pocket of his waistcoat and squinted at it. Silver it was.

I'd never seen a watch close up so I said, "Can I take a look at your watch, please, Ervan?" It was fastened on his weskit with a chain. Undoing the chain he handed it to me. Real fancy it was. When I turned it over I saw a message carved on the back: *To Ervan with much love.*

"Who gave you this, Ervan?"

"One of my wives."

"Where is she?"

He smiled like it was a big secret and tapped the side of his nose, so I didn't ask about her no more. I can take a hint.

"Let's make a fire outside," he said. "Food tastes better when its cooked and eaten outside. Learned that during my goldmining days."

"You found any gold, Ervan?"

He put his finger to his closed lips. "I did, but don't tell anyone."

"I won't."

He gave me a hatchet and I plucked the rooster then chopped it up with the hatchet. Fried the pieces with the skin on, in a cast-iron skillet over the fire until the skin was crispy. The meat was tough but mighty tasty.

"You got any kinfolk, Ervan?" I asked while I was chewing a piece.

"I got a son. He sees me but once every three or four years."

"Why don't he see you more often?"

"He went out west to California. Takes him an age to travel from there to here, and he ain't up to doing it more'n once every few years, and I don't blame him."

"Don't he miss you? I'd miss my folks if I moved west."

"I'm sure he does, son. I miss him too. But sometimes you got to make sacrifices."

"Why you gotta do that?"

"To be who you need to be."

I didn't get what he meant but I never asked him to explain. I could tell it was upsetting to Ervan to talk about his son so I left it.

"Thank you, Ervan," I said when my belly was full of wild rooster. "I better be heading home now."

"Drop in sometime, and I'll boil up some coffee, and we can have us a good old yarn," he said.

"That I will!" Feeling right grown up I headed home. Ma warn't impressed I was late to getting the chores done, but she didn't cowhide me. I never told her about my meeting with Ervan, and she looked at me kind of suspicious when I didn't eat as much corn-bread as usual.

"What's the matter with you, boy? You've got no appetite, are you sickening for something?"

"No Ma, I just ain't hungry today, thank you."

"This is the first day since you was born you ain't been hungry. Still, I suppose I oughta be grateful. It means there's cornbread left over for tomorrow. Not often that happens."

A few days later the sky got heavy with cloud. Then while I was walking through the woods the trees began to rustle. I waited for them to stop, but they kept right on rustling. The wind had got up, and it warn't gonna stop. That told me an Illinois storm was brewing. Luckily it was that time of year when you can pick up acorns, so I picked some up like Ma and Pa had taught me to. I picked up thirty-nine of them and carried them home in my hat. It was a straw hat bent at the rim but good enough to wear. Put thir-teen in my shed and thirteen in Ma and Pa's house and lit out to Ervan's homestead.

Arthur ran to me, but he didn't growl, just barked

and licked my hand. Ervan heard him and looked out the window. His windows had glass in them like the schoolhouse. He opened the door before I got to it.

"Joe, it's good to see you." I held out my hat with both hands, upside down. He looked in it. "What you got there?"

"Acorns, thirteen of 'em. Keep 'em in your house. It'll stop the lightning from striking it."

He smiled. "Thank you, I will." Taking the acorns from my hat he said, "Would you like to come in for a while? I could boil up some coffee."

I looked up and saw the clouds had turned black and covered all the sky. "No, thank you, Ervan, I ought to get home before the storm breaks, and it's gonna be a-breaking soon. I'll come for coffee some other time if the offer's still open."

"It's open anytime for you, Joe."

I smiled. "Thank you, Ervan, I 'preciate that."

As I was getting home the first spots of rain fell on me big as clay marbles. I went to my shed and lit a candle and sat on my mattress. Then I saw a flash of lightning through the gaps between the planks of my shed. After that the thunder rolled and it rained like all fury, too, and I never heard the wind blow so. Next day when the storm was all blown out my shed and Ma and Pa's cabin was still standing so I figured the acorns done the job I got them for well enough for our family. I went to see Ervan and found his place was also still in one piece, so the acorns musta worked for him, too. He came to the door and grinned.

"Last night there was enough lightning for a year of storms, but none of it hit my home Joe. I have you and your acorns to thank for that. I'm gonna boil up some coffee for you. It's the least I can do. Come inside."

"Don't mind if I do, Ervan, thank you."

I was glad Ervan was still around. I would have missed the ornery critter if the lightning had kilt him, and he made a real good can of coffee.

When I next went fishing the river was higher than usual because of the deluge. Swollen so much it was damn near bursting its banks. A log was floating downstream. Often happens when the river is high. Right away I stripped off my clothes and dived in. The water was calm and deep, slow-flowing by the bank but fast when you got to the middle even though the surface was smooth as a looking-glass. I grabbed hold of that log and kicked my legs hard, steering it toward a river beach downstream of me. The current was so strong it took me and the log further than I wanted to go. I rolled underwater a couple of times and damn near drownded, but still I clung on to that log and got to the bank with it, spurred on by the thought of getting nine dollars for it from the local sawmill. It's what they'd pay for a log that size. I'd learned that lately. But it was about more than just money with me. Way I saw it was if I got that log to the sawmill, it was one less tree the lumberjacks would cut down.

The bank was purest mud, and it took everything I had to land that log on it. By the time I was done I was coated in mud from head to toe, and it struck me I had no way of moving my treasure to the sawmill and what's more I didn't have a stitch of clothing on me. Snuck back through the woods keeping a look-out for folks as I didn't want to be seen butt naked. Not that anyone was likely to see me. You could trek from one end of those woods to the other without seeing a soul. I always remember that day. Something about being butt naked in the woods covered in mud seemed natural, the way a body was supposed to be. When I got back to where I'd left my clothes, I washed myself in river water to make myself look halfway human before putting them back on.

Up till then I hadn't given much thought as to how I was gonna get that log to the sawmill. When I finally did think about it, I realized I had a big problem. No way could I move it on my own, and I couldn't get Pa to help me because he'd take all the money for hisself. Nor could I use our horse because Ma would know I was up to something, and she'd end up taking the money. In the end I went to see Ervan.

"I got a proposition for you, Ervan."

He smiled turning his face into a mess of lines. "What's that, Joe?"

"It's a business deal. I have a log to take to the sawmill. I reckon I'll get nine dollars for it. But I need some help. If you help me, I'll split the money with you. We'll get four dollars fifty each. What do you say?"

Ervan scratched his chin. "That sounds like a good deal. Wait here while I get my horse and a length of rope."

Five hours later we was counting the money. "They only paid us six dollars," said Ervan, "better than nothing, I suppose, and it makes it easier to split. Three dollars each. Here's your share." He handed me the notes. Made me feel like I was rich for once in my life.

"Will you help if I get any more logs?"

"Sure I will, Joe."

We did three more logs that summer and earned more cash than I'd ever seen in my life before. There was a hole in my mattress big as my fist with straw poking out of it. I shoved my cash into that hole and pushed it sideways. It was easy enough to get it out when I wanted to. Hiding it there kept it safe. There was two people it needed keeping safe from, Ma and Pa.

First time I showed up with Cath at Ervan's place, Arthur got to barking before we were within a hundred yards of Ervan's cabin. Cath's eyes was big to start with, but they got even bigger when she saw Arthur.

"That dog looks evil, Joe. You'll protect me, won't you?"

"Sure I will, Cath. Don't worry, he's harmless." Felt good that Cath wanted me to protect her. Seemed I'd become a man all of a sudden. I jumped down from my horse. Not really my horse, it was one of Mr. Purdy's. He'd got to letting me and Cath borrow his horses when we wanted to get around. It warn't for free, mind. I had to agree to keep mucking out his stables to get the use of a horse now and again. Arthur bounded up to me. "Okay, boy," I said, "you know who I am." He licked my hand. "You get down, Cath, let him smell your hand."

Cath was wary, but she got off her horse and let Arthur get close enough to smell her fingers, then we walked our horses to Ervan's cabin and tied them up outside.

Ervan opened the door and raised an eyebrow at me. "Who's your friend, Joe?"

"This here is Cath. We go to school together."

He nodded. "Does her pa know you two are out here together?"

"Yes, he does."

"Then I guess you better both come in, and I'll boil up some coffee."

We went inside, and Ervan showed us into his parlor as he called it, the room where all you did was sit around and not eat in it, or cook in it, or sleep in it.

"Mighty nice place you have here, Mr. Foster," Cath said.

"Call me Ervan. Joe does."

Ervan left the room to make coffee for us. Cath got to poking around in his sideboard.

"What you doing, Cath?"

"Nothing, just curious."

"Well, don't be. Poking around in Ervan's things is bad manners, you oughta know that."

She stopped and smiled at me then opened a drawer in the sideboard, looked inside, and shut it.

"Just stop that now, you hear me?" I said.

"Sure, Joe, sorry, I didn't mean to offend you."

"I'm not offended, but Ervan might be. He trusts me and he wouldn't want me letting anyone root through his things, not even you." She gave up and sat next to me.

You might have thought we'd be fooling around while Ervan left us alone, but we didn't. We was very young, and didn't really know what to do beyond holding hands and kissing now and again, but I knowed inside we was heading for some way of behaving that was different. I just didn't know what the difference was.

Ervan brought back the coffee. Cath finished hers before me and Ervan and excused herself. She seemed to be gone quite a while. I hoped to God she warn't looking in any more of his things. When she came back we talked for a while, then it was time to leave, and we went back to town.

Her pa met us at the door. "Have you two had a good time?"

"Yes, Mr. Purdy."

"I'm glad to hear it. How was Mr. Foster?"

"He was very hospitable." Cath went indoors and didn't once look back. Her pa smiled. I'd been hoping he or Cath might invite me into the Purdy family home, but I could see that warn't gonna happen. It never happened, but that was fair in a way as I never once invited Cath to Ma and Pa's cabin. No one would have appreciated Cath seeing how we Wilds lived, least of all me.

I can't remember how many times me and Cath called on Ervan but it was quite a few. You wouldn't have thought he was the type to have secrets. Turned out he was.

4.

PA GOES OFF THE RAILS

THE THIRD THING THAT MADE 1861 SPECIAL concerned Pa.

Pa was short and skinny as a polecat. Thomas Wild he was called. When I was knee high he took me to one side and said "Son, it's time you learn to fend for yourself." Don't know if I answered him or if I could even talk at the time. He took me into the woods and showed me a bush with a heap of berries on it. Took one of them off and gave it to me so I put it in my mouth. "That's chokeberry," he said. "Eat as many as you want." Later I tried to eat bittersweet and he caned me with a hickory stick. "Don't let me ever see you touch that stuff, Son." I cried and he dropped the stick and picked me up and hugged me. "I'm sorry Joe, I didn't want to hurt you but I had to. I never want to lose you, and if you eat that stuff it might be the end of you, so I gotta put you off eatin' it ever again the best way I can."

Pa taught me what fruit and berries and mushrooms to pick and what would make me sick and likely kill me. We harvested blackberries, crowberries, dewberries, and every other kind of berry in our neck of the woods. Same with acorns, black walnuts, pine nuts, and other nuts. Some weeks it got so I grew sick of nuts.

Sometimes he had me dig up thistle root then boil it over a fire. Pa told me you have to be careful with digging up the root because the thistle can give you an awful scratch. He showed me how to push it sideways with my foot and tread it flat to make it safe to dig up. The root tastes good when you boil it and makes you healthy, he said. Ma agreed. I never got on with the taste myself but I still drink it for health reasons. I reckon it works just like Pa said it did. I know plenty of people been a lot sicker'n me in my time, anyhows.

Pa got me catching birds big and small, taking eggs from nests, and tracking animals. He said some animals are more trouble than they're worth so we left them alone. Others we caught with snares. There's different kinds of snares and I reckon Pa knowed every one of them. He could catch a deer with a snare. Hunters who have to use a gun don't know how to hunt he'd say, so Pa never took his musket when he went a-hunting. Not even when he hunted bear which he did one time. Not that his old musket woulda been much use against a bear.

When we tracked bears we found out the places they liked to go, such as a fishing hole they used, and this one time Pa dug a pit and filled it with stakes he'd whittled from branches. Then he covered the pit and we hid nearby, thinking a bear would come along soon. One did, and it fell in Pa's pit. He'd caught hisself a bear. Me and him grinned at each other and jumped up and down slapping each other's hands. The bear howling with pain or rage or maybe both made us stop. "Bear ain't dead Pa." "Wait here Boy. I'll brain it with my axe."

Pa ran over to the pit to find the bear climbing out of it. It took a swipe with its paw and knocked the axe clean out of Pa's hand. Made a nasty gash on his forearm with a claw. Pa ran back to me. "Let's make ourselves scarce Son," he said. "I ain't never seen a bear that riled up before. No telling what it'll do once its clumb outta that pit." That was the first and last time Pa went hunting for bear meat.

You might have heard tomatoes are poisonous. Most folk think they are, anyhows, but they're not. Me and Pa ate wild tomatoes every time we came across them, and they never did either of us any harm. In fact Pa reckoned they was good for you, and I ain't got no reason to doubt him on that.

Pa taught me how to fish with a line and how to fish with your bare hands when you didn't have a line. We stalked bears sometimes just for the hell of it. Had to keep downwind of them. If they knowed you was around and they had food or little ones near them you'd be a goner. By the time Pa had finished teaching me I knowed all there was to know about living off the land, and I'd been beaten on every part of my body with that hickory stick of his. Pa warn't known for his patience. But he was a good teacher, I'll give him that.

It was easy to get meat in the summer. Easier than in winter anyways. So to provide for winter Pa would do his best to catch some fat deer in the fall. You got real fat ones in the fall, but when winter came there was no fat ones to be had, they all went skinny because they couldn't get enough food to fatten up with. Same as us Wilds.

Near my shed back of the cabin was another bigger shed. More a tower than a shed, like a chimbly. It was made of half-logs and had a door on the front with hemp loops for hinges and a length of hemp to tie it shut with. There were shelves in it made of branches woven together like nets and loops of hemp hanging from the rafters. When Pa caught a deer he'd feed us fresh venison and cut up the rest of the deer and salt it and put in on the shelf of his shed which he called his smokehouse. If it was a big deer he'd hang some of it from the hemp loops. By burning hickory on the floor which was made of dirt and burning it the right way so it smouldered he got a mess of smoke going over the venison.

"That smoked venison will stay fresh no matter what," he told me once. He was right, too. Kept us in meat most of the winter when he caught enough. Always puzzled me why the smokehouse was bigger than the shed that I lived in, but I never dared ask the reason for that if there was a reason.

Pa stretched the skin of those deer and made moccasins for us to wear when the weather was cold. Mostly though we went barefoot. Folks in town mostly wore boots. I didn't know that till I started school and got laughed at because of my bare feet. My feet was brown on top because of the sun getting to them most the time and black underneath because of the dirt getting to them all of the time.

Don't recall how old I was when Pa found an anthill in the woods. Not very. Maybe four or five. Finding anthills in the woods warn't hard, by the way. I saw them most days I was a-wandering among the trees.

"Roll up your pants, boy," he said.

"What, Pa?"

"Watch me." He got hold of his pants at the ankle and rolled them up above his knee. "Do what I've just done."

I was puzzled. Pants rolling warn't anything we'd done before 'cept when we was wading through streams, and I couldn't see a stream anywhere so I couldn't see the point of it. But by then I knowed better'n to argue with Pa, so I did as I was told.

He pulled off his footwear and held it in his hand. "Now take off your moccasins." That must've been one of those rare times I had moccasins. As I've been at pains to make clear I mostly walked around barefoot. Pa said barefoot was good for me. Toughened my feet and every damn other part of me. "Footwear makes you soft," he'd said. Give him his due, he practiced what he preached. Walked barefoot hisself a lot of the time.

"Now watch me," said Pa as he walked straight at that anthill and waded right through it like he was wading through a deep puddle. When he got to the other side ants was hanging offa his legs. It looked mighty painful. He let them hang there for a minute or two, holding on by their jaws most likely. Ants got big jaws for their size. They're little critters with a big bite. When he decided he'd been ant-bitten for long enough Pa swept them off his legs with his hands and looked at me. "Now you," he said.

"What's that, Pa?"

"You heard me. It's your turn. You gotta walk through that nest of ants."

"I don't want to, Pa, I'm scared, and I don't want to get hurt by those ants."

"Don't worry, son, it don't hurt you none. Not much anyways. You know when I switch you?"

"Yes, Pa."

"It don't hurt anything like as bad as that."

"Those ants look real mean, Pa."

"Don't mind those mean old ants, just do it."

"Why we doing this?"

"It's good for you. Now get over here or I swear to God I'll kick you over, and you'll end up crawling on your belly through that anthill."

Crawling on my belly with ants biting me warn't something I wanted to do. I soon figured it was better to have them biting my legs than biting my belly so I waded through.

The anthill came up to Pa's knees, so it was almost up to my waist. But because Pa had trod it down some, I didn't get too many of the critters around my privates. Even at a tender age a boy knows he don't want anything biting at his privates.

"Now stand there, and let them bite you." All right for him to say. He didn't have any above those bony knees of his.

I reached into my pants to scratch them off. They'd got in through the holes around the crotch.

Pa raised his hand. "What'd I tell you, boy?"

Reckoning Pa's hand would hurt more'n the ants, I left them to it. After what seemed like the proverbial eternity he said, "Now you can get rid of 'em."

I couldn't get rid of them fast enough. Danced around crazier than a wild horse when it's being broken till they was gone.

Pa laughed. "I ain't never seen such a fuss over a few dozen ants," he said.

When I'd got rid of the ants I had a rash over my legs. So did Pa. I pointed at his. "What good's that gonna do you, Pa?"

He raised his hand again. "I ought to slap some respect into you, boy." When he saw me cowering, he decided against slappin' me for once and put his hand by his side. "I'll tell you what good it'll do. When winter comes all the folks around town are gonna be coughing and getting runny noses, and they're gonna get aches and pains and fevers. One or two of the rich ones who can afford it are gonna take to their beds. But not me and you. Ain't no sickness gonna get the better of us Wilds, and it's all because of them ant bites we just got."

Darned if he warn't right. When I joined the army one of the first things I was introduced to was the army cough. It started first thing in the morning at reveille. When reveille sounded and everybody got up the coughing drownded out the bugle, and sometimes when there was a drum going and two or three other instruments I'm damned if they warn't all drowned out, too. But I never coughed myself. Not one single time. So in spite of everything I got to be grateful to my Pa for what he did for me. I still walk an anthill at least once a year. If you're reading this, you're the first person I ever told about it. It's not something I'm minded to talk about because folks think you're touched if they hear you do things like that.

When I was six years old Pa said, "Come with me, boy, I need to train you to shoot," and he grabbed his musket from the shelf and took me outside. Took me down to the river where he found a boulder and drew a circle on it with a rock.

"That circle's a target," he said.

We walked away from it maybe twenty yards which I later found out was all that musket was good for, and he put the weapon to his shoulder and pointed it at the target. It made a noise like all hell had broken loose right next to us. There was smoke and flame and the target got a mark on it near the middle.

"This here is a Springfield Flintlock Musket," Pa said. "I'm gonna show you how to use it." He got

a length of metal he called a ramrod and pushed it
down the barrel then dropped a measure of gunpowder down it from a piece of horn and tamped it down
with the ramrod. Finally, he got a round bullet in a
small piece of oiled cloth and rammed that down on
top of the powder. "It's too heavy for you, boy, so
you're gonna have to rest it on a boulder," he said.
We found another boulder for me to rest the barrel
on, and he showed me how to aim, and I shot at the
target. I hit it, too. "Good boy," Pa said.

"What do we hunt with this, Pa?"

"Only animal worth hunting with that is a person.
Always remember that, Joe. I keep that musket in
case I have to hunt a person."

When we finished our shooting lesson we went
home, and Pa showed me how to clean out the barrel
with boiling water and oil it and make bullets from
lead with a mold. He loaded up the musket and put it
by the door.

"Anybody comes to visit I don't like the looks of
I'll let 'em have it," he said.

We had regular shooting lessons after that till Pa
got useless. The lessons was to make sure we both
kept our eye in, he said. Thinking about Pa brings a
tear to my eye. He could be an ornery bastard, but I
know he loves me and always did love me in spite of
it all, and I love him.

Might as well tell you about Ma while I'm on the
subject of Pa. Ma kept us in greens some of the time.
Pa had built a fence. He made it from branches tied
to split logs, so it formed a yard next to our cabin big
enough for a garden. Ma grew radishes, carrots, peas,
beets, peppers, potatoes, cabbages, sweet potatoes,
rutabaga, wintergreen, and a heap of other stuff in it.

Not enough to feed us year round but her efforts gave us a meal or two now and again. I helped her with digging and planting and pulling and picking insects off when they was the wrong sort of insect. Pa swore blind Ma's veg didn't taste as good as the wild stuff he found in the woods. He still ate it, though.

Pa warn't one for church. That drew comments on Sundays. I never heard what folk said about Pa, but I knowed they was saying it. I could tell the way they looked at me when Ma dragged me to church. They gave us pitying looks, some of them. Others looked down their noses at us. But Ma always held her head up proud.

"Everybody's equal in the eyes of the Lord, son," she'd say.

"How come churchgoers don't hold with that way of thinking?" I said once, and she slapped me hard across the face.

"Don't you dare bad mouth good Christians, boy."

I never said it again, but I sure thought it often enough.

Ma kept a bible in the house that she read every day. Sometimes she read things from it and forced me to listen. They never made any sense so far as I could see. They still didn't make any sense when Miss Larsen made me read them out in class.

It's thanks to the church I got some schooling. Pastor Graham said kids needed educating, and he chose Miss Larsen to ram education down our throats. Miss Larsen forced it down my throat best she could, though a lot of it got stuck halfway. But at least she taught me to read and write, so I got something to thank the church for. I wouldn't have gone to school but for Ma's bible-thumping, so I got Ma and her religion to thank, too.

I must have been six when Ma swole up. Pa acted like he was real glad that happened.

"He's mine," he said, patting Ma's swollen belly.

I didn't see what he was getting at. "Who's yours, Pa?" I said.

"Never you mind, boy. You'll find out soon enough. Come with me."

We went outside. It was winter and a deep layer of snow covered the ground. We hadn't got but five paces from the cabin before I saw animal tracks in it. Snow's good for tracking in. I've had plenty of good meals I got through following pawprints in the snow. But those tracks had been made by something I'd never want to eat. Bobcat. Pa told me when he was desperate once he'd kilt and eaten a bobcat. He said he was lucky the cat didn't kill him first. It damned near scratched him to death before he slit it open with his knife. The meat tasted like he expected cat to taste, which was like cat piss, and that put him off but he forced it down because he was starving. Then he had to put up with the taste of cat piss inside him for the rest of the day. Only thing to be said for eating bobcat is if you're desperate and it's all you got, it can keep your body and soul together till you find something better to eat. More than once in my life I'd have entertained eating bobcat if one had been to hand.

Anyways, Pa took me into the woods. Lots of tracks there left by all kinds of critters. "What we hunting today, Pa? Are we gonna get us a white-tail?"

"I seen some tracks. We'll hunt deer later," he said. "We're hunting something easier today."

"What's that, Pa?"

"Red Osier Dogwood."

"What?"

"You heard me." He pointed. "Some over there. Help me gather it up."

"We collecting firewood?"

"Nope. Watch me and do what I do." He found the thinnest branches and cut them off near the ground. Couldn't have been thicker than my little finger. It made no sense to me. We never collected dogwood before. You couldn't eat it and branches that thin was no good for burning. When we had a good pile Pa tied them up in bundles, and we carried them home. Ma looked pleased when we took them indoors.

"You're gonna help me make a crib, boy."

"What's a crib?"

"You'll find out." He wove the dogwood sticks together and showed me what to do to help him here and there. I doubt I was any real help. Pa just wanted me to feel I was part of it, whatever it was. A crib turned out to be a tiny bed. When we finished it the crib looked pretty good, and I wished I had one to sleep in myself, a bigger one of course. It was made of green wood, which was real bendy. Pa dried it out in the cabin, and it stopped being so bendy.

Ma swole up bigger'n ever. Then she was crying, and so was Pa. Only time I'd ever seen him do that. Something was in the crib wrapped in a blanket. Pa wouldn't let me go near it. When I did he cussed at me, and I knowed if I tried to see it I'd get a taste of the hickory stick, so I kept my distance after that.

The next day we all went to church, even Pa. The thing from the crib was buried next to the church. Turns out it warn't a thing at all, it was a he, and the he was my brother or should have been. Ma and Pa had stopped crying by then, but Ma started again in the church. The churchgoing women held her and said comforting things—even the ones who looked down on us. The men shook Pa's hand in a sad way and murmured politely to him about loss and such. Pa didn't look like he was taking it in, he just looked dazed.

My late brother was buried in a Christian way with Pastor Graham making a speech over his grave. Pastor said my brother would have brought richness into this world if he'd lived, and he'd brought joy into Ma and Pa's lives while he was around, and he'd be sorely missed even though he'd been but a baby when the good Lord had taken him from us. He'd gone on to greater challenges that lay ahead and would have everlasting life, Amen. Just like the bible his speech made no sense to me. Life ain't everlasting. You only have to look around you to know that much. And I can't see as there's any greater challenge for anyone than surviving in this world of ours. All the same I was glad Pastor Graham said nice things about my dead brother. It made me feel good, and I could see Ma and Pa appreciated it, too, even though it made Ma cry again.

Later I learned most of the women in town had lost more than one child. Some of them had lost half a dozen. But I guess Ma and Pa warn't very good at cooking up children, so losing one hurt them more than it did other folks. My brother was the last they had as far as I know, and I was the only one came before him. That makes me the last in the family line. Some family.

It was after my brother died that Pa took to drinking whiskey. Strictly speaking it warn't whiskey, it was shine that Pa stored in a half-gallon jug. Every time Pa emptied the jug he got it filled again by Mr. Beaker who had a secret still. Mr. Beaker used it to make cheap liquor that he sold to Pa and other folks in our neck of the woods. Mr. Beaker's liquor business warn't strictly legal because the guv'ment had said you warn't allowed stills of your own. The guv'ment wanted to make money from any liquor going, and they warn't gonna make any money out of the likes of Mr. Beaker, but he got away with his lawbreakin'. Folks got away with a lot of lawbreakin' in our town so long as they warn't breaking no laws that could lead to a lynch mob going after them.

Ma said it was the whiskey made Pa useless. I don't know about that. If whiskey was the cause and she knowed it, why did Ma take to drinking it herself? I never drunk it personally 'cept when I had to, when people died and such. Then I had whiskey days and whiskey nights, too, if the loss called for it, and time permitting. Like when Ervan died.

Pa spent most of his time drunk after my brother passed, and when Pa warn't drunk he was fixing to get drunk or earning money to get drunk with. He was a poor drunk just like he was poor at everything else 'cept living like a wild animal. Some men make good drunks, I seen them. They're friendly to begin with, and they get friendlier and funny with it when they drink. Other men are poor drunks. No matter how friendly they start off when they're sober, they end up getting real nasty when they're drunk. Pa was one of those. What made it worse was his way of being drunk was very friendly to begin with. It took you in, and you expected him to carry on that way. Then when you was all relaxed he'd give you a look and call you a bastard or something worse and go for you right out of the blue. Didn't need nothing to provoke him. It was something inside of him provoked him.

In one of his sober moments Pa came home with a couple of lengths of rope and said, "Grab some of those rutabaga you got, and come with me, boy."

"What you doing with that rope, Pa?"

"Don't ask any of your damn fool questions or I'll take my stick to you."

"Why do I need rutabaga?"

"Ain't I just told you not to ask any more damn fool questions?"

I shut up after that knowing the stick was just round the corner, and I was lucky I hadn't felt a taste of it already.

We followed a trail me and Pa called the valley trail that right enough led to the valley. It warn't a trail in the sense folks used it. No one could see anything resembling a trail there unless they was a tracker like me and Pa. Me and Pa knowed the route because we'd done it a hundred times before. Pa had found it before I was born, he was fond of telling me.

"I seen two pigs yesterday in the bottom of the valley," he said. "We're gonna catch 'em and take 'em home."

"Ain't that gonna be dangerous, Pa?" I ducked after I said that, expecting him to take a swing at me with his open hand like he sometimes did, but he let it go.

"I studied 'em real hard," he said, "and soon enough worked out they must've come from one of the homesteads. Not that long ago, looked like."

I hoped Pa was right about it not being long ago the pigs left their homestead. Pigs soon go wild when they escape, and some of those wild pigs are real vicious. Even tame ones can be. Pa didn't have his musket with him, but even if he had it wouldn't be no help against a pig. All it was good for was shooting rabbits, and you'd miss with it most of the time if you tried it. A pig was a bigger target, but you could miss even a pig with that musket of Pa's unless the pig was real close. Or the musket might not shoot, and even if it did shoot it was likely not to kill anything as hardy as a pig. Just enrage it. Then when the pig charged at you, you'd have no time to reload, what with that gun being a muzzle-loader and firing round balls of shot. If that happened, best you could hope for was to beat the pig with the buttstock and drive it away. Good luck with that.

Ain't nothing in this world scarier than a pig. A pig is worse than a grizzly bear. A bear will only attack you if you annoy it or if it's real hungry and desperate. But pigs like eating people. They like the taste of us as much as we like the taste of them. When a pig sees a man, woman, or child walking by, what it sees is dinner on legs. It'll attack and kill you so as to enjoy a good, tasty meal. Even tame pigs have been known to do that. Pigs are cleverer than bears, too. Bears ain't stupid, I ain't saying that. But pigs are real smart. That's another thing that makes them so dangerous. A pig can outsmart a man, so oftentimes they give you no warning they're coming for you. A hog can knock you down before you even know he's there. First you know of a pig attacking you is when you're on the ground and it's tearing lumps from you, but a bear will always let you know he's coming.

Theodore Gibbler found that out the hard way when he had a run-in with a wild pig. It knocked him clean off his feet and took a bite outta one of his legs.

Made a hole like a half-moon in his thigh. Liked the taste of it so much it took another bite soon as it'd finished chowing down on the first one. Lucky for Mr. Gibbler a group of us kids was nearby and heard his screams. We managed to drive the pig off by throwing rocks at it. Kept our distance, mind. Then we helped Mr. Gibbler back to town. Left a trail of blood in our wake so obvious any tenderfoot who knowed not the first thing about tracking could have followed us all the way there. Soon as we could we got Mr. Gibbler to Euclad Bonham's house. Euclad Bonham was the closest thing we had to a doctor in those parts. He never done any formal doctor training, but he was in the Indian wars, and he learned how to fix up wounds on the job, you might say. Knowed how to splint up a broken leg, too. He put a tourniquet on Mr. Gibbler's leg, but by then we all knowed it was too late. Too much blood had leaked out of him. We buried Mr. Gibbler the next day.

Me and Pa followed the trail to a flat grassy area in the valley bottom. Trees was more spaced out there for some reason. Nature's reason, whatever that is.

Pa pointed. "See those tracks?"

"I see them, Pa."

He said nothing else just followed the tracks, and I followed him.

"We're making a lot of noise, Pa."

"Didn't I just tell you those pigs are fresh from a homestead? This is the easiest game to trail you'll ever find, boy. You don't need to keep quiet, and you don't even need to be good at tracking to catch 'em."

He was right on both counts. Trail those pigs left was easy to follow as the Mississippi, and when we got to those pigs they paid us no heed. We walked right up to them, and I fed them rutabaga while Pa fastened ropes 'round their necks. Then with a deal of pulling and encouraging them with Pa's switch and feeding them rutabaga we got them home. Pa tied them up to a couple of trees by the cabin. The trees was far enough apart and the tethers short enough that they could never get tangled up with each other, but the pigs could get close enough to touch snouts if they had a mind to. I ain't never seen pigs tied up like that before, and didn't think it was a good idea, but I didn't say anything. I knowed I'd been riding my luck on saying things, and one more comment was liable to get me a switching worse'n either of those pigs had got.

"Don't scare those pigs now," Pa said. "If you do they're liable to run and hurt their selves. We gotta keep them real calm while they're tied up."

"How we do that?"

"By keeping them well fed."

"What 'bout if a bear comes in the night to eat them, Pa?"

"I got that covered, boy. Soon as I hear those pigs squealing, I'll come out here with my musket and blow that bear to kingdom come."

Only way you'll do that is by putting the muzzle of that musket of yours right up against the bear's head, because that musket ain't worth a damn, and it don't shoot straight. And as for waking up, you might do that right enough when you're sober, but what 'bout when you're drunk? The school bell wouldn't wake you up if you was drunk, not even if I was to put it right next to your head before ringing it. I didn't say those words out loud, I knowed better'n to risk sayin' them out loud, but I thought them.

"If you hear those pigs squealing at night you make sure I'm woken up, boy," Pa said. "I don't want no bear eating our dinner."

"Got that, Pa." So it was down to me to make sure he woke up when the bears came. That order was as tall as orders get. I seen corpses livelier than Pa when he's sleeping off a skinful. Looked like it was gonna be down to me to scare any bears that came our way. If I didn't and the pigs got eaten I'd be in for the switching of my life. I hoped to God we'd be slaughtering the pigs before any bears showed up.

Ma and Pa was hoping those pigs would have piglets we could sell but they never did, so Pa said we'd feed them up, and he'd turn them into bacon and salt pork. The feeding up was my concern, and because Ma and Pa had no money to buy feed, I had to find it. I was meant to get it from the woods, but that would've taken too long, so I got it from the fields 'round about the edge of the woods, rutabaga mostly. Got the rutabaga at night when no one was around. Sure must've pissed off a lot of farmers in those parts.

Regarding the liquor, it didn't seem to do much to Pa when he first took to it. He just drank it and got drunk and slept it off. But by and by he got to being a wide-awake drunk. Then he got to being a wide-awake ornery drunk and hit me and Ma pretty regular, mainly me. He had leathery hands that came of living off the land, and although he was skinny his slap was like the kick of a mule. Sent me reeling cross the cabin more'n once. I was watching him filling a can from that half-gallon jug of his once when he turned on me.

"What you looking at, boy?"

Scared of what he might do, I didn't answer.

"I said, what you looking at, boy?"

"Nothing, Pa."

He set down his can and came striding over to me, then Bam! Before I knowed it I was on the floor senseless. My head throbbed for hours afterward. After that I'd leave the cabin whenever I saw Pa getting drunk. Took to spending most of my time in my shed with just my thoughts for company. Seeing as it didn't have any windows in it I'd lie around in the dark or light a candle when I could get one. A candle made it nice and homey and gave a body comfort.

I wouldn't say Pa was right good before he took to drink, but he was a sight better than he was after he took to it. Before he was a drunk he'd teach me things and be nice to me some of the time. He was what you might call tolerable. Likeable, even. I got the impression he loved me even when he was tanning the hide offa me. After the drink got him I counted myself lucky when he warn't downright nasty. And the only time he warn't downright nasty was when he was asleep or not around. Absence makes the heart grow fonder, they say. Well, when Pa was someplace else it didn't make my heart any fonder of him. It did make me rest easier, but I dreaded him coming back. Ma loved him, but even she found him hard to stomach.

"This keeps up I swear to God I'll slit Pa's throat next time he passes out in fronta me," she'd say. Then she'd look guilty, and I knowed she was thinking of God and working out whether she had any chance of getting to heaven when she'd been harboring such thoughts as those about Pa.

I harbored them myself. More than once when he was lying on the floor snoring I thought about getting the sling blade and using it to separate his head from his body. But although I thought about it, I knowed I couldn't do it. He was my Pa after all, and in spite of all I loved him, and somehow I knowed that in his own strange way he still loved me. There's something special about a pa to his boy and about a boy to his pa, even though it didn't often feel that way in our family.

My worst fear happened one night when I heard a pig moving about. It warn't squealing so I knowed a bear hadn't attacked it, but I also knowed that the pig had been affrighted. I could tell by the way it was moving it was likely it'd smelled a bear. Most likely the bear had tried to creep up on the pig from downwind, but the wind had changed. Springing out of bed I left my shed and ran to Ma and Pa's cabin. Didn't stop even to pull my pants on. Pushed open the door and grabbed Pa's musket from the shelf he kept it on then walked quietly to where the hogs was tethered. Bears can see better'n people in the dark. One mistake and the bear would be eating me rather than a hog. It'd be disappointed if it did. Warn't any meat on me to speak of. Last thing I wanted was to end my life as a disappointment to a bear.

Crouching low I stole out the gate. Pigs was getting real excited now. Where was that bear? One piece of good fortune was the moon was bright, glinting silver against the edge of a gray cloud. That gave me something to see by at least, not much, but a drowning man is grateful for any straw, so they say. Pa's old musket was too long and heavy for me to carry against my shoulder. I had to hold the barrel in the crook of my left arm with the stock under my right. Even then it was a burden for me. No way could I aim it like that. If I was to shoot at anything with any chance of hitting it, it'd have to be point-blank.

Soon enough I heard a low growl and damn near wet myself. I was near enough stark naked and felt like I was well on the way to becoming a meal for a bear. Ain't no feeling like it, and I can't say I recommend it. Bear came a-walking steady at me on all fours. I heard it on the soft earth. Bears are quiet but when you've lived in the woods all your life you can hear just about any animal if you listen out hard enough for it. Was the bear gonna charge? If it did, would I get it before it got me?

Our cabin was in a natural clearing. Around it was the fence Pa built when he was still capable of building things, and all around that was the edge of the woods. Tied to two of the trees at the edge of the woods was the pigs. Damned if that warn't the stupidest thing we coulda done with those hogs. Only thing we got going for us was pigs are intelligent. They knowed better than to stray among the trees at night, and they kept close as they could to our fence. So Big Ol' Bear would have to show hisself if he wanted to eat one of them. I just hoped that's what he'd do, and he wouldn't come after me. Quiet as could be I stole round the outside of the fence toward the pigs, every now and again stopping to listen out for the bear. I heard him only a few yards away and shivered, knowing I could hear him so he could hear me, and he'd be a-listening on my every footstep. Even with the pigs squealing he'd hear me. I was hearing him after all, loud and clear.

The pigs was straining at their tethers as far away from the trees and as close to our fence as they could get, their tethers pulled tight. The tree trunks was dark poles sticking up into the night sky, and the gaps between them black slits that anything could have been hiding in. I knowed for a fact a big ol' bear was hiding in one of them. Which one was he gonna come out of? He had a choice of at least three. Creeping up close to the pigs I got them covered as best I could. Wondered if I might not be better off going back to my shed and hiding till the bear was gone. Maybe a certain switching was better'n a chance of death. Why hadn't I thought of that before?

Then it was too late to go back to my shed. Big Old Bear came out looking for his next meal and came right at me. He might've been going for one of the hogs, but I was between the hog and Mr. Bear. Teeth gleamed in the moonlight. His mouth was wide open and ready to take chunks outta me.

How quick do you think a bear charges? Think again. It charges a whole lot faster than that. You ain't gonna outrun that ol' bear, not even on a horse. It was at me like a bullet from a gun, and I ain't got no time to think. *Just wait till it's on me and pull the trigger and pray to God it goes off,* I thought. Swear to God the muzzle of that musket was touching the bear inside its mouth no less before I pulled the trigger. The noise it made would've woken up the whole town if I'd been standin' on the main street, but seeing as I was miles away everyone slept soundly in their beds not knowing of the hell I was going through. Smoke erupted around Mr. Bear's head, and he growled some more, came right at me, and knocked me over. Just when I thought I was dead he fell sideways. Pa slept through it all. It was morning before he learned what'd happened. Ma came out to see what all the fuss was about. My legs was trapped under the bear, and I couldn't get out. With her help I managed.

"You did good, Joe," she said. "We can eat bear

for weeks now, maybe months."

"Sure thing, Ma. It's too big to drag in the yard. We gonna have to butcher it out here and carry it in in pieces. It'll have to wait till daylight."

"I know that, son. You and me and Pa can do it together. It's gonna take all three of us to butcher that bear and salt it for the winter."

Even Pa was impressed when he saw that bear. Didn't say anything. Just patted me on the shoulder and nodded. Made me feel real proud of myself.

Ma went to town and got some salt and barrels. She had to beg, borrow, and steal to get them. Promised the storekeeper she'd give him some salted bear meat in return for the goods. Me and Pa skinned and cut up the animal and took the pieces into the yard. You can't take any chances with bear meat. It can make you real sick. So we salted and cooked the meat in big pots over an outdoor fire and let it cool before preserving it. We put some in barrels just in its own fat. They call that a confit. It tastes good and lasts a long while. We put the rest in barrels and added lotsa salt. That tastes almost as good as a confit and lasts forever, or for a very long time, anyways. Pa kept the barrels in the cabin. No telling what would happen to them if we didn't keep them safe like that.

The barrels disappeared before me and Ma got to taste much bear meat. Pa disappeared with them, but he came back before long. Later I heard he'd made a pile of money selling salted bear round town. Spent it all in the saloon.

I've just realized I still haven't told you the thing about Pa which made that year special, at least for a while. I got back from school one day, and he warn't around and nor was the pigs. I thought nothing of it other than I knowed it meant we wouldn't be eating pork any time soon. Next day when I got back from school I said to Ma, "Where's Pa?"

"I don't know, son. It looks like your Pa's disappeared someplace and taken our pigs with him."

She was sad but not as sad as she ought to have been at losing her man. I knowed how she felt. I was sad, too, but I should've been a lot sadder at the loss of my Pa. Truth is, I could see the advantages of Pa disappearing, and try as I might I couldn't see much in the way of drawbacks. I began being happy at home and stopped worrying about Pa getting drunk and making my life hell.

There was one nagging thought back of my mind, though. Pa had become so unpredictable there was no telling where he might be or what he might do.

5.

EVEN MORE SECRETS

FOURTH THING MADE 1861 SPECIAL WAS MR. Purdy.

Took me by surprise when I called for Cath and he said, "You know how to shoot, Joe?"

"A little, Mr. Purdy."

"A man oughta know how to shoot. I'll take you out of town, and we'll do some shooting together."

I would've rather seen Cath than go shooting with her pa, but I wanted to keep on the right side of Mr. Purdy so I said, "I'd like that."

"We'll take the cart. Help me get a horse between the shafts, Joe." We got the cart sorted, and he said, "I got some bottles." I musta looked puzzled because he said, "To shoot at, it's fun. They explode when you hit 'em."

I couldn't see how that was as much fun as shooting rabbits would have been, plus, you'd have got your dinner as well as having fun by shooting rabbits, but I kept my views to myself. It was always the best way when speaking with grownups.

Mr. Purdy opened a wooden crate back of his stable. It had more bottles in it than a body could shake a stick at. Handing me a sack he said, "Help me carry them."

I filled it with bottles while he filled another sack.

He winked at me. "I get 'em from the saloon. Drunks get through a lot of liquor in these parts."

That was one thing he didn't need to tell me. We loaded them on the back of his cart, and he put a couple of muskets and six guns and some powder and bullets on the back, and we set off. A few people who saw us asked where we was going. "Just out of town to do some shooting," Mr. Purdy said. "I'm giving Joe here shooting lessons."

Once we was far enough away from town that the noise of gunfire warn't gonna scare anybody, he stopped the cart and we got off. Mr. Purdy set up ten bottles on a big rock and we walked away from them to another rock.

He showed me how to load a musket, which I already knowed, of course. Only thing I didn't know was how to put powder in it, because Mr. Purdy's musket worked different from Pa's old musket. Mr. Purdy didn't have a horn full of powder. He had paper cartridges you bit the end off before pouring the powder from them into the barrel. It gave you the same amount of powder every time. Not like when me and Pa loaded up his musket with powder. When we poured it from the horn it was guesswork how much went in.

Mr. Purdy tamped down the powder with a ramrod and tamped the bullet on top of it. "Watch me, Joe." Standing tall he put the butt of the musket to his shoulder and squeezed the trigger. There was a powerful noise and a whole lot of smoke and a bottle at the end of the row exploded just like he'd said it would. "Your turn now." The musket was too heavy for me to hold to my shoulder and aim. "You rest the barrel on that boulder, son," he said. First time he called me son. It felt kinda good, even though I already had a pa. Taking careful aim I squeezed the trigger and the bottle next to the one Mr. Purdy shot went into the air in tiny pieces. "That's good, son, you're a natural."

I never told him his musket was a sight easier to hit anything with than Pa's. I reckon if you could shoot Pa's musket and hit a target you could hit any target with any old musket. So Pa trained me well probably without even knowing it.

As we worked our way through Mr. Purdy's bottles Jessee Elliott came riding by. "What's going on, Corman?"

Mr. Purdy winked at me. "I'm having a shooting contest with young Joe here. He's whipping the hide offa me. Show him, Joe."

My musket was loaded, so I took aim and blasted a bottle.

"How far is that?" Jessee asked. "Must be a hundred yards at least. That boy can really shoot. You taught him well, Corman."

"Hell, this boy's a natural, I ain't taught him anything." Jessee touched his hat and rode off. Mr. Purdy said, "I'm gonna get me one of those new Springfields before long."

"What's that, Mr. Purdy?"

"The new Springfield musket. Takes a conical ball and shoots it accurately four times farther than this old thing."

When we'd had enough of shooting muskets we shot the six-guns. Good thing about six-guns is you don't need to load up after every shot. Bad thing is you couldn't hit the proverbial barn door with one unless you was right up against it, and even then you might miss.

We shot for a few hours. I got to fire more bullets

than I'd ever shot in my life before. I guess Mr. Purdy could afford for me to use up a mess of bullets and not think about it. Ma and Pa and me, we always had to think about anything that cost us so much as a cent.

When we was done with shooting Mr. Purdy said, "You're good, Joe. You can shoot like a man."

I have to admit that made me feel real proud, like the door of manhood was swinging wide open for me and all I had to do was walk right through it. I realized then I'd enjoyed shooting with Mr. Purdy almost as much as spending time with his daughter.

Back in town whenever we bumped into anyone Mr. Purdy told them what we'd been up to then gave me a wink and told them how I'd whupped him at shooting bottles. I thought nothing of it at the time, other than I was proud of it, of course. And a bit embarrassed, too. My face reddened when he told folks, but I didn't mind none.

Mr. Purdy was another of those men you would've thought didn't have no secrets he kept from anyone. Turns out he did.

I thought that afternoon I spent shooting with Mr. Purdy was one of the best things that ever happened to me, but I was wrong. Turns out it was one of the worst.

6.

RIGHT AND WRONG AT THE SAME TIME

THE FIFTH THING THAT MADE 1861 SPECIAL WAS Cath's brother Max Purdy. Max was twenty-five and tall as his pa but slim. Always wore the finest clothes, which was black mostly. They must have come from St. Louis or someplace like that, they had so much style about them. Max had a dangerous cast to his eye, but that didn't put no one off him. Seemed to make him more interesting, somehow.

I was doing some chores for Mr. Purdy one afternoon when Max came out of their house, leaned against the door frame with his long legs crossed, and lit up a cigar. As he was smoking it Mrs. Guyler came by with Miss Sidney. Mrs. Guyler was twenty-five and newly wed, and Miss Sidney was nineteen. Max looked at them both from under the brim of his hat with those dangerous eyes of his and gave them a smile that put me in mind of a timber wolf. Both those ladies smiled back, and Miss Sidney turned redder'n a ripe tomato. After they'd walked by the two ladies whispered to each other, and both of them giggled. I sure wished I coulda had that effect on women. Hoped I would someday. Max noticed I'd seen what'd happened, and he gave me a sly wink that seemed to say, "I did that just for the hell of it, Joe."

When I got back to doing the chores I tried my best to look easy and casual like Max always looked while I was at it. Don't think I managed. Next time I saw him he was going into the saloon with a group of men, rough types, all of them laughing and joshing. I sneaked in while no one was looking. Easy enough when you duck under the swing doors and run like hell bent double. I hid under a table watching them drink whiskey, play cards, and smoke. Max was the one who did all the joshing, and his friends did all of the laughing. Whenever he talked, they listened. Struck me that when I talked folks got deaf at least half the time, and the other half their hearing warn't too good. I wished I could be one of Max's friends and be close to him so that some of what he got might rub off on me.

A week later Max said, "I saw you under that table."

"What table?" I was trying to bluff it out.

"The one in the saloon."

No point in bluffing any more. He'd got me, and he had me real affrighted. Was he gonna tell my ma and Miss Larsen I'd been in the saloon? We kids had all been warned by Miss Larsen never to go in there. Ma didn't have to warn me. I knowed where she stood on the saloon without being told, and I knowed that me being seen in a saloon would earn me the granddaddy of all leatherins.

"Don't look so worried, Joe, I ain't gonna tell on you. Truth is I enjoyed watching you crouch there. Gave me something to take my mind off the conversation I was havin' when it got boring. Those friends of mine are okay, but one or two of 'em talk an awful lot without sayin' too much. Ever known anyone like that, Joe?"

My tongue wouldn't work, so I couldn't answer. It felt like such an honor that Max had even noticed me, let alone was talkin' to me, that I was all excited and tongue-tied.

He slapped his arm around my shoulder. "You don't have to tell me right away. You can think 'bout it if you need to."

The way Max had got his hand on my shoulder made me feel better somehow, and my tongue started working again, and I got to feelin' I could do things easy like him. "Don't know if I do know anyone talks that way. Maybe Fraser Tuski. He's the only one."

"We all meet bores, Joe. The world's full of 'em. You shouldn't be nasty to 'em, but avoid 'em if you can, they make life miserable. Important thing is not to be a bore yourself, don't you think?"

I found myself nodding. "Yes, I do think that, Max."

"You're growing up real fast. I noticed how you changed since you started seeing my sister. You got a lot more 'bout you now than you did a few months back."

"Thank you."

"Tell you what. How'd you like to grow up some more?"

"What do you mean?"

"I got a bottle of whiskey, real good stuff. You could share it with me. Would you like that?"

I thought about it. Ma didn't want me to drink, not that she'd said so, and I knowed she'd find out if I did. There was no hiding that smell. I'd smelled it on Pa often enough to know that. Was it worth Ma's anger to share a bottle of whiskey with Max? Didn't have to think too long, maybe half a second.

"That'd be great, Max, thank you."

"Let's go somewhere nice and private then. You

climb on the back of my horse."

I clumb up, and he rode just out of town, and we found a couple of tree stumps to set on. He had a swig from the bottle and passed it to me.

"Not too much now, you hear?" he said when I put it to my lips. It tasted warm and smooth. I just had a sip. "That's good, Joe."

We talked some I don't recall what it was about, but it kept me real happy and interested and in among the talking he and I kept on sipping his whiskey.

And then he said, "That's enough, Joe."

I was enjoying it mightily by then. "Why can't I have more?"

"Because you wouldn't thank me if I gave you more. Part of being a man is knowing your limits, Joe. Nothing manly 'bout rolling around drunk and throwing your guts up all over your clothes." I wondered if he was talking about Pa. He glanced at the sky. When he saw where the sun was, he said, "We better go," and we both rode back into town on his horse. I felt like I'd just made the best friend in the world. Turned out I was right and wrong at the same time.

7.

LIGHTNING FROM A CLEAR SKY

NOW COMES THE TRAGEDY, THE THING THAT made 1861 my worst year.

It was close to the fall of 1861 when I finished school and headed over to Ervan's place on a cold day. My feet was covered in soft boots made of deerskin greased to keep the water out. Made them myself the way Pa showed me. As I headed down the trail I heard gunfire in the distance. Two shots, one of 'em muffled. Didn't pay much heed to it as you hear sounds like that in our neck of the woods all the time. Bob Finn and Lowrie Cheetham, a couple of trappers from Wisconsin, was trigger happy and was always letting their guns off. And Mr. Purdy was on the trigger-happy side, too.

When I got to Ervan's I was surprised Arthur warn't guarding the place like he usually was. Hardly a day passed without I saw Arthur on Ervan's land when I passed. I didn't think anything of it because oftentimes Ervan had Arthur inside his cabin for company. A man living on his own treats his dog like a person. Talks to it even though there ain't no way on earth a dog can hold up its end of the conversation. I've seen it many times.

I had to get home to do my chores, and if I was late Ma would be mad at me, and one thing I didn't want was Ma mad at me. She'd cowhide me, then she'd start pecking at me. And she pecked at me enough when she was in a good mood, so I had no wish to get her in a bad one. Even so I decided to call on Ervan just to check up on him. I started walking across his land toward his cabin expecting Arthur any second to jump out at me a-barking, but he never did.

Before I got to the cabin I found him lying in the dirt among bushes, and he warn't moving. His head had a hole in it with blood in the dirt next to it. He'd been shot. The blood hadn't dried out so he ain't been shot long. My heart beat louder than a drum in battle and faster, too. I ran to Ervan's cabin, opened the door, and saw Ervan giving me a mean stare. He scared the hell out of me, and I stepped back breathless, the wind all gone from my chest not from running but because of Ervan. *You gotta go in there and do something, Joe*, I told myself and went back inside. Now I looked at Ervan properly.

He was lying on the floor next to his kitchen table, what was left of his head twisted to one side with his eyes and mouth wide open. I knowed right away from the burns on his face a bullet had gone through it. His Samuel Colt six-gun was lying next to him. When I walked around him I saw the bullet that kilt him had made a real mess of his head. I didn't know if I should be scared or mourn the passing of a true friend. In the end I did both and burst into tears. That went against Pa's teaching.

When I was done crying, I didn't know whether to go back to town to tell folks what'd happened or go to the cabin to tell Ma first. After some dithering I decided I better see Ma first and said my goodbyes to Ervan most respectfully even though he couldn't hear me or answer back, then I left his house. Right away I saw Jessee Elliott riding his horse on the trail toward town. He stared at me, eyes narrowed. I set off running home and waved at Mr. Elliott, and he stared at me even narrower eyed, then he touched the brim of his hat with his hand. Got to the cabin and told Ma about Ervan. Took a while to get her to listen as she was hell-bent on leatherin' me for getting home late, but in the end she listened.

"Run to town and tell the Pastor," she said, "he'll know what to do."

So I ran to the church fast as I could, burst in, and found Pastor Graham. Blurted out my news. "Ervan Foster's dead, Pastor Graham. I just seen it with my own eyes."

Pastor looked at me and raised his eyebrows and his mouth dropped open. "You sure, Joe? You sure he's dead?"

"That I am, Pastor. I saw him lying on the floor with a bullet through his head."

"A bullet? You mean somebody shot him?"

"Looks that way to me."

It was a long time before Pastor Graham replied. Finally he said, "We better go out there and see what's been going on. We need to get Corman Purdy. He's public-minded, and he'll help us move Ervan to a place where we can get him ready for a good Christian burial." The Pastor was already thinking of putting Ervan under the ground next to the church where my dead brother was buried. That warn't what I was interested in. But I didn't say anything. I'd learned it's better folk don't know what you're thinking most of the time.

"Sorry to hear that, Joe," said Mr. Purdy when I told him about Ervan. "I'll get a cart ready." He fastened his best horse between the shafts of a cart, then the three of us sat on the bench seat up front. With a wristy flick on the reins Mr. Purdy got his horse moving. Rain fell as soon as we set off. It was a bumpy ride to Ervan's place, and we rode it in silence, the rain seeming to speak for us. The only noise came from the horse and from rocks grinding and slipping beneath the wheels. We got there soaked to the skin and all went inside shaking ourselves dry as we did.

"It's just like you said it was, Joe," Pastor Graham said, staring down at the floor. "Looks like Ervan was bushwhacked." He glanced around the room then went to the other rooms and came back a minute later. "Ain't none of his stuff gone missing, looks like. Why would anyone kill Ervan and not take any of his things?"

Mr. Purdy meanwhile walked around Ervan's body, looking at it every which way, then picked up Ervan's six-gun and smelled the end of it. "It's been fired," he said, "and not that long ago. Could be he was defending hisself. You say his dog Arthur was shot, Joe?"

"That's right, Mr. Purdy."

Mr. Purdy shook his head. "Looks like someone kilt the dog then came after Ervan. Musta been someone pretty handy with a gun because Ervan warn't a man to be trifled with. He knowed how to take care of hisself."

Pastor stroked his chin. "Whoever kilt him ain't taken anything, not that I can see anyways. Why do you think they kilt him, Corman?"

Mr. Purdy stood with his feet planted real firm and his hands on his hips. "Could have been someone from Ervan's past out for revenge. Most likely though it was someone wanting Ervan's gold who warn't interested in taking anything else. The gold was probably worth more than everything else put together, so it warn't worth taking anything else. Probably took the gold from wherever Ervan had hidden it without messing the place up."

Pastor nodded, looking as if lotsa wheels was going round in his head, making him dizzy. The thought came to me I shoulda looked for tracks outside Ervan's house as soon as I found him dead, but I never did. Now it'd be too late. Rain woulda washed the tracks all away.

Mr. Purdy, sounding real angry, said, "We could get some men together and look for Ervan's killers."

"You mean a lynch mob, Corman?" said Pastor Graham. "Two wrongs don't make a right."

"No, I mean justice, Pastor. But don't worry it ain't gonna happen. I reckon it's too late for that. Those bastards have too much of a lead on us."

"If you change your mind, just make sure the person you catch gets a fair trial. We've already had too much summary justice in this town." Mr. Purdy didn't say nothing to that.

The pastor closed Ervan's eyes and crossed hisself and said a prayer, then between us we loaded Ervan's body onto the cart and headed back into town. "We'll put him in the church for now," said Pastor Graham, "to show him respect. Then I'll tell Fred 'bout what's happened." Fred was the undertaker. He was also the owner of the general store. He was also the mailman. He would have been the judge, too, if we'd had call for one, that's what folk reckoned anyways. But as we didn't even have a sheriff it would've been jumping the proverbial to appoint a judge.

We carried Ervan to the church wrapped in a

blanket so no one would see what had happened to him. A couple of people watched us, and I knowed they'd be asking the pastor what was going on first chance they got.

Mr. Purdy said, "I'll leave everything in your good hands now, Pastor."

Pastor Graham took Mr. Purdy by the arm. "Could I have a word with you in private, Corman?" he said and led Mr. Purdy to a small room at the side of the church.

I stood outside and did my best to listen to what they was talking about, but all I could hear was hushed murmurings, then the two of them came out both of them looking very serious. Me and Mr. Purdy said goodbye to the pastor, and I said a private goodbye to Ervan in my head, and we left.

I was about to set off walking home when Mr. Purdy said, "Jump up next to me on the cart, Joe." So I did. Gave me a look with his eyebrows crossed, flicked the reins in that way of his, and the horse set off. The way his face was set he looked just like Pastor Graham had done like he had wheels goin' round in his head.

He pulled up the cart outside his house. I said, "Thank you for the ride, Mr. Purdy," jumped down, and headed home.

8.

BLUE PAINT MOURNING

WHEN I GOT BACK TO THE CABIN, I SEEN MA filling a can from Pa's whiskey jug when she thought I warn't looking. She took a good mouthful and put the can on a high shelf I couldn't reach. She told me to peel a sight of potatoes for a stew she was making and went outside to sit on the porch while I got them peeled. Soon as she was gone I stood on a chair and got the can down and looked inside to make sure I was right about it being full of whiskey. It was dark in the front room so I couldn't tell if it was whiskey or not. The light caught it, and it rippled, but water would've done the same. So I smelt it. It sure did smell like whiskey, but I needed to test it some more, so I put the can to my lips and took a good swig. It felt like a bush fire burning in my mouth. That's when I knowed for certain it was whiskey. It warn't like Max's whiskey though, it had more fire in it than his. So much I could hardly drink it. But I'd heard it made you feel good when you was feeling bad, and I was feeling bad as I'd ever felt on account of Ervan, so later I filled up a can myself and took it to a cornfield where Ma wouldn't see me. Finished off the lot of it even though I hated the way it burned my insides. Wanted to feel better about things than I did, and I was miserable as hell. Not long after that I got to feeling good and lay on my back among the corn looking up at the sky. The blue of it looked bluer than usual, if that's possible. I told myself, *Now I know why people like whiskey.* Soon as I said that to myself the sky above me started to spin and it made me scared, so I got to my feet and found I couldn't walk straight no more. Now I knowed why the town drunk staggered the way he did. I thought I better get along home and lay down in my shed till I felt right.

Ma caught me outside. "You been drinking!" she said as soon as she saw me.

"How do you know Ma?"

"You're walking like a drunk, Goddamnit. I ought to take the strap to you, but there's no point being as you probably wouldn't feel it. Go sleep it off, and don't dare touch that whiskey again!"

I turned to go to my shed and before I went two paces I got ridda my last meal and all the whiskey I'd drunk. It came outta my mouth and went two yards through the air before landing on the potatoes in Ma's vegetable patch.

"Lucky for you it warn't the lettuce," she said. "If it had been I woulda made you eat the one you threw up your guts on."

I didn't bother thanking her for her leniency in not forcing me to eat the leaves of the potato plants that got covered in my throwings-up. I just rinsed out my mouth with water and went straight to bed.

My shoulders shook. Opening my eyes I saw it was Pa. He was back. The good life was over.

"I hear you've been at my whiskey," he said.

"What if I have? You sold both of the pigs, and one of 'em was mine."

"How d'you work that out?"

"I helped catch 'em both, and I fed the both of 'em. I did more'n half the work, so I'm entitled to at least half the bounty."

Grabbing me by my shirt he hauled me to my feet. "You'll shut your mouth, boy, if you know what's good for you. Those pigs was all mine. The whiskey is mine. And you're mine. You touch that whiskey again I'll leather you till you wish you was dead." Letting me go he dropped his hands to his sides, then he raised one of them again and pointed a grubby finger at me. "You hear me?"

"I hear you, and I'd rather be dead than have a pa like you."

His face was a picture and not a pretty one. Black as an Illinois thundercloud and just as menacing.

Knowing what he'd do next I pushed him in the chest. He warn't expecting it, so he fell over. "You owe me, Pa," I said. "Give me what's mine. Half the money you got for the pigs."

"Why . . . you . . ." he said, getting up, and I ran from my shed.

Spent the next two days hiding out in the woods to keep away from Pa. Only when the coast was clear did I come back.

"Where is he?" I asked Ma. I didn't have to say who she knowed who I meant. "He's gone, but he'll be back. That's the way with drunks. They come and go in your life."

Pa had left a few things behind. A wood box of cigars. A pair of leather boots. A railroad cap. I listed them in my head.

Ma's eyes softened. "I know why you got drunk on that whiskey. It was over Ervan, warn't it? What a turrble tragedy. You shouldn'ta done it but at least you had good reason." She crossed herself and went outside to the place she thought I didn't know about where she hid what little money she had to keep Pa from getting his hands on it. Came back a short time later and pressed some cash in my hand. Crossed herself again. "Go to the general store and get some blue paint." That was another job for me to do. Two jobs if you count the paintin'. As if I didn't have enough on my plate already.

"All right, Ma."

Wagging her finger in my face she said, "And be quick 'bout it."

"Okay, Ma, I'll be right quick." I warn't, though. Dragged my feet somewhat. Felt like things had been getting me down since Ervan got hisself kilt. Anyways, I bought the paint and brung it home.

"Paint the doorframe blue," she said. "We ain't got no porch so that'll have to do." She handed me a stick with a heap of rags tied to the end of it. Looked like my pants tied to the end of a stick, only smaller. "We ain't got no brush. Use this."

I did the best job I could of painting our doorframe blue. It warn't no expert job being as I didn't have the right tools, and the lines warn't straight as they might have been, but it was the best I could manage. I took a real pride in it being as I was doing the job for Ervan in a manner of speaking. When I was done I shut my eyes and bowed my head and said, "Rest easy, Ervan, I'm thinking 'bout you, and I'll never forget you." As God is my witness I meant it. Still think about Ervan to this day. I can see him now in my mind's eye.

Not much to tell you about Ervan's funeral other than the whole town was there like they always were for funerals. It was raining, and we got soaked through standing around the grave while the coffin was lowered in. It felt like some of the townsfolk were looking at me out the corners of their eyes and muttering about me, but I paid them no heed. Told myself it was the way they treated us Wilds, and nothing I did was gonna make any difference. I'd just have to ignore them and do my best to keep my dignity.

When I saw Pa a week later he didn't mention leatherin' me. Just came in the cabin and helped hisself to the bottle of whiskey he'd somehow gotten from somewhere. Ma was busy sewing. When he came in she put it to one side and went to tend her vegetable patch.

I ought to have found an excuse to leave the cabin myself but instead I said, "Where did you get the cigars, Pa?"

"Bought them with the money I got for the pigs."

"Funny, they look just like the cigars Ervan used to smoke."

His mouth said nothing, but he got lines in his forehead.

"That cap you got looks like the cap Ervan had."

His forehead got more lines on it. "What you saying, boy?"

"I'm saying Ervan's dead, and you got his things, and I want to know how you came by them."

His lip curled and a snarl came outta his mouth like a grizzly with a headache. Made me jump so hard I crashed into the wall at the back of me. He laughed out loud, and that's when I got mad. Don't know what got into me truth be known. Something been building up inside of me for years, I guess. Whatever it was I went for my Pa. Ran at him swinging both fists. First one caught him on the side of the head. Took him by surprise but it didn't hurt him none. It put an end to his laughing, though. He raised an arm and blocked my second swing. Then we got to rassling, and I might've thrown another punch that did nothing at all to stop my Pa. Like me he had no meat on him, but unlike me he got some strength in him. Man strength, you'd call it. Picking me up he threw me at the window, and I flew right through it as if it warn't there into the sheet Pa had nailed on to keep the wind out. Sheet tore off the nails and wrapped around me. I landed on the dirt at the side of the house. It'd been a hot summer and that dirt was baked hard as iron. It knocked the breath right out of me, and for a while I couldn't even think let alone move. After a while my senses came back to me little by little, and I pushed the sheet to one side. My head was spinning, but at least I could think, and what I thought was, *One day I'm gonna get my own back on that evil drunken murdering sonofabitch.* Not that I really knowed he was a murderer. It was one of those thoughts you get in the heat of the moment. But still, he might have been, and it was preying on my mind.

Not really thinking I headed into town. Walked by the Purdy place wondering if I might see Cath, but I didn't. I hadn't seen her for a while and was missing her. As I went past I stared at the window and saw Cath staring out at me. When she caught my eye she looked away, and I knowed from the expression on her face that whatever we had between us it was over. Funny how just one look like that that lasts no more than the time it takes you to blink can tell you so much. I felt tears coming to my eyes, but they didn't get there. Sort of stopped before they came out. Pa had told me not to cry when I was growing up, and by the time I was twelve I couldn't cry no more no matter how much I was hurting. All my cryin' came later, apart from when Ervan died. But believe me when I tell you my heart was broken by Catherine Purdy that day even though you might not have known it if you saw me. It was broke so bad it felt as if I'd never put it back together.

I hung around outside the Purdys' house for a while hoping maybe Cath would come back to the window and give me a smile, or she'd open the door and tell me she'd made a big mistake and wanted to still be my girl, but she never did. Deep down I'd knowed she never would. That look of hers she'd given me through the window was final, if you know what I mean. It was closing off whatever had gone before. You can know such things even though you've never had experience of them to tell you what they mean.

Further along the dirt track we called our main street I saw Pastor Graham. He turned away from me. I hurried up to him and said, "What's wrong, Pastor?"

He made the sign of a cross. "You know what's wrong, Joe."

"No, I don't, tell me."

He stopped and stared me right in the eye. "The more I think 'bout it, the more I think I know who it is kilt Ervan." He crossed hiself again. "Not just me who thinks it, either."

The way he was acting made me kinda queasy. "So who is it kilt Ervan?" I asked, my voice all shaky because I was worried he was gonna say Pa kilt Ervan. Pastor Graham's answer made my insides squirm some more. Pointing at me he said, "You, Joe. I think you kilt Ervan Foster."

My insides damn near turned to water.

Pastor lowered his finger. "Something I didn't tell you 'bout, Joe. I didn't see no call to at the time, but now I see it's real important. Before you came to tell me Ervan Foster had died I saw Jessee Elliott. He told me he heard gunfire at Ervan Foster's spread and when he rode past he saw you coming out of Ervan's house. Said you looked mighty shook up like you was guilty of something. Since then I've been putting two and two together and speaking to Mr. Purdy and some of the other folks around town. Turns out you saw Ervan all the time and went to his cabin all the time. If anyone knowed where his gold was hidden, you did. You know how to shoot, you're an expert. If anyone shot Ervan it was probably you so you could help yourself to some of that gold of his. But you shot his dog first so it wouldn't be no danger to you."

My feet walked me backward away from the pastor without my even wanting them to. "I didn't kill him!" I shouted. "I didn't kill Ervan, you got that wrong, Pastor. I never kilt Ervan. I wouldn't have done that. He was my friend."

All of a sudden the pastor and I warn't alone. The fuss I'd kicked up brought a few of the townsfolk out of their cabins. Storekeeper came and stood in the doorway of his general store. Saloon owner came to the doors of his saloon. Everybody looking at me. Going by their faces it was clear enough what they was thinking. They was, to a man, woman, and child, judge, jury, and executioner rolled into one, and they'd decided the verdict without looking at the evidence. They'd found me guilty of killing Ervan. The sentence was death. I saw it in their eyes and heard it in their murmurs. I was in an awful peck of trouble. If I didn't get out of there powerful quick they'd form a lynch mob to string me up from the nearest beam or branch of a tree. I knowed it because I'd seen it done. But that's a story for another time. I never gave them a chance to lynch me. Soon as I saw which way the wind was blowing, I turned and ran fast as I'd ever run in my life. It was a dry day, thank God. If it'd been raining that main street of ours would've been too slippery to run fast. So you could say my luck was in for once if you ignore the fact I had the whole town baying for my blood.

When they saw me running a cry went up. "Get him! Get the murdering little sonofabitch!" I might have heard the words "String him up! String him up!" in and among the hue and cry, but that could have been my imagination. Then again maybe not. Folks in our town liked their justice summary. Didn't care for it to be drawn out. We didn't have a courthouse in our neck of the woods, only law was gun law, and the closest thing we had to a judge was a length of rope. So you'll understand why I was so eager to make myself scarce.

9.

'BOUT THE WAR

GOT TO TELL YOU SOMETHING ABOUT THE WAR
now since it comes into my story.

Folks was speculating 'bout the war for a long
time before it came. At least a year before it started
the townsfolk was wondering if it was gonna happen. Then the Rebs attacked Fort Sumter, and we all
knowed it had begun. Nobody died in the battle for Fort
Sumter, which gave us ideas about what sort of war it
was gonna be. A short and bloodless one. It also gave
some folks ideas 'bout joining one of the armies. In
our town we was close enough to the southern states
that we could have chosen to enlist in whichever army
we wanted North or South, which put some folks in a
quandary. They had kin in the South. They didn't want
to fight their kin, but they didn't want to fight for the
South either. Then there was others couldn't wait to
fight their own kin. They'd held grudges against their
kinfolk for years, and at last they had an excuse to do
something about it.

But not many in our town went to fight. Not in
1861 anyways. They mostly thought it warn't worth
it. It was gonna be such a short war there was no
point getting involved. It'd all be over before a body
even got sight of a battlefield.

I had no idea what the country was meant to be
fighting about. People talked about keeping the Union
but that meant nothing to me. The Union hadn't done

anything I could point to by way of making my life better, so I warn't bothered about the Union, and I warn't bothered about the Confederacy either. Couldn't see how a branch lopped offa a tree could be any better than the tree itself.

Miss Larsen had views, and she made 'em clear. The Union was bigger'n any person she said, it was a cause and a just cause at that. The North was bound to win the war against the South because it had more men and more money and more industry and pretty much more of everything else. About the only thing it didn't have more of was slaves. She said the most important thing was the North had a just cause, and therefore it had God on its side. I agreed with her about the God bit. In my experience God is generally on the side of the strong against the weak. Very rarely does he hop over the fence to help the weak against the strong. So the North was bound to win just like Miss Larsen said it would.

Mr. Purdy thought war was gonna be fierce, and that was good. "Bloodletting gonna provide opportunities for a man who knows how to look for 'em, Joe. Mark my words this war is gonna make a lotta people miserable and a lotta people dead, but it's gonna make a lotta people rich as well, and I aim to be one of 'em."

"Yes, sir. How you gonna do that, Mr. Purdy?"

He scratched the stubble on his chin. "I don't rightly know at the moment, because I don't know what opportunities is gonna be offered. But I'll keep my eye out for the main chance, and when it comes I'm gonna grab it with both hands. A man might only get one main chance in life, Joe, that's why you gotta look out for it and make the most of it when it comes your way. You got me?"

"I think so, Mr. Purdy."

The Battle of Manassas was a big shock to most of us. To Miss Larsen in particular. She turned pale when she told us about it. "The North lost a battle," she said, "but it warn't important. Only thing that's important was we was fighting a just cause. The Good Lord made us lose Manassas to test us. We will pass the test, and then we will win." She was always harping on about the Good Lord testing us. So was Pastor Graham. Don't know about you but I'd rather the Good Lord didn't test us. Got enough on my plate being tested by life without the Good Lord putting his spoke in.

A few of the young men in town got a touch of war fever. Got to talking about how it'd be a fine thing to be in a battle and give the Rebs a whupping for what they did to our fort. They gave me ideas. I'm not saying I was in a hurry to join an army, but listening to them planted a seed you might say. It made me think one day I might join the army to get away from Pa. It'd have to be the northern army of course. I had no desire to fight on the losing side.

10.

I'M RUN OUT OF TOWN AND HUNTED LIKE AN ANIMAL

IT TOOK ME LESS THAN A MINUTE TO REACH THE edge of town, it being a small town and me being very eager to get out of it. As I ran past the last house I realized I'd made a big mistake. The trail I was on ran through a long stretch of cleared land. No trees to be found anywhere. Nowhere to hide till you get to the woods three miles away. Soon as anybody on the lynching mob saddled up a horse he could gallop out and have me. I couldn't outrun a horse. I could out-walk one given time, but time was a commodity I didn't have. So I stopped and turned, heading back the way I'd come. No one was running after me, but there was a commotion around the stables. That meant someone—more than one person probably—was saddling up to get me. Down the far end of the street where the church was, a group of folks had gathered together. Pastor Graham was in the middle of the group. No doubt he was preaching a sermon about God wanting me brought to justice right quick or some such flapdoodle.

On my left was the saloon, a ramshackle place with the sort of noises coming from it only drunks can make. All along the front it had a raised board-walk so you could get to the doors without having to dip your feet in mud. The walkway had railings in front of it you could tether your horse to. Three horses was tethered there. Nobody ever stole horses from in front of the saloon even though they would have been easy pickings. Horse theft was the worst crime you could commit in our town, worse than any other kind of theft, worse even than murder. Steal a horse from outside our saloon and you'll get yourself kilt by a mob in our town. Seeing as a mob was gonna kill me anyways that consideration didn't deter me any. I eyed up the horses and loosened the tether of the middle one knowing it was likely the best of the bunch. When you grow up around animals you get a nose for such things. Quick as you like I jumped on, turned him with a twist of my hips, and rode him the hell out of there. Dust went billowing up at the back of me, and a couple of folks ran from their houses suspecting something was wrong but not knowing what so they didn't try to stop me.

In under an hour I'd gone from being an innocent boy to being a criminal and a hunted one at that. I was a murderer and a horse thief. That made me lower than a rattler's belly. I admit to being a horse thief, but that was forced on me. As you know I never kilt Ervan. Nothing I could say would change things, though. I could have sworn on every bible in town I was innocent, but no one would have believed me. Partly that was because the people accusing me was the top people in town who always got listened to, and I was at the bottom of the heap. When you're at the bottom your voice don't get heard. It gets stifled by the pile on top of you squeezing the air outta your lungs and making you desperate for whatever little scrap that falls off the table you can get from life.

The other reason folk warn't minded to listen to

me was they liked a good hanging. It's an occasion, a cause to celebrate. Some of them was disappointed they didn't get more excuses to hang a body and celebrate. Now they'd got one they warn't gonna let it go, not easily. They was minded to get the hanging done and make the most of it. There was little else to enjoy in a town like ours. I warn't far out of town before I heard a commotion at the back of me and looked round over my right shoulder (as looking over the left one is guaranteed bad luck) and saw a big dust cloud a-following after me. That could only mean one thing. A power of men on horses was chasing after me. Hot as that day was I got the chills running right through me like you get with a bad fever. But I warn't ill. I was scared to death. Next thing I knowed a bullet whistled past me. One of those boys in the posse must've dismounted and loosed off his musket my way. That was the last chance he'd get to plug me. By the time he reloaded I'd be out of range. I had a feeling he wanted to miss anyhow. Probably only shot at me to exercise his trigger finger. Nobody wanted me dead by a bullet. Ain't no spectacle in that.

The horse I'd stolen was a good one. You could say that was another stroke of luck, but I did use my skill to choose it. Plus, I was a skinny little runt. That gave me an advantage over the men following me. They all weighed a lot more than me. It was the first time in my life I felt grateful for never having been fed properly.

The woods beckoned. They was my only chance, and I took it, by God. Headed straight in at a gallop and followed the trail but not far. The trail soon got dangerous to follow on a horse. You might follow it slowly, but try to gallop and before long your horse

will put a leg down a hole and break it. I had no intention of heading down a trail anyhow. Ain't no surer
way of getting yourself caught than that one. So I dismounted and turned the horse around and slapped
its behind. "Off you go, boy!" I said. It ran back the
way it'd come, and I left the trail heading deep into
the woods. No way was any of those men in the posse gonna get the better of me in the woods. I knowed
how to track better'n anyone 'cept Pa, and I knowed
how to cover my tracks better'n anyone 'ceptin Pa. So
I had something else to be grateful for. Having the Pa
I'd got. Last thing in the world I ever expected to feel
grateful about.

That reminded me. Pa had those cigars in the
cabin and Ervan's hat and boots. Those fellers who
was looking for me would likely go to the cabin once
they'd decided they couldn't find me. They'd search
the cabin in case I was hidden there and find Ervan's
things. Then they'd likely hang Pa instead of me. Or
they'd decide those things of Ervan's was proof I'd
kilt him. Not that they needed any more proof than
they'd got already. Only proof they needed was somebody's say-so, and they'd already got that.

Did Pa kill Ervan? Or did he loot things from Ervan's house after Ervan got kilt? Either was possible, but I didn't want my Pa to be kilt by a lynch
mob whatever he'd done. I wanted the truth to come
out, if only to me. So I circled 'round, keeping myself
low. It was easy to avoid the necktie party crew that
was after me. Not one of them had any real woodcraft. Noise they made woulda woken the dead three
states away while I was quiet as a ghost. I led them a
trail to a stream so obvious a city boy coulda followed
it, then I doubled back leaving most no tracks at all

and hid in the undergrowth. Soon enough I saw the necktie party boys at the bank of the stream deciding what to do. They split into two groups. One lot waded upstream with their horses, and the other waded downstream. I went the other way completely on dry ground to the cabin.

Ma was out in the yard tending her few greens. Ignoring her I went inside and saw Pa slumped in a chair snoring. A whiskey smell was on his breath, and it got stronger every time he snored. Ervan's hat was on his head slanted to one side. Pa's gray hair was sticking out from underneath it right down almost to his shoulders. I took the hat from him gently as you like. His snores turned into grunts, and he opened an eye.

"What you doing, boy?"

My arm went quickly behind my back out of sight with the hat in it. "Nothing, Pa." I was shaking now. Last thing I wanted was a fight with Pa. I just needed to get away before the necktie party arrived. If they found me and Pa together with Ervan's things they'd string us both up.

Pa watched with his one open eye as I backed away. The cigars was on a shelf behind me. "What you hiding, boy?"

"Nothing, Pa."

"You're lying, you got something behind your back."

"No, I don't."

He opened his other eye, and the way he looked at me was the way a grizzly looks at you just before it charges. I knowed right away I had to get outta there but I couldn't go without the cigar case. Turning around right quick I grabbed it and headed for the door. Pa's feet thudded on the floor at the back of me which told me he was drunk. He was quieter than a cat when he was sober. I opened the door with my free hand. He lumbered into it slamming it shut. I had nowhere to run.

"Thought you'd get away from me, didn't ya?"

Holding up the cigar box and hat I said, "Pa please, I got to get these things out of the house. And those boots you got. The townsfolk are saying I kilt Ervan Foster. If they find these things here, they'll kill the both of us." That's what I meant to say anyhow. I got as far as the word *Ervan* and I didn't even finish that because Pa's hand walloped me round the side of the head. My knees buckled, and I fell to the floor. The hat flew from my hand and so did the cigar box. Lid came off and cigars flew everywhere.

"What kind of son are you? That was nothing but a slap. If'n I'd a punched you, I could understand you falling down. But a slap? You must be soft. I didn't bring you up to be soft, but you are. And you're stupid. You thought you could come here and steal from your Pa. I ought to leather some sense into you, but I'm gonna let you off this time. Pick up those cigars before I change my mind."

My ears was ringing, and I was in no state to argue. I grabbed the cigars and stuffed them in the box. Picked up the hat, too.

He sat hisself back on his chair and held out his hand. "Bring me my hat and one of the cigars."

That was when I saw my chance. I picked up the boots, opened the door, and fled. Ran past Ma while she was hoeing. Trod all over her skirrets. She looked at me with poison in her eyes.

"Sorry, Ma, no time to explain. There's cash in

my mattress you might as well have the benefit of it." She got a look as if I'd just told her the sky had moved to beneath her feet, so I took Ma's shoulders and shook them. "I left some cash hidden in my mattress all stuffed inside of it. Make sure you get the benefit of it, Ma, and don't let Pa know 'bout it. Gotta go now."

Pa came running out shouting, and she looked as though she understood, sort of. "Run, Joe!" I didn't need no telling. A group of horsemen had appeared on the trail. They saw me running and Pa running after me trying to catch me.

"Get him, Thomas!" one of them shouted, Thomas being my Pa's name.

"Murdering little sonofabitch shot Ervan."

Pa was too drunk to take it in and too drunk to catch me, thank God. I got to the fence well ahead of him. The horsemen saw me throw away the hat and cigar box and boots before climbing over it. It gave them the idea those things was mine. One good thing was it put Pa in the clear. They saw Pa had no chance of catching me, so they gave chase. I headed for where the undergrowth was thickest. It was thick enough to stop the horses, so they had to dismount there. They ran after me, and credit where it's due a couple of them could run. They soon got so close I could hear their breathing behind me. Didn't dare turn my head to see how much distance there was between me and them. Their heavy footsteps was crashing through the bush only a couple of steps away it sounded like. My spine tingled and not with excitement. I was affrighted as I'd ever been. Don't think a grizzly could've made me feel any worse or run me off any faster. A hand grabbed my collar and pulled me back. I was done. Soon I'd be swinging from the branch of a tree or a makeshift gallows in the middle of town. Straightening my legs I wrenched my body hard as I could.

There's a first time for everything. That was the first time I was grateful I was always dressed in rags. My smock tore, and the man who'd grabbed it was left holding onto a piece of cloth. Free from his grasp I got running, and being small and skinny I had an advantage over the people who was out to get me. I could squeeze through gaps in the undergrowth quicker'n they could. They had to fight their way through obstacles I could almost run through.

It was hard work, mind. If you've never been chased by anyone out to kill you, you won't know what I'm talking about. You'll think you've worked hard dragging logs from one place to another or building a barn or ploughing a field or whatever you do for a living. You'll think you've had days when you've given it all you've got and you've nothing left to give. But I guarantee that if, on one of those days, a group of men had come at you wanting to hang you, you would've found something extra in your legs, and you would've made the best effort you could to run away. That's how it was for me. The effort I put forth was the most effort I'd ever put forth and then some. It warn't long before my lungs was on fire, and I needed to stop but I didn't. I carried on running without slowing up. Behind me the voices of the men from town and the neighing of their horses faded into the distance. I was moving too quick to look out for bears. Those animals generally leave you alone if you leave them alone, but running like I was I could blunder into one then my number would be up, because I'd end up getting kilt and eaten by a bear. Worse still, I might bump into a pig. Seeing as I've told you all about the dangers of pigs no point in repeating myself here 'ceptin to mention I stood to be eaten alive. When that thought hit me I decided I'd sooner hang and slowed down enough to watch my step a little.

After a good long while I stopped and listened hard. All I could hear was birds in the forest canopy, the wind rustling the leaves, and the trickle of water from a stream. Couldn't hear the hanging party at all. They must've been a long way behind me because those boys warn't quiet. They didn't know how to be quiet in a wood.

I soon got going again. My legs could barely carry me after all that running, but I forced them to walk at a fierce pace. South I went, opposite direction to the moss on the tree trunks. I also took note of the sun in the sky when it showed itself, but most of all I was guided by the feel in me. I got a feel for where North is. Pa got the same. He taught me how you get it. I used to think it warn't nothing special till I found out me and Pa are the only ones I know who got that feel. While I was heading south the ground got shadows on it now and again, moving around letting me know high up in the air a wind was a-blowing even though it was calm all around me.

When I'd slowed to a walk I took more note of the trees. Folks that don't live in a wood don't know one tree from another and think they all look the same, more or less. That type of person easily gets lost in the woods. Having been born and bred among trees, I could see each one was different like you and me. If I needed to get back from where I'd come, they'd be my guide.

Pa told me trees been around thousands of years since before even the first man walked this earth, and he said they'll be there long after man is gone. When I'm alone in the woods it feels like he was right. It sure did that day.

Every now and again I'd pause for a second or two.

First because I wanted to listen out for the noises so I knowed whether I was being followed. All I heard was the sounds the woods make. Leaves rustling in the breeze, birds with their bird noises, animals passing by me outta my sight.

Second because I wanted to take in the lie of the land. The way it rose and fell and the shape of the rocks when I saw them and streams I crossed or walked beside. All that I stored in my head so I could bring it out again and find my way home if I needed to. Force of habit, mind. I warn't fixing on going home.

It was Pa taught me how to know your way in the woods or anywhere else you found yourself. But specially the woods. Being in woods was like being in a church to him. You could call it his religion. He was a woodsman through and through. Sometimes he'd look at me and say, "Too many lumberjacks these days. One lumberjack is one too many. I feel like taking my old musket and blowing the lot of them to kingdom come." When I was a boy I didn't understand what Pa was talking about, but over the years I've come to feel the same way he did about lumberjacks. He used to take me deep in the woods before he got useless, and we'd spend days at a time living off the land and sleeping under the stars.

Once I asked him how he got so clever as to know all this stuff. "People I grew up with and people I lived with, boy," he told me. "Hillbillies and Indians."

"You grew up with hillbillies and Indians, Pa? What was that like?"

"Not easy."

"What was Indians like?"

"Better than people say."

"What do you mean?"

"I've said enough. Don't go spilling the beans to anyone what I told you, you hear?" He put his finger over his mouth.

Shaking my head I said, "I won't, Pa."

My plan was to head north, but first I headed south to take the hanging boys in the wrong direction. Hopefully when they followed my trail they'd lose me at some point and keep going the way they was headed. Meanwhile I'd be headed the other way.

It got to dusk, and the woods didn't seem so friendly anymore. Trees turned into gray shapes that could have come from my nightmares, and the heat of the day drained away so that the woods grew cold as the night air. I might have found a way to light a fire and keep warm, but that was the last thing I wanted to do. Nothing would get me caught sooner than a fire in a wood. But I sure wanted one. It was getting hellish cold. I wanted my shed and my mattress, too, with a pile of blankets on it and a lit candle to make me feel good. And I wanted to know Ma and Pa was close by to protect me if I needed protecting. But all I had was myself and the trees for company.

It got so dark I could barely see the trees at all. They was just black shapes in a black space with blackness above them and black beneath my feet. Wind was making them rattle and hiss, and I don't mind admitting to you I got real scared. First, I was scared because it was dark and I was on my own, a hunted boy. Second, I was scared because I knowed bears could see better'n me in the dark. They warn't likely to come after me, but they might, and if they did I wouldn't even know it was happening till it was too late. I always carry a knife. That's another thing Pa taught me. Bastard though my Pa could be sometimes he had my back, and he did teach me some useful things. I carried my knife in a leather sheath threaded through my belt at my hip. Made the belt and sheath myself from cowhide. Pa bought the knife or traded something for it at the general store. Traded furs probably. He caught a lot of furs at one time though he said he didn't much care for killing animals for that purpose and gave up after a while. "You shouldn't kill more animals than you need to feed yourself and put clothes on your back and shoes on your feet in winter," he used to say. I pulled the knife from the sheath and held it in my right hand. It made me feel better even if it wouldn't have stopped a pig or a bear. Not in my hands anyhow. Maybe if you was the size of Corman Purdy you could take on a pig or bear with a knife in your hand. Maybe, if you was very lucky and it was your best day ever. But if you was a runt like me? No chance. Pig'd bowl you right over and so would a bear.

I went to the nearest tree and scratched about with my hands piling up dead leaves and moss to set myself on. Warn't many of them because it warn't fall, but I found enough that I didn't have to set my behind on bare earth. Then I sat with my back to the tree trunk, pulled my jacket tight around me, and did my best to fend off the cold and forget my empty belly so's I could nod off with my trusty knife close to hand. When I slept, I slept with one eye open, if you know what I mean. Heard all the noises going on around me. Warn't a leaf blown by the breeze without I knowed it was happening.

And I did some thinking, too. About Pastor Graham for one. Couldn't help but wonder if he was the one that kilt Ervan. Why else would he go filling Mr. Purdy's head with ideas that I was the one who did it? I thought about Mr. Purdy also. Wondered if it was him who kilt Ervan. He mighta fixed on it from the beginning. All those times he took me out a-shooting could have been to make sure the townsfolks knowed I could handle a musket and a pistol. The praise he'd heaped on me for being a good shot could have been to make doubly sure folks would pin the blame on me when Ervan breathed his last.

Thought about Pa as well. Why did he hate me? For he surely did. And at one time he loved me or seemed to. Ever since my brother died he'd been different to me. Why? I tried to work it out, something I'd never done before. I'd always pushed it to the back of my mind because it warn't a subject I wanted to deal with. But now I was dwelling on Pa whether I liked it or not. The woods can do that to you when you're alone. You think about things when you're not busy tracking animals.

Upshot was I faced facts for the first time. Facts was Pa had changed since my brother got buried. Pa's change was eating away at me and had done for years. I'd been pretending things was okay. It was time to stop pretending. Pa hated me. *Deal with it*, I said to myself. Then I remembered about the cigars and railway cap and boots. Had Pa kilt Ervan just to spite me? Or maybe to steal from him? Then I got too tired to think and my head rolled to one side and I slept some, but I kept myself alert. It was mighty cold, but I was used to being cold. Birds making a racket woke me up. Opening an eye I saw hints of daylight and listened carefully but I didn't hear no men stamping about. That meant I was still safe, at least from lynching mobs. Rubbing my eyes I stretched and got to my feet. My belly was empty but that was nothing new to me, so I ignored it and shook myself off like I was shaking off rainwater to get the blood flowing into my cold arms and legs, then I set off walking again, all thoughts of Pa gone from my head. Figured I'd carry on south for a while. Warn't sure whether I was headed toward Missouri or Kentucky, but I knowed I was headed for one of them. I also knowed I was in no danger of crossing over the state line into enemy territory because there was a river in the way.

The more I thought about it the more I thought my best bet of keeping my neck out of a noose was to join an army. That way I could disappear among thousands of men if not tens of thousands on whichever patch of land the army was camped, and the folks back home would never find me.

I'd fight in the Union army of course. If I fought for the South I'd be on the losing side. I knowed that because of what Miss Larsen had told me. I wanted to be on the side God was on. The one with most men and guns. Plus, if I fought for the South, I might have to kill some of my own townsfolk, and that didn't sit right well with me, even though they'd been trying to take my life. Thing is I wanted to kill them for the right reasons. For trying to string me up if they tried it again. Not for being on the other side in a war. Killing them for fighting on the other side wouldn't feel like justice. It would just feel like doing a job.

Trouble was I couldn't join the army in Illinois because there was no telling how far word had spread that I was a lawbreaker. If I showed up at a recruiting station in Illinois I might be arrested and tried and hung for a crime I didn't commit. Murder. Or one I did. Horse theft. It seemed to me I had to sign up for the army far, far away from Illinois. Best place would be Washington because it's about as far away as you can get, so that's where I decided to go.

With a rumbling belly I trekked past more trees and bushes and thickets than a body could count, and the day got warmer. My belly stopped feeling hungry after a while. It does that if you take no notice that it's empty. But I did get a thirst on, so I found a stream and had a good drink from it before walking down the side of it. Best way to make sure I had a supply of water on hand when I needed one. I could maybe go a day without eating, then I'd have to get something down me to keep my energy up. When you're skinny as I was you got no fat to draw on. That means you soon get sluggish if you ain't had enough to eat. And I couldn't afford to get sluggish. Not with the prospect of a posse on my tail.

The stream dropped into the bottom of a valley where it joined a river. To follow it I had to do some hard scrambling down a steep hill with a slippery rock face. Had to be careful. One false move and I'd injure myself, and out there being injured was as good as being dead. There warn't no one to come running if I needed help. Chances was that if I injured myself, I'd end up as food for the first wild animal that happened on me. Even a bobcat would finish me off and eat lumps from me if I hurt myself bad enough. Luckily, I got down the rock face in one piece and was able to pick my way along the valley bottom. I was glad to be there because I was sure I'd find something I wanted real soon. And I was right. I happened on a bunch of pecan trees and picked myself as many wild pecan nuts as I could eat and more besides. Lots of energy in those nuts. I filled my belly with them and stuffed my pockets, too. Reckoned I had enough to keep going for a couple of days if need be.

Birds woke me up next day. I was cold and stiff from sleeping on the ground but pleased I'd survived another day, and that gave me reason to celebrate. Plus, I had my breakfast of wild pecan nuts. I got some down me and drank near enough a pint of fresh clear water from the river then followed the valley. Judging by the trees I was going east, and before long I'd be joining the Wabash River. I aimed to follow the Wabash to the Ohio river then head to Washington. That's where the army was, I'd heard. Once I was in the army I'd be safe from anything, 'ceptin war of course.

I reckoned I didn't have to rush so anymore. Townsfolk would've given up hope of finding me by now and all gone home, hoping maybe some other poor bastard would do something they could find an excuse to hang him for. Plodding along I enjoyed the scenery. I'm never so happy as when I'm in the woods. Only when darkness falls do I feel any different to that. Comes of growing up wild I suppose, or as near wild as you can be, in these strange times we live in that some call civilization.

Apart from survivin' on what the woods could give me and circling north I didn't have much of a plan, but I didn't need one. All I had to do was keep out of harm's way.

I soon got to the Wabash River. It was wide and smooth, deep and clear, glistening in the sunshine. Made my heart sing. Right about when my heart started singing, dogs started barking at the back of me. I couldn't see them, but I knowed by the sound of them they couldn't be far way. Those crazy townsfolk hadn't given up the chase. They'd gone home and put together a dog pack to track me down.

I knowed if I kept moving I could see off those dogs because they'd tire and give up. The same was true of the townsfolk. Ain't none of them could keep going the way me and Pa could. Only thing was, I had to make sure the dogs didn't get too close and put on a burst of speed and catch me.

And they was already real close. Barking got louder. Four dogs, I reckoned, with two men. Only two I could think from our town who had what it takes to follow me day and night through the woods were Bob Finn and Lowrie Cheetham. Bob and Lowrie was grizzled old fur trappers. Plied their trade in Wisconsin, and when they got sick of trapping in Wisconsin they came to Illinois to have a go at farming. Not that farming in Illinois was a whole lot easier than trapping according to Bob. Someone must've offered them money to come and get me. Can't see as Bob and Lowrie would've gone to such lengths as following me this far just to get justice for Ervan Foster. Neither of them were much interested in justice as far as I knowed. And neither of them had been too friendly with Ervan. No one had been friendly with Ervan, other than me and Cath Purdy.

Anyhows I knowed I could escape if I just moved quicker than a dog could move for longer than a dog could. But I also knowed I had my work cut out. Bob and Lowrie had hunted game and knowed at least some of the tricks I knowed. Not as many, though. There's a sight of difference between hunting with dogs and hunting with your own nose and eyes. Everything they could do I could do better. So I was confident I had the beating of them.

There was a crashing through the undergrowth. One of them had let one of his dogs go. It would've been their strongest dog, the one with the stamina to run me down at the end of a long chase. Rest of their dogs would be too tired by now to run. Bob and Lowrie was no doubt hoping it'd bite a lump out of me and stop me running away. Their dogs was vicious. Heard tell they was Spanish hunting dogs part bred with wolves. Big and mean, they had slavering jaws and knowed no such thing as mercy. They'd been bred to be ruthless. And now one of them was only a few yards behind me, and it knowed zackly where to find me. If it sank its teeth in me I'd be finished. Dropping into a crouch I faced the direction it was coming from and pulled out my knife. Trees was close together. I moved back a couple of steps to encourage it to come at me between two trees. Now I knowed its line of attack I steadied myself. Held out my left arm bent at the elbow to give it something to fasten its teeth into. Right arm bent at my side, blade up at the ready. Breathed deeply the way Pa taught me to when I had some killing to do. Then I saw it. The dog from hell, all teeth and savagery and a growl fit to make a body keel over with fright. It was coming right at me quicker'n you would've thought possible. Unless you was me, that is, and you'd seen animals close up killing other animals.

Best way to kill something is when its coming onto you. Dog didn't know that. I offered it my left arm, and it went straight for it. Those teeth would've stripped the flesh offa my arm and broken the bone it if I'd let them. But at the last second I whipped my left arm away and stuck the knife into its throat. Dog gave a surprised yelp and fell at my feet. It was still alive, so I stabbed it a couple of times to finish it off. Didn't want it to suffer. There was no pleasure in killing the dog, only relief. I don't like killing animals unless I plan on eating them. You gotta respect life. Taking it without you have to is evil. Another thing I learned from Pa.

Now the dog had found me it was only a matter of time before Bob and Lowrie caught up with me if I let them. Following the river I moved east at a good lick aiming to outpace them. Bob and Lowrie was skinny like Pa and used to hunting, so they had a better chance than most at keeping up with me. But a chance was all they had, and a slim one at that. They was old boys, and I was young. That was one thing in my favor. Another was they had to move at the pace their dogs set. A dog can't keep up with a man over a long distance. No animal can.

I'd gone but a hundred yards when I heard a dog and a man up ahead. Someone had come downriver of me on a skiff with his dog. Phil Tetcher most likely, known as Big Phil on account of being the shortest man in town. He warn't much taller'n me. Phil owned a skiff, and he fancied hisself a hunting type. Hung around with Bob and Lowrie a lot of the time. Warn't no good at hunting, though. I swear I could hear him a mile off in the woods when he was meant to be lying in wait for a deer. Only reason he caught anything worth a damn was because he had a good dog. Dog got more brains in its head than Phil had.

I hadn't reckoned on Phil Tetcher being involved. He gave me a real headache. Dogs to the back of me, dogs to the front of me meant I was cornered worse'n a rat in a barrel. Next thing I knowed, Tetcher's damned dog was standing right in fronta me. Fresh it was, too. It hadn't had to trek through miles of trees and valleys to reach me. It'd been relaxin' on a skiff. No outpacing that hound. Being near enough the riverbank, I dived in the river thinking I'd swim to the other side so as not to have to kill the dog. Turns out that was a crazy idea because Phil Tetcher had a crazy dog. It jumped right in after me. Looking over my shoulder when I was swimming—right shoulder of course—I saw it paddling along behind me. Only one thing I could do, the thing I'd been hoping not to have to do. I trod water and pulled out my knife. A dog in the water is easy meat, much easier than on dry land. All you have to do is stick your knife in its throat when it gets near. That's what I did, and it made me sick doing it. Blood clouded the water, and the dog sank with a yelp. Phil Tetcher came bursting out of the undergrowth and saw his dog disappearing beneath the waves. Must've wondered what'd happened to it as he wouldn't have been able to see the knife. I slid it back in my sheath.

That stretch of river was about fifty yards wide. The current was strong in the middle, weak at the edge. I was near enough the middle, drifting downstream fast. Tetcher put a musket to his shoulder and pointed the muzzle at my head. That surprised me as I'd thought they wanted to take me alive. Now I knowed otherwise. Whoever had paid them musta told them he wanted me dead or alive. Tetcher was going for dead. Holding my breath, I dipped underwater and swam with the current then bobbed up briefly downstream. Heard a bullet and saw a splash by my head. Tetcher had loosed off his one shot and missed. That meant I was safe. By the time he'd gotten reloaded the current woulda carried me downstream well outta range.

Phil started shouting. "Bob! Lowrie! I found the little bastard!"

It warn't winter, it warn't even fall, but the leaves was getting ready to drop and the water was so cold it was making the insides of my arms and legs numb, so I was keen to get out the river soon as I could. Up ahead was a beach where the river bent in a lazy half circle. A skiff was on the beach. Musta been Phil Tetcher's. Right then and there I changed my plan. Instead of swimming to the other side I headed for the beach. It took all I had in me to get to it. The current wanted to pull me further downstream, and fighting it was like rassling a grizzly. Somehow I got the better of it and got to shore. By the time I did I was gasping like one of the sorry fish me and Pa had caught over the years, and I warn't fit to stand let alone walk. I just lay there with my chest rising and falling hoping to God Bob or Lowrie or Phil or any of their dogs wouldn't happen on me while I was helpless.

When I got my strength back I grabbed the back end of the skiff and hauled it into the water. Soon as I got it there I clumb in. It was about ten foot long and packed with goodies. I'd look at them later. First order of business was to get the hell out of there. Crawling to the middle I picked up the oars and got a-rowing, looking back the way I'd come. The beach I'd been on was clear as a bright day, but there was shouting and barking from thereabouts. Then three vicious looking dogs came bursting through the trees onto the beach and ran to the edge of the water snapping at me, not that it did them any good from so far away. Brought a big smile to my face. First time any dog snapping at me ever done that. Snapping dogs always made me uneasy before. Bob and Lowrie burst through next, both of them carrying muskets. By this time I was a good way off, but still in range.

"Stop, boy, or we'll send you straight to hell!" one of them shouted.

"Seeing as I'm going thar anyways I don't see why I should stop!" I shouted back.

Both of them raised their muskets. I'd rowed to the middle of the river where the current was strongest. It caught hold the skiff and swept me away. Meanwhile there was flashes from the muzzles of Bob and Lowrie's muskets and a pile of smoke came out of them. A bullet hit the water next to me and another whooshed past my head. Heard the bangs of the muskets next, and knowed I was safe. The skiff would be well outta range before they could load up and shoot at me again. Things was looking up. I gave up rowing and let the current carry me down the Wabash.

Good news and bad. The good news was I soon left Phil and Bob and Lowrie far behind. I'd been moving on the river a sight quicker'n they could move through woodland. Bad news was I was cold. My clothes was wet, and a chill wind was a-blowing. I'd catch my death if I didn't do something. Paddling to the bank I caught hold of a low branch and tied the stern of the skiff to it. Then I looked at what there was on board that'd help me. Turned out I had lots that would be useful. A couple of dry blankets, good warm ones. Salted meat wrapped in paper and a water canteen. Dry clothes, too. They didn't fit me of course. But I took off my own clothes and put the pants on I'd found in the skiff and tightened my belt to the very last notch which was the way I always wore it. Then I rolled up the pants at the bottom. Didn't have to roll them up too much because of Phil being short. Guess his legs was what made him short. My privates got warm for the first time in months, because Phil's pants didn't have any holes in them. Put on his shirt and jacket and once I'd rolled up the sleeves it felt all right on me. A bit roomy on the shoulders and baggy around the middle but I figured I'd grow into it if I kept it long enough, and it was better'n any jacket I'd had before. I got the things outta my clothes I needed and put them in the pockets of my new outfit. Pa had told me I should carry those things with me wherever I went. They would keep me alive, he'd said. Namely a couple of flints a handful of dry grass a good length of twine and a fishhook My grass was no longer dry, of course. But I reckoned I'd soon get it dry or find some more. Also I had a knife. Pa was big on carrying knives. Strung my leather sheath with my knife in it through my belt and I was good to go. Wrapped a blanket around me, and now I was warm and dry. Reached over to the salt meat and got me a good-sized chunk that I chewed and swallowed, and boy did it ever taste good. I got some more and filled my belly with it.

What with having spent the better part of three days on the run and then getting my belly brim-full I got to feeling dog tired and decided I'd take a nap. Knowed I'd be safe because Phil and Bob and Lowrie was at least a day's trek away, the rate I'd been moving downriver. I could afford to have a good long rest. Folding one of the blankets into a pillow I put my head on it and sandwiched myself in the other, which I folded in half. Then I lay down in the bottom of the skiff. I was in a shady spot which I found very restful. The water lapped against the hull, rocking it gently. I was just like a baby being rocked to sleep by its ma. Soon as you like I was dead to the world.

What did I dream of? Cath Purdy and Ervan for some reason. In my dreams me and Cath was rolling together in a pile of hay in the corner of her pa's stable on a hot sunny day. She wouldn't stop kissing on me, and I didn't want her to stop. I wanted the roll in the hay to go on forever and ever Amen, but it did stop, and I don't know how or why it did or how I got there, but all of a sudden I was in Ervan's front room. We was sitting on his chairs both of us holding a can of coffee he'd made for us. He was sitting sorta hunched like he always did and looking at me with sad gray eyes in a gray face from under gray hair. Struck me as odd because in real life his face was the color of a nut from being out in the sun all day.

"Joe," Ervan said to me, "you gotta find out who kilt me."

That's when I realized why Ervan was so gray. It was on account of his being dead. I was talking to a dead man. A shiver went through me from my toes to the top of my head and back again. Then I stood up. "I gotta go, Ervan. I can't spend no time with a dead man. It ain't right." My voice had an echo to it like it did when Pa took me to the big rocks and made me shout. But there warn't no rock face for it to echo off. I knowed that so I shivered again.

Ervan looked at me pleading. "Find him, Joe. It ain't right what happened to me."

"I would if I could, Ervan, but I'm only a boy and I'm up against a heap of men, all of them armed. I'd love to help you. Hell, it'd be helping myself much as you, but there ain't nothing I can do, sorry."

Raising his arm he pointed his finger right at me, and those gray eyes of his saw right through me. "Be a man, boy. Don't be a coward, and don't run away from your responsibilities."

"It's too late, Ervan, I am running away. They'll kill me if I don't."

With a flash and a rumbling Ervan's house started collapsing all around me. Smoke billowing everywhere. That's when I knowed I was in hell. I ran to the door but was too late. Lightning flashed in fronta me, and the roof fell in, sealing me up in hell forever. Then I opened my eyes to see it had been a dream, thank God. And lightning really was flashing. And more thunder rumbling. Sky was black, it was night, and my skiff was loose from the tree I'd tied it to. The branch had broken. Shoulda chosen the branch more carefully. How long the skiff'd been loose I didn't know. The branch was trailing in the water still tied to the rope.

The skiff had drifted to the wrong side of the river. The bank had been on my right before. Now it was on my left. The river was so wide I couldn't see the side I shoulda been on. Got the impression I wouldn't have seen it even in daylight. Trees on my side was blacker than the sky, and the river was shining like a coal-black mirror in the night. Black against black everywhere I looked. While I was busy admiring it, rain began to fall. Drops big as bullets plopped into the water all around me. I rowed to the bank to shelter under the trees. There was but half a dozen of them in a tight group. I was a long ways from the woods that was my second home. Maybe my first in some ways. They was on the other side of the river. A long way to row and I warn't trying it till the rain eased up. I didn't want to risk getting caught out in a storm in the middle of a fast-flowin' river.

I couldn't tie up to any of the trees because they was too far from the bank, so instead I clumb from the skiff and waded onto dry land dragging the skiff behind me. On this side of the Wabash I was in the state of Indiana.

I got my legs wet all over again but sooner that than stay on the river in a storm—especially in the dark. If the storm got up I could get capsized, and if I had to swim to safety it might be touch and go in that current. The current is weak by the bank of a river but strong in the middle even when its smooth as glass. That current will carry you a quarter mile outta your way even before you got time to realize you're going anywhere.

Once I got on land I pulled off my pants and wrung them out dry as best I could and put them on again. Then I sat in the skiff and chowed down on salt meat. Got to thinking about Ervan. I didn't know whether I'd been dreaming when I'd seen him or if somehow I'd really visited him in hell, but whichever it was, he was right. I'd let him down. I should be doing something to get justice for him. Instead, I was covering my own tail. It didn't sit right with me, but I put survival over justice.

Then I thought it doesn't have to always be that way. I was gonna learn how to fight in the army, and how to kill people. I knowed how to do that already of course, but then and there I determined to get real good at it. Then, when I was all growed up, I'd go back to my old town and clear my name and shoot Ervan's killer in the head from point-blank range. Make sure he knowed I was about to pull the trigger and end his life before I did, and make sure he knowed zackly why I was ending his life. I'd prove to ever'one I never kilt Ervan and get an apology from them all. Most of all from Pastor Graham and Mr. Purdy. And as for anyone who got in my way or tried to lynch me, well they'd be taking a very big risk because I'd be an expert in the killing department. Wouldn't be anyone better than me when it came to taking a life in the blink of an eye.

Also I thought about Cath. Wished I hadn't seen her in my dream because I'd managed to forget her. Now I couldn't stop thinking of her, and she broke my heart all over again. Wished I could cry to get the sadness outta me, but I couldn't. Just sat there in the skiff with tears wanting to come outta my eyes, but I couldn't even get them to well up.

The storm was one of those that blows over real quick. Just a downpour of rain and it was gone, and the clouds opened, and the moon shone through full and bright. Sky lightened so I could see better. I got to wondering where I was and how long I'd been asleep. Couldn't figure it. Anyways, I knowed I had to head north and decided I oughta get my bearings first. That way I'd have an idea of how long it might take me to get where I wanted to go.

11

WELCOME TO HELL

LOOKING 'ROUND THERE WARN'T NOTHING TO tell me where I was. All I could see was a mess of tall plants getting' in my way. They was eight foot high maybe ten. Far higher than I was tall so I couldn't see over them. But there was a way I might be able to. I was right next to some bluffs. Getting out the skiff I clumb them by moonlight. It warn't hard because I found an easy route up. The bluffs made me tall enough to see over the plants. Stood on top of the bluff taking in the scene and saw a town in the distance, or squarish shapes that looked like a town, anyhow. It was a good way off. I couldn't see the town when I'd gotten off the bluffs because the plants was so damn tall, but I knowed which direction to go. Trouble was the Goddamn plants was in the way. Solid wall of them. No point in even trying to get through them because I couldn't. They was only inches apart, and if I did squeeze through even I'd lose my way, and I have a better sense of direction than most. I walked alongside the edge of the plants figuring I'd find a way through somehow, and I was right. There was a path about three foot wide cut right through the middle of them. It went the direction I wanted to go so I followed it, figuring I'd ask one of the towns-folk where I was. It might seem like a crazy idea doing that seeing as I was wanted for murder, but I was pretty sure news of my crime wouldn't have gotten to the town ahead of me.

It turned out the tall plants was hemp. More hemp than you could have shaken a stick at. More'n I'd ever seen in my life, and I was walking right through it by the light of the moon. The moon got lower, then the sky brightened. That brightness warn't dawn, it was the light you get before dawn spreading slowly 'cross the sky.

The path through the hemp took me onto a plain with some woods on one side, which was a welcome sight. But I could tell right away by seeing some stumps that someone had been clearing them, and that didn't sit right well with me. Guess I was my Pa's son even though me and him hadn't been getting on these last few years. As I got nearer the town I saw it was nothing like the town I knowed back home, but that didn't trouble me none. It stood to reason one town would be different from another, same as me and Ma and Pa being different from other folks. I had to admit, though, this one was more different than I would have expected any town to be. It was more like two towns with a big gap between them. One of the towns was small and rich. It had a big grand building made of stone with columns on the front. Much grander than anything I'd seen back home. There was smaller buildings around it, some of wood and some of stone, and all of them looked perfect. Clusters of trees dotted here and there. Those trees would give the folks living in that rich town shelter from the hot sun in summer.

The other town, which was way over to the right of the grand one, a good distance from it, had no trees to give its folk shelter from the sun. It warn't none of it built from stone, just a peck of big wooden sheds.

The town I came from had cabins big enough to fit a family in them, unless you was rich like Mr. Purdy in which case you got a cabin big enough for two families or three in a pinch. In my town a big cabin meant you must be rich. These sheds was big enough for lots of families, so you woulda thought the owners was rich. But the sheds was old and tumbledown, so they couldn't have been owned by rich people. Owners must have been as poor as me and Ma and Pa. So why did they need such big houses to live in? And why didn't they have no windows? Only thing I could think of was the menfolk was all useless like Pa and couldn't be bothered to give their families windows. That didn't explain why the menfolk had gone to the trouble of building big cabins, though, and then not repairing them so they got to being all tumbledown.

I headed toward the grand stone building. Before dawn had even broke the people who owned it got to moving around the front of it, sweeping up and cleaning and going in the stables and sorting out the horses like they was really house proud. Funny thing was they was all black. I never knowed there was rich black people. I thought all of them was poor like me and Ma and Pa. Truth is, I never saw many black folks, so I had no idea how they lived.

I saw one once who came out of the woods back home. He was called Benjamin and was a runaway slave. When he landed up in our town he was nine-tenths starved. Told me he'd been only half-starved to begin with and said he was looking for work. He'd come to the wrong place. The smallholders in our neck of the woods found it hard enough to scratch out a living for their selves. They didn't have no call for someone to help them. A hired hand was another mouth to feed when they could barely grow enough to put in their own mouths.

Some of the townsfolk said we should run him out of town. Others said he was someone's property, and we oughta give him back. Said there might be money in it. Miss Larsen said she wouldn't let them do either because it wouldn't be Christian, and seeing as we thought of ourselves as good Christians we oughta treat him well. Mr. Purdy was standin' right next to Miss Larsen while she was saying these things. He had his hands on his hips, his feet planted firm, and a six-gun in his belt; he glowered at the crowd. Mr. Purdy didn't say anything, he didn't have to. It was obvious anyone who wanted to get to Benjamin would have to get through Mr. Purdy first. No one in their right mind in our town was willing to attempt that. Knowed the odds were they'd come off badly.

Pastor Graham, who hadn't said anything till Miss Larsen piped up, agreed with her. Miss Larsen got Pastor Graham to give Benjamin what she called sanctuary in the church, and she and Mr. Purdy fed him, and by and by some of the town folks got to feel shamed by Miss Larsen and fed Benjamin, too. Between them, Miss Larsen and the other folks who fed him got him looking like he had some meat on him, and he made hisself useful by doing a few odd jobs for them. Then he had to move on because he was looking for regular work, and there warn't none to be found in our town. Before he left, he told me he'd been aiming to get to Cairo because he'd heard there was a underground railroad there he could catch. Made no sense to me. Warn't no such thing as underground railroads so far as I knowed. Anyways, he got lost before he got to Cairo and fetched up in our town.

When he left us Benjamin headed for Canada, which he called the Promised Land. That made no sense either. Miss Larsen had taught us Israel was the Promised Land.

"How did you get here, Benjamin?" I asked him.

"I crossed the Ohio river by clinging to a log and got through the swamps on the other side, then I ran into the woods."

"Those woods are dangerous if you don't know 'em," I told him. "Didn't you know that?"

"I sure did, son. Reason I snuck into the woods was because I was worried I'd get caught by slave catchers if I stayed out in the open. More slave catchers your side of the river than you can shake a stick at. They make a good living from it."

"What's a slave catcher?"

"They catch runaway slaves and gets paid a bounty for it."

"Bounty?"

"It means money and good money at that. Do you have any idea what I'm worth, son?"

"Worth? What do you mean?"

"I mean that a white man would pay good money to have me as his slave. I'm a valuable commodity in the South to be bought and traded like so many bales of cotton. Do you know how much I'd trade for?"

"No, I ain't got no idea."

"Eight hundred dollars, if not more. Heard tell a slave on the market sold for fourteen hundred dollars t'other month."

I whistled. "That's an awful lot of money, Benjamin."

"It sure is. It means there's a price on my head, son. Person who paid for me gonna pay to get me back and likely sell me on after he done whipping me for running away. That's if'n I get caught, which I ain't fixing to do. Anyways, I lost my way in them woods and kept a-wandering and a-wandering without knowing where I was going. Thought I'd die before I stumbled on your town. Must have been other slaves like me went through those woods. Have you seen any of 'em?"

I didn't have the heart to tell Benjamin that if there had been other slaves in the woods like him none of them had made it out, and they'd likely ended their days as hog food. He was lucky he hadn't fattened up a hog or two hisself.

But all that's by the by.

I felt it better not to show my face right away in that odd town. If those black folks was as welcoming with me as some of our townsfolk had been with Benjamin, I could expect them to run me out of town. Having just been run out of my own town I didn't care to be run out of another, so I fixed on making sure I'd get a good reception before talking to any of them. I decided to watch the rich black folk for a while and see whether there was any white folks with them. If there was, I figured I'd be all right showing my face. If there warn't I'd move on rather than take the risk they didn't care for white boys like me.

Waiting till the coast was clear, I slunk round the back of the grand house then moved forward through a cluster of trees and stood with a tree between me and the house. The sky was brightening more so than before, so I knowed dawn was breaking. Moment the sun peeked over the horizon there was a hollering from the woodsheds in the distance. I paid it no heed and ran to the wall of the grand house, pressed myself against it, and moved sideways like a crab. Then I heard the most Godawful scream. It was the scream of just one man, but it was as loud a scream as you could expect ten men to make, and it was coming from a stone outhouse across the yard. Made my blood run colder than the Wabash River in the midwinter. Felt like I'd gotten pure ice in my veins. Only other time I heard a sound that affrighted me so much was when Theodore Gibbler got attacked by that pig I told you about. When it took that chunk outta his leg he made a noise which would've put out a window if he'd been anywhere near one.

I was minded to run away from that grand house. When you hear such a-screaming you don't want to hang around, no sir. But then I wondered if someone had had an accident and needed help. Making my way along the wall I peered around the corner into the yard. It was paved with stone slabs, real fancy they was. The black folks had finished sweeping them and had gotten on their hands and knees scrubbing the slabs clean. Thin people they was, like me. And ain't one of them went rushing to help the poor soul who was crying out. One or two looked over in that direction shaking their heads, but that was all they did. It didn't sit right with me so I decided to see what was going on for myself and help if I could.

I took a chance and ran to the outhouse where the screams was coming from. Snuck to a window to peek through. What I saw made me think I was asleep and dreaming I was in hell again. There was a black man with his wrists tied together by a rope thrown over a beam high above his head, so that he was all a-dangle. He warn't wearing nothing. Naked as the day he was born. He had his back to me, and that back of his was like a ploughed field. It had furrows in it so big and deep you could stick your finger in them right down to the top knuckle. Some of them had blood coming out of them. A white man was behind him holding a whip. He said something, I didn't hear what, but I could tell it was awful nasty, then he cracked the whip and ran at the black feller, lashing him across the back with it. Whip might have made a new furrow or opened up an old one, I couldn't tell which. Either way the black man howled again. "Mercy!" he cried, and more blood showed on his back.

That was when I realized I'd gone further south than I thought. I'd drifted clear down the Wabash River to the Ohio River and was in Kentucky on a plantation. Those black folks I saw warn't rich. They was poorer than me and was slaves. That's why they was up a-scrubbing and a-cleaning before the sun had even showed a glint in the sky, and that's why the black man in the outhouse was being whipped. If I had to guess whether he was gonna live or die after that whipping he was being given my guess would be he was gonna die. I couldn't see how a body could lose that much of the flesh offa his back and survive it. White man turned 'round, and I ducked outta sight. A short time later I heard another scream and knowed the black man was another whiplash closer to death.

Miss Larsen taught us about slaves. She taught us they had slaves in ancient Greece, and they had slaves also in Rome who did all the work because they had to. Slaves was given no choice in the matter. They had slaves in all the states down south, she said, and we had them up north, too. Folk had slaves in Illinois, but they warn't supposed to. It was against the law in Illinois but the law looked t'other way when it was supposed to be looking at slavery. We didn't have no slaves in our town. She expected that was because we was mostly too poor to have slaves. You couldn't make money from slaves unless you was growing cotton or some such crop. 'Round here it was all hardscrabble, so slaves didn't pay. Even Mr. Purdy couldn't make money out of slaves, and he was right clever when it came to making money.

Slave labor didn't make no sense unless the slave was making more'n he cost you to feed, Miss Larsen said. That's why oftentimes they was fed hardly enough to keep a hen alive. Most folk in our town could barely feed their selves, so they warn't gonna get no slaves to feed. Miss Larsen wagged her finger. But they surely would if they could, some of them. Only thing stops 'em getting slaves is the ee-conomics of it. She was against something called the cotton gin. It had a lot to answer for. Made it real easy to make lots of money outta slaves if you grew cotton. It got more people owning slaves and wanting to own slaves than ever before, and more slaves was more misery in this world. As if there warn't enough misery to be going 'round already. Miss Larsen wouldn't have been surprised to hear the cotton gin had been invented by the Devil. She was what they call a "abolitionist." She taught us it was wrong to have slaves, and God frowned on it. I frowned on it, too, because sometimes it felt like my life was one of slavery, and I didn't much care for that state of affairs, so I saw how slavery was wrong. Miss Larsen never taught us what they did to slaves. Treated them worse than you'd treat your worst enemy's dog I was finding out.

As God is my witness I woulda helped that poor black man in the outhouse if I could have done. But

I was a twelve-year-old boy, unarmed, and a Yankee at that, in a place where they might not care over-much for Yankees. This was enemy territory in a manner of speaking. Kentuckians was of two minds. The Union mind and the Reb mind. No telling which of their minds was gonna win out. If the Reb mind had won out here, on this plantation, then if I so much as showed my face I coulda been taken prisoner and kilt for being a spy. So I took the coward's way out and did nothing. Sometimes it's all you can do, unless you have a death wish. That's what Pa told me when I was little. I never understood it at the time, but I understood it now.

I didn't have a death wish. For all the hardship I'd endured in my twelve short years on this earth I wanted to live. That's because I always hoped for better things coming 'round the corner. They never came of course, but I never stopped hoping. That was the difference between me and the slaves. They hadn't got nothing to hope for coming 'round the corner. All they ever had coming to them was more of the same. I saw that clear enough. The one faint hope they had in hell was escapin' to a town like I came from, that likely didn't want them and had no use for them. If I had anything to thank God for, it was he made me a white boy. If he hadn't, it coulda been me strung up from a beam in an outhouse somewhere crying out for mercy that never came.

The white folks that owned the grand house warn't up yet, most of them. But the ones that ran the farm was up, and they was making sure their slaves was working hard as a body could work. It was what you might call death work. Many of them was close to death even those that might not have had the lash. I went back into a tobacco field. Tobacco plants was planted wide enough apart for me to hide in, so I moved between them and stole over to the sheds I'd seen. When I got to the first one I opened the door and peeked in. It had no furniture to speak of, just bedding on the floor to sleep on. No telling how many families had to sleep on it. Out in the fields those families was working hard, though I did see some of the young-sters running around and playing like I used to. *Make the most of it*, I thought. *You won't be doing that for long. Soon as the rich master decides you're old enough to work you'll be joining your Ma and Pa in that field and dying a slow death the same way they are.*

Now I knowed I had a long way to go there was no point in hanging around. I couldn't go back the way I'd come so I found another route. It took me through another tobacco field, where I gave a wide berth to the pickers and their overseers. Heard the overseers talking real nasty to the pickers and did my best to ignore them. It warn't no concern of mine. My only concern at that moment was to get back to northern soil in one piece.

12.

WHY AIN'T YOU SAVING ME, BOY?

WHEN YOU'VE BEEN BROUGHT UP LIKE ME YOU know animals can stalk and kill you, and you learn to watch out for it. There comes a time when you don't have to watch out for it because it gets to be natural to know whether some animal is tailing you hoping you'll be its next meal. If the animal is a bear you can't help but know it, because a bear makes its intentions clear. If the animal is a pig you know it also. A pig is smarter than a bear, but if you listen out you can tell by the noise a pig is stalking you. And if the animal is a man, you can't help but know he's stalking you because men are the clumsiest animals in the woods. I'm talking about town men and farmers of course, not folks with woodcraft like me and Pa. If you was in the woods I could sneak up on you until I was standin' right next to you, and you wouldn't know I was there unless you turned your head and looked my way.

Crouching down among the tobacco I got the feeling I was being stalked, so I stopped moving and listened hard. Behind me the tobacco plants crunched then stopped their crunching. That told me someone behind me had been following in my footsteps and stopped moving a second or two after I had done, so I pulled out my knife. Then I got to walking forward again in my crouch and made a point of leaving a real big trail the man behind me could follow without barely looking for it. Moving quickly I got well ahead of him then slipped sideways and doubled back, dropping into an ambush crouch. I waited still as a rock in the desert. Tobacco plants crunched, and a black man came by, bent double, wearing a long shirt and raggedy pants, no shoes, bony shoulders sticking up through his shirt, bony knees with the skin all flaked like the scales of a lizard sticking out of the holes in his pants. Stealing to the side of him, I wrapped my left arm round his neck and pressed the sharp edge of my blade up against his throat like Pa learned me to do with a pig.

"What you up to?" I said.

The way his eyes widened told me he was as scared as I felt. "I saw you watching Isaac get a whipping," he said, "and I knowed by the look on your face you was shocked, so I figured you don't come from these parts and you must be a Yankee, and I figured I'd follow you home."

"I want to get home in one piece," I told him. "It's gonna be hard enough for me to save my own hide without having to think about anybody else's." All the while I was talkin' I kept my blade against his throat. He gulped. Blade damn near cut his skin when he did, because I always kept it good and sharp like Pa taught me.

"Help me," the black man said. "You saw what they did to Isaac. If they catch me I'll get it worse'n he did. I'll be whipped to death to set an example to the others."

Putting my knife back in my belt I shook my head. Then I changed my mind and said, "Follow me if you must. But keep quiet and keep down, damn you."

"Thank you," he said.

I said, "Keep quiet!" so he shut up.

As we got 'round the farthest of the tobacco pickers and overseers I wondered how long it'd be till he was missed and the hue and cry went out for him. When it did, what would the search party be like? Would they come after us on horses? If they was gonna be horsebacked, we needed to put a good distance between them and us as soon as possible. A horse will run down a man over a short distance, no doubt about it. But over the long haul the man wins out. We needed to make sure it'd be a long haul, so long that their horses wouldn't be able to catch us. Would they send dogs after us? When I thought about a pack of big hunting dogs running at us through the baccy, my belly turned over and made me feel right sick. After that I tried not to think about dogs too much. Even so I couldn't help but think we was in a big hole. Only thing we got going for us was that for now we hadn't been seen, and my new friend, if you could call him that, hadn't been missed. We could take care so as to make sure we wouldn't be seen, but sooner or later someone would notice my runaway friend was gone, and the posse from hell would come after us. Those slave catchers Benjamin told me about would be leading the charge. What would they do when they found me with him? I warn't no use to them. No one gonna pay money for a twelve-year-old white boy. I'd just get in the way so they'd kill me soon as they'd look at me. Or take me back to the slave owners for them to whip me to death to make an example of me to learn folk not to have any truck with helping slaves escape their masters.

I knowed what I had to do. I had to make sure that if my friend was caught I warn't caught with him. The only way to be sure of doing that was to cut him loose.

Leave him behind to fend for hisself first chance I got. And that's what I was fixing to do.

The sky was blue, and the clouds had mostly gone, but it warn't too warm. I reckoned my new friend would be shivering, both with the chill air, and with the fear of gettin' caught. It made me feel bad for him but not bad enough to help him get away. My hide was too important to me to risk it saving another.

The path I made through the tobacco field was silent, but behind me there was lots of noise. I stopped and turned my head, put my finger over my lips. The black feller following me raised his eyebrows and shrugged.

Taking my finger offa my lips I stole over to him put my mouth to his ear and whispered, "Keep quiet when you movin', Goddamn you. You'll get the both of us kilt." He looked kinda hurt, but I ignored that and got going again. Not gonna feel sorry for telling the truth when the truth was all that stood between us and death.

Tobacco pickers was way over to our right, and their overseers was standing over them making sure they was breaking their backs a-picking tobacco, which was good for us. It meant none of them was likely to look our way. Even if they did, so long as we kept low, made no noise, and didn't shake the plants too much, we wouldn't be seen. In the distance was a bunch of trees I headed for, same trees I'd sheltered under during the night. As I got near them I moved quicker. My black friend being taller'n me found it hard to go as quick as I did. He had to bend double where I just had to move in a hunter's crouch, which I'd done many times before when I'd gotten close to game. His back and legs musta hurt like hell bent up the way he was. On top of which he'd been eatin' barely enough to keep his body and soul together. One look at him told me that much. So he wouldn't have the energy I had. I was starved right enough, but he was starved and then some.

I burst out the tobacco plants near the hemp plants, went in my crouch to the riverbank, and followed it over the bluffs back to the beach where the skiff was. I ran to it, pushed it in the river, jumped in, and got to rowing hard as I could. Didn't take me long to clear the shore. A wind blowed, and the water got choppy. The bow of the skiff bobbed up and down. I rowed looking over the stern back the way I'd come. Current was taking me downstream and I did my best to fight it and go in a straight line towards the other side. It was a battle I could never win. No matter how hard I rowed I ended up drifting downriver. Over on the shore my new friend came down the side of the bluffs. His head turned right and left looking for his savior who warn't there. Then he lighted on the lines left in the sand by the skiff where I'd pushed it onto and offa the river beach. His head followed the lines to the river, and he raised it until I seed his eyes looking into mine. Never seen so much despair written on a feller's face as I saw on his that day. It twisted up into a mess of lines and every one of them said, "I'm gonna die a horrible death soon, why ain't you saving me, boy? Can't you see you the only hope I got? Why you running out on me? What did I ever do to you?"

My life had become a trail of broken hearts. My brother broke my heart though I never admitted it to myself, then Pa broke my heart, then Ma did, then Ervan, then Cath, then near enough the whole damn town. Now I'd broke someone else's heart for a change, my new friend's heart. But he got his own right back on me, because that look on his face broke my heart into such tiny pieces I thought I'd never put 'em back together again if I had my whole life to do it in. But my broken heart didn't stop me from rowing. I was too affrighted of the slave catchers and slave owners to stop, having seen what slave owners could do to a body with a whip. I didn't want 'em doing it to anybody at all, but in particular to my body.

Next thing I knowed my new black friend goes running up to the river and dives in after me, and that's where things started going wrong. I knowed right away from his splashing he couldn't swim worth a damn. Probably never got near water deep enough to swim in very often in his life. Too busy cutting hemp or tobacco or some other work dawn to dusk to learn swimming, so he had not gotten the least idea of how to keep his head above water. Arms flailing and water flying he was carried downriver. You couldn't call what he was doing swimming, but it got him away from the shore. In other words, in a place he had no business being. Farther away from land he got, the more trouble he was in, and it warn't long before he was in a heap of trouble. His flailing got more desperate, and he cried out, "Save me! I'm drowning!" Luckily the tobacco pickers and overseers was a good way out of earshot of his cries for help. Hearing him tore up the tiny pieces of my heart into tinier pieces still, but I didn't stop rowing. I had to get away and save my skin. Way I saw it was it was every man for hisself. Credit where its due he couldn't swim, but he did his darndest to get across the water to me, and he made some progress with it, too. Just not enough.

In my head I was saying, *You're crazy, head back*

to the riverbank! Then I shouted it.

He was close enough to hear me, and somehow he shouted back, "I'm gonna die if I do, I might as well die of drowning here in the river as die of a whipping on dry land."

"Alright, die if you want!" I said, pulling on the oars harder. Next thing was I seed him bobbing under the water, and it made me want to wet myself but I didn't. He came back up after a while, and I felt mighty relieved and put more space between me and him, and he splashed more desperate than before, and bobbed under a second time. I waited for him to come up, and he did, but I knowed if he bobbed under again, it would be his last. Ever'body knows you only got three chances at it. Three times you go under and the third you stay under. Drowning man goes under only three times.

He kicked up a hollering fit to wake the dead. He warn't asking for help no more. He was just affrighted of dying, and I knowed I couldn't let him die. I'd done my best to turn my heart into stone, but it warn't made of stone, it was flesh and blood and love and hate and all the other ingredients our maker if there is one put into our hearts, and the love such as it was in me for humanity won out. Turning the skiff 'round I rowed upstream of the hollering so as to end up near enough where he was. All the while I was rowing that direction, I was praying I'd get there in time. Rowed so hard my arms felt like they was dropping off, but I kept pulling on those oars hard as I could until my lungs got fit to bust with the effort. Burning in my chest felt like my ribs was on fire. I got to gasping like I'd spent more time underwater than the man I was trying to save.

When I reached him his head was beneath the waves. He was going under for the third and final time. I got the skiff up close to him and one of his hands latched onto the rope that was still trailing from the stern. In my hurry I hadn't gotten hold of it and pulled it back on board. He still had the strength to close his fingers round it and pull hisself back to the surface. Believe me when I tell you I was grateful he did that. I hadn't wanted him with me, but I hadn't wanted him dead, either. Deep down I knowed he'd be a dead man if I left him behind on dry land, but it wouldn't have been entirely on my conscience, because someone else woulda done the killing of him, and it wouldn't be happening right in front of me. But I couldn't watch him drown, I had to save him from that. I found out something about myself that day. Can't say I'm proud of what I found out, but we all got something to be ashamed of.

I pulled in the oars and let go of them, so they lay flat lengthwise in the skiff. Then, crawling to the stern, I did my best to haul him in like a fish on a line. He came above the surface gasping worse'n I was with his mouth wide open and his eyes blinking the river water out of them. He got one hand on the stern then t'other and pulled hisself up. I got my hands under his armpits giving him such help as I could. He got an elbow over the stern then another elbow and sorta crawled on board dripping wet, his shirt or smock or whatever it was clinging to his skinny frame. Those shoulders of his poking out put me in mind of the pointy triangles Miss Larsen used to draw in her geometry class. Soon as I knowed he was safe, I rowed for the opposite shore. Not long after I started rowing, a couple of men appeared on the beach I'd left the skiff on. They was a good way off, because the current had carried us downriver. They looked at the marks the keel of the skiff had made in the sand, and looked over at us, and saw a black man with a white boy. I cursed myself for not making my passenger lie down in the skiff soon as I'd gotten him aboard. If he'd been lying flat they wouldn't a seen him, and if they hadn't seen him, they wouldn't have known for sure he was with me. They would've suspected it, but not knowed it. But now, sure as eggs ain't nothing else but eggs, they knowed we was together. What, though, could they do about it?

One of them decided to do something. He raised a musket to his shoulder and aimed it right at me. We both knowed at this distance he was as likely to hit my passenger as he was to hit me, especially as we was sitting close together, the skiff being so small. And being as a black man young enough to work for a day was a valuable commodity in those parts, he thought the better of it and lowered his musket. They would both be back, no doubt, and they would bring with them whatever they needed to catch us. That was the safest bet a body could have made that day, take it from me. Knowing that, I rowed like hell to get to the Illinois side, and when I couldn't row no more I put the oars in the bottom of the skiff and crawled to the back making it do a deal of wobbling.

"Swap places with me," I said to my new friend. He ain't never been in a skiff before, I could see that by the look of horror he got on his face. But give him credit, he made his way on all fours to where I'd been sitting and grabbed the oars without being told, and pulled on them hisself. "Row like hell! Both our lives depend on it!" I said.

"You think I don't know that, son?" He warn't no good at rowing, but still he pulled that skiff good and hard, using nothing but man strength and a good dash of ignorance.

I just hoped no other boat would come along while he was sitting up making hisself plain for all to see. Chances was if that happened someone would try to make some bounty money. No boat came, and between us we got close to the Illinois shore. The effort wore us both out, let me tell you. When it was my turn to row I let the current drag us so far downstream the men on the river shore lost sight of our skiff, and we lost sight of them.

When we were close to the Illinois riverbank, with the last of our strength we got out the skiff and got the skiff out the water. Then we got the provisions such as they was out the skiff.

"Help me get the skiff back in the river," I said.

My friend looked puzzled but helped me push it back in. The current caught it and swept it away.

I gave him the blankets to carry, and I carried the salt meat and the canteen. Filled the canteen with fresh water from the river and hung it over my shoulder by the strap.

"What's your name, son?" he said.

"Ain't no time for knowing names now," I said. "We gotta move fast. Might be time for exchangin' formalities later." That was true. But what was also true was that I didn't want to know his name, nor for him to know mine. Names would complicate things, and I didn't want complications. Certainly I didn't want no truck with the complication of getting to like a man I was aiming to abandon to his fate first chance I got.

Picking up a couple of fallen branches off a tree, I gave one to my friend. "Watch me," I said, using the branch to wipe away the marks our skiff had left in the mud on the riverbank. He soon got the idea and did the same. Then I showed him to walk backward hiding the marks his feet had left, wiping them away with the branch he was holding as he walked.

"Follow me," I told him when we got to the tree line, and we hightailed it into the woods but not so fast that we couldn't keep going. We did a steady walk quickly. Best way to move if you want to outpace an animal, which is what I figured we'd have to do. I took us west, reckoning what we needed was to get deep into the woods fast as we could. We'd be safer there than close to the river. When I judged it right I'd take us north.

After an hour near as I could tell I stopped. "We oughta eat to keep up our strength," I said.

He nodded and I gave him half the salt meat I was carrying. He ate it like he'd never had a scrap of food in his life before. I was no better. Chowed down on mine like it was about to run away from me even though it couldn't. Also I took the opportunity to study my new friend some. He was thirty looked like, with a face that would've been pleasing to the eye if it but had more meat on it. His sunken cheeks put me too much in mind of a corpse that died of starvation to feel I could call him good looking. In height he was about five foot six inches and in weight not much more than Pa, who was a good four inches shorter than him, which tells you all you need to know about how skinny he was. His shirt garment was still sticking to his skin here and there. It would be some time before that water dried off it properly.

Within minutes of me unwrapping it, most of our supplies of meat was in our bellies. Slave or ex-slave as you might call him swallowed a piece and looked at me. "I'm called Billy."

"What's your last name?" I said right quick, before he got the chance to ask me for my name. I didn't want him asking that. It'd make things too personal.

"Don't have one," he said.

"Don't have one?"

"I was given my master's name, which is Colston, and I'm known as Billy Colston, but that's a slave name so I'm figuring on changing it. I'll still be Billy. My Ma gave me that name. But I'm not gonna be called Colston no more."

"What you gonna be called then?"

"I don't know. I ain't decided yet. What's your name, son?" he asked, chowing down on our last piece of salt meat. My heart sank like a rock in a river when he asked me that. Someone who's just a face don't mean nothing to you, and you don't owe them nothing. But when you know their names and get on friendly terms, all that changes. Knowing his name would make it harder for me to cut him loose when the time came. It'd feel like I was letting him down. Worse, it'd make me feel like that there Judas Miss Larsen told us about in Bible class. Bible was the main class she was interested in teaching us, I don't know why.

Anyways, I looked at Billy and told him, "Joseph Wild, but you can call me Joe."

He smiled holding out his hand, so I took it, and we shook hands. Something else I would rather not have done. "You're quite the little man, Joe," he said, still smiling all wide.

"I don't know 'bout that," I said, not smiling because I didn't want to get too friendly.

By pulling him out the water and feeding him had I done enough for Billy? If I had, could I leave him to his fate? That's what I was thinking.

The way I figured it was Billy was wanted for being a slave, and I was wanted for being a murderer. That meant we needed to go far enough north without being seen that when we were seen folks who saw us wouldn't know who we was or what we was, and wouldn't even have heard tell of us. That in turn meant we would have to spend a long time hiding in the woods while heading north before we could risk going out into the open and letting folks see us.

Another thing I figured was I oughta lose Billy as soon as possible because slave catchers would be out looking for a white boy and a black man together, and also they would be telling folk in these parts to look out for a white boy and a black man together. We would stick out like a thumb that's been hit with a hammer if we showed our faces anywhere, and I'd be heading for the noose before you knowed it, while Billy would be heading for a death whipping just as quick. Either that or if he was lucky he'd be sold on to a place where life was no more than a living death. Had to admit I'd rather be hung than whipped to death. But the point was I wanted to live. Most sensible way of making sure I did was to survive in the woods on my own, because Billy was a magnet that would bring trouble our way, and like as not a dead weight for me to carry. A dead weight will slow you down when you need to move quickly. He'd likely not survive if I left him behind of course. He'd lose his way in the woods and go 'round in circles and starve or end up as a hog's dinner or a bear's. I didn't want that to happen to him, but I had to harden myself and let it happen. It warn't my fault he ain't got no woodcraft. It warn't my fault he'd been a slave and got slave catchers on his tail. Whose fault it was I couldn't rightly say. Maybe God's, if anyone's.

We drank a little water from a stream and set off again. There was a way of moving Pa schooled me in from an early age, and it had become a habit with me. It was near silent. Usually when I moved that way I could hear all the sounds in the woods I needed to hear. But all I could hear that day was Billy's clumping footsteps at the back of me even though he was barefoot. Guess he'd had no call to ever walk real quiet and had never learned how. Stopping, I turned round with my finger over my lips. He got the message. Then I was able to hear at last. Above us birds was crashing through the treetops. A scratching on a tree trunk told me there must be a squirrel nearby, or a pine marten, maybe even a fisher. I listened harder. Definitely a fisher. Anyways nothing to worry me. No hog sniffing in the dirt. No bear sniffing for a hog or a man. Waving my arm to say "Follow me," I walked some more, cussing up a storm in my head as I did, about how I couldn't hear a damn thing with Billy at the back of me. I was getting real mad at him. That warn't fair of me, but it was good in a way. It'd make it easier to rid myself of him when I got my chance.

We trekked uphill a good while through trees and more trees. They was watching us in their own way. Pa always said trees talk to each other. When he first told me that I didn't believe him, but you spend a lot of time with trees and you can see the truth of it. I only wish I spoke their language. I reckon I could find out a few things that'd make you wonder.

The land fell, and we trekked downhill. A gurgling sound told me we was dropping into a valley with a river at the bottom of it. The river was a small one. If it had a name, I don't know what it was. When we got to it I kept my eyes peeled for pecans, and sure enough I found some and stopped.

Pulling one off the tree I said, "We gotta eat some of these pecans, Billy. I don't know when we'll get the chance to eat again."

He looked at them kinda curious, and I could tell he ain't never eaten a wild pecan like we got in the woods before. Probably never even seen a pecan tree deep in a wood. All he'd ever seen in his life was tobacco and hemp and cotton and similar, and the inside of a big shed and a whip maybe, too. It didn't make for someone who'd do well in the woods. The woods can be your best friend if you know what you're doing, but they will surely be your worst enemy if you don't. The woods will feed you, but they'll also kill you. You gotta tread real careful to be fed rather than be kilt to feed something else.

"This is the kind of thing we gonna have to eat for a while," I said. "We can't afford to waste any time trapping animals for their meat. Gotta live on nuts and berries and such so we can keep up a good pace."

He nodded.

When we'd had our fill I said, "Pick more and stuff your pockets with 'em, Billy."

"I ain't got no pockets," he said pulling at his shirt to show me. Damned if he didn't. I rammed what I could in mine and had him fold a blanket into a sorta bag so he could carry some pecan nuts hisself.

The river was some twenty-foot wide and fast

flowing but not too deep. Rolling up my pants I found I could wade it. When I got to t'other side I waved my arm at Billy, and he followed me across. We kept moving till dusk. Then I scouted round for bear tracks. When I was satisfied there was none I found a tree trunk to sit up against, and we wrapped ourselves in our blankets, sat with our backs against it, ate some pecans, and drank some water.

"When you sleep, sleep with one eye open," I said. "If you hear anything don't call out, give me a nudge or something."

"Sure thing, Joe," he said. Then the night closed in, and I fell asleep knowing I would wake up first and head north, leaving Billy to his fate.

13.

THE VANISHING

IT WAS A LOW GROWL THAT WOKE ME UP. RIGHT away I knowed a bear was nearby. *No point in hanging around,* I thought. The bear might wander over and not take kindly to me. Mostly they'll leave you be if you ignore them, but you never can tell. If they decide you're food they'll charge you like a train and knock you down, then they'll eat you like as not while you're still alive. They like their dinner fresh. Naturally I wanted to put a good distance between the bear and me. Billy was wrapped in his blanket sleeping soundly. I got to my feet without disturbing him just as I'd planned. I'd done my bit for Billy. It was up to him to save hisself now.

I shoulda made myself scarce right away, but I didn't. I just stood there looking at Billy sleeping and wondering if I was doing the right thing, and if I could go through with it. If I left him he was surely dead. When I thought about it not one in one hundred folks who didn't know the woods could go in one end and get out the other side in one piece. They'd all die by the hand of the woods and the things that lived in them. The few that didn't die would need the luck of ten lifetimes to stay alive. I was fine because I was a thing that lived in the woods, or near to being one as made no difference. Billy was a thing that didn't. He had no idea about the ways of the trees and the critters. No doubt he could knock me into a cocked hat when it came to something like picking tobacco. But he had not got the first idea how to survive in my world.

While I was rassling with my conscience I warn't walking away from Billy or the bear. I was still as one of those statues they got outside of cigar shops. Billy rubbed his eyes. This was my last chance to go before he opened them. I took a step back. All I had to do was stand behind a tree, and he'd have no idea where I was, then he'd panic and make a lotta noise. The bear would hear him. Depending on what kind of bear it was, he might be all right. But if it was a hungry bear or a grizzly whether hungry or not, he'd be in a heap of trouble. Not my concern I told myself. With footsteps soft as those of a pet cat I glided across the forest floor to hide behind a buckthorn. I could see Billy through the foliage. Opening his eyes he looked right at me but didn't see me. His head turned to where I'd been sitting next to him. The panic on his face made me want to throw up at the thought of my bad behaviour in letting him down, but I convinced myself it warn't all that bad. It was just what I had to do to survive.

Billy jumped up and the blanket he'd been wearing dropped to his feet, and he turned his head this way and that, his eyes getting wider by the second. Moved away from the tree. When I tell you not one man in a thousand knows how to get about in the woods without making a hell of a racket I'm not exaggerating. Not being one man in a thousand, Billy made one hell of a racket. The bear heard him and decided to investigate. It came into view. Worst news possible for Billy. It was a grizzly. Black bears ain't really so dangerous 'ceptin very rarely. Grizzlies you always got to watch out for. Best thing you can do is steer well clear of them. But it was too late for Billy to do that.

Billy looked at the grizzly, and the grizzly looked at him. I kept hid behind the Buckthorn, breathing long and deep and slow and quiet, making not a sound, twitching not a muscle. Billy sorta froze. Best thing he could do, in a way. At least he warn't gonna rub that grizzly up the wrong way by standing still like that. Grizzly stayed on all fours watching what Billy was gonna do. If he'd stayed the way he was, it mighta got bored and wandered off, found some berries to eat, or gone fishing or whatever. But Billy made a big mistake although he warn't to know it was a big mistake.

"God help me!" he cried, loud as anything. "God help me!" Waving his arms around, he did a little skip and ran away from the bear fast as he could.

It ain't worth running from a bear because a bear can run faster than any man that lived. It'll get you if it wants to. Only difference if you run is you'll be tired and out of breath when it mauls you. The real reason you shouldn't run though is if you keep still you got a chance of the bear leaving you alone. If you run the bear is more likely to go for you. Maybe not if it's a black bear, but likely it will if it's a grizzly, because when you run you look more like food to a grizzly, same way a deer looks like food to it.

So the bear takes an interest in Billy now. Billy charges toward me not knowing I was there, screaming about God and saints preserving him, and all sorts of things, and I can see the grizzly is thinking about going after him. Next thing it did, its paws like thunder on the ground as it ran. Billy musta heard it behind him. I sure did. *He's gonna die*, I thought, *but at least it means he's luring that ol' bear away from me. So long as it's chasing Billy it ain't gonna be chasin' me. Probably won't even notice me.* So I fixed to keep low and quiet and still and let Billy run right past me. The bear would follow, and I'd be safe.

But just as Billy came past something happened. I got what you might call a wobble inside. I just couldn't stick to my plan to let Billy go his own way without me. My head knowed it was the right thing to do for my survival, but my heart begged to differ, and my heart won the argument. My heart made me stick out my leg as Billy came a-running past me. He went backside in the air and fell on his face. Knocked the wind right outta him. At least that meant he stopped screaming. Before he had the chance to get up I dived down next to him and slapped him on the back with my arm to get his attention. "Lie down and keep still if you want to live, damn you," I whispered, "and cover the back of your neck with your hands and play dead. Don't you dare so much as move an eyelid till I tell you to." I played dead myself.

I heard the grizzly slow to a walk. Its walking got nearer until it was right next to me. Felt its breath on the backs of my hands. A paw the size of a man's head sorta prodded at me, curious. Next to me Billy making noises same as those a drowning man might make, gasping and desperate. I wanted to shout at him to be quiet! But had to stay the way I was. Bear pushed against me with its paw, and I made myself all floppy as if my bones had turned to jelly. It rolled me over like I weighed nothing and sniffed at my throat then it turned itself around and wandered off. The sound of its paws got fainter and fainter. When the sound disappeared altogether and had been gone a good few minutes I raised my head just enough to look in the direction it went. There warn't no sign of it.

"Billy, don't make a sound," I said. "Quiet as you can and slow as you like, stand up. We're getting out of here." We got up and moved off like we was at the bottom of a lake of molasses. When I judged it safe to talk I said, "That bear gave me one of the closest shaves I ever had."

"I saw it out the corner of my eye," said Billy. "Scariest thing I seen. Don't know how you stopped yourself from getting up and running."

"I don't, either," I said, and we both laughed so we could barely keep on our feet. Big belly laughs bending us double. We stopped laughing, and Billy wiped a tear from his eye. Then his eyebrows came together, and his eyes they narrowed, and his lips pursed.

"What was you doing hiding behind the back of that bush?" he asked. "Where was you thinking of going?"

He got me there. My face turned bright red, I'm sure it did. I had no way of seeing it but I felt it prickling and getting hot like a campfire. "Nothing," I said. "Just foraging."

He gave me a stare fit to poke a hole through a stone wall. "Uh-huh," he said, but he kept his stare on me.

I looked away. No point in having an argument with him. I'd already had the argument with myself and come to a decision on it. Upshot was, I was gonna look after Billy and take as much care over keeping his hide safe as I was my own.

"Better get going," I said.

"Uh-huh," he said again.

We headed north, and I kept my eyes peeled for bear tracks. No point in asking Billy to do it. Even if I showed him what to look for, he'd never spot them. Not unless we crossed a patch of mud or soft earth where the trail was clear. Mostly trails aren't clear. They're a disturbed line in the leaves with maybe a few depressions, and a bush missing some berries, and the remains of a kill, and a whole lotta other things including the poop and stuff like that that tell you what it was went ahead of you through the woods, and how big it was. You can't explain such things to a body in two minutes, and even if you could, it takes a lotta experience and training to make use of it. Pa and me got years of that experience. Ain't nobody better than Pa at that kind of thing. But he brought me up so I'm almost as good as he is. Funny how I keep finding things to be grateful to the old bastard for.

We made fifteen miles a day, I reckon. No way of telling for sure. Whatever number of miles we did we shoulda done more, but we was hampered by Billy. He just couldn't go no faster than he was going. He was bigger'n me but was also skinnier, which is saying something. Looked like he'd never had a square meal in his life. I hadn't had too many myself, but I'd had more'n Billy. The difference showed when it came to covering a distance. Billy was always struggling to keep up each day when we'd gone a few miles. I did my best to keep up his energy by finding us supplies of hickory nuts. We stumbled on a persimmon tree, and with Billy's help I shimmied up it and got us some fruit. It warn't altogether ripe, so it tasted sour, but it filled our bellies, and that's all we was after. We stuffed ourselves with curly dock whenever we came across it. "Your belly is like a fire," Pa always told me. "You got to keep a log," by which he meant food, "burning in the fire." He never lived up to what he said about logs and fires, not really. But his words sunk in me, and I sunk them in Billy.

After five days Billy was looking none too good. Whatever he'd done or had done to him all his life hadn't got him half ready for this sort of thing. The way he looked put me in mind of Benjamin when he came outta the woods into our town. Benjamin had been on the brink of death. Miss Larsen saved him by looking after him and giving him a chance to rest and feeding him up. Warn't no way I could look after Billy and feed him up and give him a chance to rest, but somehow I'd have to try.

I'd been wondering how we was gonna cross the Skillet Fork River when we got to it. In view of Billy's health, I decided not to, at least not for a day or two. Instead I found a level spot leading up to the bluffs overlooking the river. With Billy's help I built a frame a bit like the letter A from dead branches we found lying around. I laid dead branches over the frame and dead leaves over the branches. Started at the bottom and worked up with the leaves to make them good and watertight. Pretty soon me and Billy had built us a shelter the way Pa had taught me to. Pa told me it was the way Indians built them. Never told me which Indians but that ain't important. Inside it we raised the floor offa the ground with more dead wood, thin sticks of it. Finally, we gathered enough dead wood to build us a fire with a pile left over to give us a good stock of firewood. I had my flint I always carried with me, and I found some dry moss to help out on the kindling front. Sparked the flint onto the moss until

I'd got a red glowing spot on it which I blew until it glowed more and flamed up. Shoved it quickly under the thinnest of the dry twigs we had. That fire roared up and made us both feel a whole lot better.

I knowed I was taking a hell of a risk. No telling if the slave catchers would still be chasing us but if they was then stopping and setting up camp like this would make it a sight easier for them to catch us. On the other hand if we carried on the way we was I could have seen Billy dying on his feet. We were caught between a rock and a hard place, you might say.

"You keep that fire going, Billy, and rest yourself up," I told him.

"I will, son, thank you," he said, sitting on his blanket in our shelter looking out at our fire.

"I'm going foraging."

He nodded.

Down at the river I took out my trusty fishhook and fastened it to the end of my twine. Then I got a short piece of twine and tied a pebble to it. I tied the short piece of twine to the main line that had the hook. Now I had a hook, line, and sinker. All I needed was bait. Dug myself a good fat worm from the ground and stuck the hook through it. The worm wriggling on that hook made me think of me and Billy if we got caught. I put the thought to the back of my mind and found an easy stretch of water with a rock I could set on and cast the line in and set myself down. The rock made a small splash and disappeared. When it had sunk so deep the twine was tight in my hand I let the twine rest against my finger, feeling the tightness. If a fish goes for bait on a line you feel something. Not a pull zackly, more like it shakes gently, so gentle sometimes you could easy miss it. You have to watch out for that shake and know what to do so as not to lose the fish. The way I held that line I coulda felt a speck of dust landing on it. I sat there on the rock good and patient for a while and ain't nothing happened.

Don't know how long I sat. Musta given it near enough half an hour. Then I pulled out the twine and tried again, aiming the sinker for a different stretch of water, just a bit farther out than the first stretch. It warn't long after that I felt something. I didn't do anything about it, just held onto my twine. You have to do that so as to give the fish a chance to get the hook deep in its mouth. Pull too soon and the hook won't be deep enough. Might not be in at all. Either way, you'll lose your fish. Well, I waited and waited and I got that feeling of the line shaking harder like someone got hold of it underwater and was dragging it away from me. That's when I pulled the line in. It turned out I'd caught a Largemouth Bass about a foot and a half long. Threw in the line again a few times and after a while I'd caught myself a couple of bluegills.

Top and bottom of it is I went back to Billy toting three fish. I scraped off the scales with my knife and cut off the heads and gutted them and sliced off the tails and fins and shoved sticks through them and cooked them over our campfire. They went down real good with some curly dock I'd collected.

"This is tasty, son, I do declare," Billy said. "Real tasty. I ain't never had fish before. Just heard tell of it."

"What do you eat then?"

"Cornmeal and such. Peas and greens. Sometimes the smallest piece of meat you ever seen in your life. So small it ain't hardly worth calling meat. Never enough of anything to fill your belly. This is the first time I ever had a full belly that I can remember." Hearing Billy say that made me real proud like I'd done something worthwhile.

"Know anything 'bout the war, son?" he said after a while.

"Only what Miss Larsen told me. She's the schoolteacher in our town."

"What do you know?"

"It's for the Union. North wants to keep the Union and South wants to break it. Miss Larsen says the Union's a good thing, and we should fight to keep it. That's why folk in the north are fighting. Folk in the South got a contrary view, otherwise there wouldn't be no fighting. But it ain't gonna be a bloody war. It's gonna be short and bloodless."

"You're wrong, son."

"What do you mean?"

"It's not 'bout the Union, it's 'bout slavery. This whole thing is 'bout slavery. And the South ain't gonna give up their slaves without putting up a hell of a fight. We're worth too much to 'em. Ever'thing they have comes from slavery. Their money was earned from it. Their fine houses built from it. Their fancy clothes made outta it. They ain't gonna give any of that up, which means blood is gonna be spilled. More blood than you can possibly imagine. It's gonna flow wide and deep as the Mississippi before this thing is over, you mark my words."

I hoped Billy was wrong about all that blood flowing because if I joined the army like I was fixing to, some of that spilled blood could be mine. But I never said nothing about that. Instead I changed the subject.

"Looks like you been living in hell, Billy," I said.

"Hell? You wrong there too, boy. That plantation you saw is paradise." I musta got a look on my face because he said, "You don't believe me? Let me tell you cutting down hemp and tobacco in Kentucky is backbreaking work but even so, it's heaven compared to picking cotton in Virginny. I've done both, I know. You pick raw cotton off'n a bool, and it's so prickly it takes the skin offa your hands after you done a few of 'em, but you gotta keep picking dawn to dusk because if you don't you get whipped. And even if you do pick all day and all night too chances are sooner or later you gonna get whipped. That's life on a cotton plantation for you, son. All they know is the whip."

I shook my head. Nothing I could say to that. Any case, me and Billy was too tired to say much else, and as it was getting late we said goodnight to each other and turned in. Best night's sleep either of us had had in quite a while, I can tell you. Swear to God that makeshift bed I'd put together from dead wood was as comfortable as my old mattress back home. Either that or I was more tired than I'd ever been before in my life, which was possible, what with all the runnin' away I seemed to have been doing lately. Next morning Billy looked a lot better but he warn't ready yet for more hard walking so I got the fire going again, and got some more fish caught, and we holed up for another day. I turned in that night hoping to God the slave catchers had given up the chase, but deep down I knowed they hadn't. Anything worth eight hundred dollars is worth chasing to the end of the earth for. Even I knowed that.

Billy woke up looking like a new man, but I didn't want to put too much burden on him just yet, so I walked him up near the side of the river for only half a day. I was planning on us moving a lot further the next day, figuring he'd be so much better then. I made a camp with a fire same as before.

"Wait here, Billy. I'll catch some fish," I said, and went down to the river and did my thing with my fishing line and caught us a couple of bluegills, nice big ones. Right proud of myself I was. I pictured Billy's face when he saw he had more good fish to eat. He'd be smiling no doubt. But he warn't. Because he warn't there.

14.

CAPTURED, TIED UP, AND TORTURED

I AIN'T NEVER BEEN SO AFFRIGHTED IN MY LIFE
as I was when I went back to the camp and saw it
was empty. Figuring Billy had been caught and tak-
en away, I got guilty because it was my fault for not
looking after him. I should've found a way of keeping
him safe. Should never have stopped in one place for
so long. When had he been taken? The fire had burnt
down low. It was no more'n a pile of glowing embers,
which told me Billy had been gone a while. If he'd
been around he woulda kept wood piled on the fire
to keep it good and strong. Where did that leave me?
It left me with the task of freeing him if I could and
getting myself kilt in the attempt if I couldn't.

Looked around for his tracks. There they was,
plain as day. Billy warn't light of foot in the way me
and Pa was. He'd left his mark on the forest floor.
No other tracks to be found, though. What had happened? Had something spooked him making him run
off? A tracker dog maybe? A white man with a gun?
Or a wild animal like a hog or something? But this
was no time for speculatin'. Billy had a head start on
me, and I had to find him. Dropping the fish I lit out
after Billy, following his tracks as good as any sniffer
dog. I ran. I had to, to be sure of catching up with him
before anything bad happened to him.

While I was running I warn't looking at anything
but his tracks and I warn't listening out for anything.

I was just hell-bent on the one thing: finding Billy. Well, I ain't gone but a couple of hundred yards when I heard something in spite of not listening. Footsteps loud as you like coming at me from the side. Turned my head and saw a man about six foot tall aged maybe twenty-five with black hair and a beard. He was carrying a musket and seemed to be a trapper type. Probably made his living by trading furs. Good in the woods but not so good as me. He had a scarred cheek which told me he'd likely been in a knife-fight, eyes burning like coals, and a face on him mean as a diamondback. He was as hell-bent on getting me as I was on getting Billy. I turned and headed away from him and put a real spurt on, but he was bigger'n me and a whole lot quicker. I heard him coming up behind me. A growed man will generally beat a boy in a fight or in a race. I zig-zagged to throw him off, because one thing I knowed I'd be better at than him was turning a tight corner. That kept me out of harm's way for about ten seconds before he threw down his musket, and I felt his weight on me and tumbled to the deck. Got a mouthful of leaves the taste of which I didn't much care for so I spat them out.

I was lying face down, breathing hard, and he was kneeling on my back. If I hadn't been used to pain I woulda said it was real painful having his knee in my back. It warn't no picnic, but it warn't as bad as being switched. He took one of my arms and pulled it behind my back then did the same with t'other and held them, and I felt rope being tied around my wrists real tight. Reaching round me he took the knife I was carrying from its sheath. Then he got offa me and hauled me to my feet like I weighed less than a skeeter that ain't got fed for a week. Stood in fronta me holding the end of a rope in his right hand. My eyes followed the rope and saw it went from his hand to behind my back. Wriggled my hands and felt it tied to my wrists. He had me in his power like a dog on a chain. All sorts of things went through my mind right then. *Was he a slave catcher come for Billy? Had he followed us all the way from Kentucky? How had he followed us? I didn't see no dogs with him. Only way he coulda followed us all that distance was with the help of a dog.* Me and Pa was the only people I knowed could track a person through woods. I heard tell some Indians had the skill, but this feller was no Indian.

"I seen that slave from way in the distance," he said. "Only reason it's here is its run away from its owner. It's what you call lost property, and I'm minded to find it and sell it back to its owner. I went to where I saw it and tried to follow it, but couldn't pick up its trail. Went around in circles I did. Then I seen you runnin', and I knowed you was following it. You're gonna get it fo' me."

"But I don't know where he is," I said.

He slapped me so hard my head spun, and my mouth tasted blood, and I spat it out. "You get him fo' me," he said again.

Shaking my head I said, "I told you I don't know where he is, Mister." He slapped me again so hard my teeth rattled.

"Are you deaf, boy? I said you get that slave fo' me. You're gonna find it whether or not you know zackly where it is. I know you can find it. I seen you following its tracks. I don't know how you do it, but you can do it. Ain't a hound in the state of Illinois could do a better job of finding it than you." Pickin' up his musket he said, "Get moving, and be quick 'bout it. If I don't get what I'm looking for mighty quick you're gonna be sorry."

I had no doubt he warn't bluffing and I headed back the way we'd come until I picked up Billy's tracks, rope trailing behind me to the mean man's hand. Felt the weight of it on my wrists even though he warn't pulling it, and it weighed next to nothing. Wondered if I could lead him on a merry dance, but then I figured he'd find out sooner or later I warn't being straight with him, and what then? Would he kill me? Or worse still torture me? I reckoned I was pretty tough, but how long I'd hold out under torture I didn't care to speculate. Not long. Upshot was I had no intention of dying or getting tortured, so I might as well lead him to Billy right away as spin it out.

Once I'd found Billy's trail it warn't hard to follow him. He crashed around like a baby bull leaving marks ever'where he went. The feller at the back of me holding the rope musta been blind not to be able to see that for hisself. But then again, everybody's blind that way, 'ceptin me and Pa.

I worked out the only way I could help Billy was by going real slow to give him a chance to get well ahead of us and that's what I did, for a while at least, hoping Billy would skedaddle. To make it look like I was having trouble seeing Billy's tracks I stopped and looked this way and that from time to time and shook my head like I was stumped before moving forward again.

Warn't long though before that mean man at the back of me planted his boot in the middle of my butt so hard I went sprawlin', or woulda done if'n he hadn't yanked hard on the rope holding my wrists together. "You take me for a fool, boy? I know you can follow a man's trail quicker'n a prairie dog can dive in its hole. I seen you runnin' after that slave, but now you doing a slow walk like you in a funeral. You'll be attending your own funeral if you don't get a move on. You undertstandin' me?" I didn't answer and his boot hit my butt again, real hard. "I said, you understandin' me?"

"I understanding you right good, mister," I said walking more quickly.

"I said, git moving!" The toe of that boot of his caught me again and damn near kicked my butt right up to my neck. "You still deef, boy? I said, git movin'." I loped forward slower than a run but quicker than a walk, like a timber wolf on a hunt. Ain't no other choice I could make, was there?

No way had this man trailed us all the way from Kentucky. He lived in Illinois same as me, but he warn't from these parts. Sounded like a Missourian. He'd been out trapping or hunting or something and seen Billy. Or not Billy, zackly. What he saw when he looked at Billy was a walking gold nugget. An eight-hundred-dollar fortune with black arms and legs on it. Then, being the mean man he was, he decided to catch Billy so he could get that fortune for hisself. What was he gonna do with me when he'd got it? I didn't like to think about that. But I had a feeling it wouldn't be pleasant. It seemed like my only purpose in life was puttin' off death by a few miserable minutes. That ain't any reason to live when you think about it. You might as well die now as in five or ten minutes or even an hour if'n you ain't gonna do anything worthwhile in that hour. But the funny thing is no matter how much you think about it, and no matter how much you know it, and even believe in it, you still want to live a bit longer even though you ain't achieving nothing more than just putting off your death. I was dying to live you might say, as well as living to die.

I suppose I coulda chosen to die right away, and if I'd done that it woulda been a way of saving Billy. He mighta gotten away and lived. Then again, he mighta gotten away and died or not gotten away at all. No way of telling. It would've been noble of me to choose death so that Billy could live. I knowed that much thanks to Miss Larsen. She was always going on about being noble and such. But when your life is on the line, are you gonna choose to be noble or you gonna choose to live? The heroes in Miss Larsen's books always chose being noble over being alive. But if the writers of those books had made the same choice their heroes made they would never have got to write their fine books because they woulda died of being noble long before they got the chance to write about it. Any road, I warn't one for dying of being noble. I'd just as soon die from being ig-noble. I ain't no hero from a book.

By and by Billy's trail started getting fresher. I don't know how I knowed that, I just did. Having trailed so many animals so many times over the years I guess I got a feel for that kind of thing. My foot caught on a fallen branch, and I fell over and cried out at the toppa my voice, "Goddamnit, that hurt!" If you're thinking I made my foot catch on that branch on purpose, you're right, I did. I ain't never hardly tripped up over anything in my life, especially when I been following a trail. I was hoping Billy would hear me and know to make hisself scarce. The rope on my wrists got yanked pulling me back to my feet so hard my arms damn near came out their sockets.

"You takin' me for a fool again, boy? Well, I ain't gonna stand for it. Try that again and I'll make sure to skin you alive afore I kill you."

Now I knowed for sure I was gonna die once we'd caught Billy, and I had no reason at all to stay alive. If ever there was a reason to be noble I had it then. But instead I followed Billy's trail in the hope the mean bastard forcing me to find Billy would at least have enough mercy in him to give me a quick death. And of course to allow me to live a few miserable minutes longer. Let's not forget that.

Time came when I knowed we was real close to Billy, so close my skin prickled. It was like I was smellin' him or feeling him. At the same time I knowed deep in the middle of my bones right where the marrow is that something warn't right. I tracked so many animals in my time I knowed what happened when you was almost on them, and man ain't no different to an animal. Not really. Folks like Miss Larsen will tell you otherwise. Man is different because he has a soul and guff like that. But folks like Miss Larsen ain't never watched animals close up the way I have.

You probably think one beaver is much the same as another beaver, or one raccoon is the same as another raccoon, or one bobcat same as another bobcat. Well, let me tell you they is all different. Not just the markings on them, and not just the shape of their faces and bodies. What I'm talking about is their personalities. All animals got a personality belonging to the type of animal they are. I'm sure you know that. Skunk got the personality of the skunk, fisher got the personality of the fishers. But more'n that, when you study them close up, each skunk got its own personality that makes it different to all other skunks. Each fisher got its own personality that makes it different from all other fishers. They're clever, and they talk to each other in their own animal languages, and most of them got the sense to know man ain't no good for them. So don't you go telling me man is different to animals and better than animals 'cause I know he's not, and I ain't never gonna believe you, not even if you keep telling it me for a thousand years. If you need proof man ain't no better than an animal, then you got it in me helping that trapper feller catch Billy. If I was truly different from an animal, I would've been noble and sacrificed my life for Billy's, wouldn't I? But I didn't. Not even when I knowed for certain I was gonna die anyways.

Knowin' something warn't right when we closed in on Billy, I got to wondering what it was, and trying to figure out what to do about it. Right here and now I should tell you Pa always told me folk got instincts, and when you get near to where a trail is being laid your instincts should be telling you that animal is right ahead of you. But my instincts warn't telling me that. My skin was prickling down one side, which meant Billy warn't in front of us, he was somewhere at the side of us. That was my understanding. If I'd followed my orders the way the trapper wanted me to, I woulda turned left and given the trapper some warning as to where Billy was, by saying he's this way. But I didn't. I just kept right on following the trail. I musta had a tiny piece of something noble in me after all, to have done that.

Next thing I knowed, Billy was behind us. It ain't no mystery how I knowed it. He was making more noise than a herd of buffalo, at least to my ears. But the trapper never heard a thing. He'd kept asking me if I was deaf; well, he musta been deaf hisself not to have heard Billy at the back of us. But then not everyone got ears good as mine. Maybe they can hear noises I can, but when they're in the woods they can't figure out what those noises mean. That's the way my ears are better'n most. Mine can figure things out and know what's making the noise. To you it's just a load of senseless scratching. To me it's a pine marten.

A crunching back of me and the rope on my wrists pulling tight told me the trapper'd heard Billy, too, and was a-turning round to deal with him. Turned 'round myself to see what was happening. Billy had a piece of wood in his hands thick as a man's arm and about the same length. He brought it down on the trapper's head. Or would have done but the trapper put his arms over his head stopping Billy's club with his musket, then he belted Billy in the breadbasket with the butt end of the musket, and Billy dropped his club, letting out a sigh like he was dying and fell to his knees.

The trapper said, "I woulda hit you on the head, slave-boy, but you're worth too much to risk damaging you."

I kicked the trapper on the back of his leg. It did no more to stop him than being bitten by a flea woulda done. He turned and hit me on the head with the butt of his musket. Felled me like a tree. Then it went dark as night in my head, and I didn't know what was going on for a while.

When I was able to open my eyes again I was tied to a tree standing up with my hands fastened by the wrists in front a me. Trapper also was in front a me with his knife in his hand. It was a Bowie knife with a blade about a foot long narrowing to an evil-looking point at the tip.

"You don't listen, do you, boy?" he said. "Didn't I tell you I was gonna skin you alive if you didn't do zackly what I told you to do?" Behind him Billy was on the ground hands tied behind his back and ankles tied together. "Now I'm gonna have me some fun," Trapper said, "tearing your skin off yo' flesh and yo' flesh off yo' bones. Think 'bout that, boy, what's it gonna feel like?"

I felt myself coming over all faint. Stuff like that ain't good to think about, let me tell you. But when you're tied up and someone is in front of you waving a knife in your face telling you to think about it, then think about it you do.

"Have you heard tell 'bout those Kansas and Missouri border wars, boy?"

"No, sir, I haven't." I thought it best to be nice and polite and maybe he'd have a change of heart. That said I hadn't seen no sign of him even having a heart so far.

"Well, allow me to improve on your education before I kill you, boy. Anything went in that war, from tarring and feathering to hacking folk into pieces so you kill 'em slowly one piece at a time, and yours truly here did some of the tarring and feathering and hacking. Right enjoyable it was. I'm just letting you know so you got an appreciation of the level of mercy you can expect from me when I git started on you."

"I'd like to hear some of those tales about tarring and feathering and a-hacking to give me an even better idea, sir," I said, hoping he'd talk me to death.

"Said all I'm gonna say on the subject. Now where shall I start? How 'bout cutting off yo' nose and yo' ears to give you a little taste of what's coming to you?" He took a hold of my right hand, giving it a squeeze that brought tears to my eyes. "Don't start crying yet, boy. This ain't even the beginning of what lies in store for you. I'm gonna start by prying off one of your fingernails." He pushed the tip of the Bowie knife just under the edge of my pointing finger's nail. "This one," he said. "That'll give you something to think 'bout." He slid the knife-tip further till it was about halfway under the nail. I ain't never knowed such pain before, not from Miss Larsen's worst canin', not from ma's worst leatherin', and not even from Pa's worst switchin'. Funny thing was, I didn't cry out at first. Just watched the blade going under my nail, feeling sorta sick in the bottom of my stomach.

Then there was this almighty crash and the trapper looked at me with a puzzled look on his mean face and rolled his eyeballs up and dropped to his knees, and behind him Billy was standing holding his club which he'd used to hit the trapper over the head with. Blood all over the end of it from where it'd broken the trapper's skin. The trapper fell sideways to the ground and lay there groaning and bleeding. I was bleeding from the end of my finger but didn't notice at the time because I was too busy starin' at the trapper.

While the trapper had been telling me all about what he was gonna do to me, Billy had threaded his legs through his arms and gotten his arms in front a him. Then he'd bitten through the rope tying his wrists together good as any beaver could've done it, untied his own ankles, picked up his club, and used it to brain the trapper, who was now lying at my feet. Billy hadn't quite knocked the trapper senseless. There was still sense enough left in him to beg for his life.

"Mercy," he said. "Have mercy on me. I'm just a po' man out to make a living and feed his family. I got a wife and young chillun. You gotta understand."

"I understand better than you might think," said Billy and he finished off the job he'd started with his club. When he was finished beating on the trapper Billy looked me in the eye. "Sorry you had to see that, son," he said, "but I had to do it. The way I see it is if we'd have let him go, he woulda done the same to someone else down the line. What I've done here warn't so much a murder as an execution."

"Folks will call it a murder if they ever find out," I said. "Let's hope they don't. We got enough problems on our plate without trying to swallow down more." Then I held out my hands. "How 'bout cutting me loose?" And that's when I noticed my finger was bleeding. Reminded me it was hurting some. At least I hadn't lost my fingernail.

Billy picked up the trapper's Bowie knife and cut the ropes keeping me captive. "Thanks, Billy," I said, dancing around to get the blood flowing back in my arms and legs. The dancin' made my head hurt from the blow I'd taken, plus, it made my finger bleed more, so I soon gave up. I tore a piece offa the bottom of my shirt and wrapped it around the end of my finger to stop it bleeding too much. "Guess I owe you my life," I said.

"I guess you do at that, son," Billy said, "and that makes us even. I'm going now. Nothing to stay for. I'll see you around." He turned and started walking away.

Running after him I said, "Hey wait, Billy! Where do you think you're going? Wait for me!" When I caught up with Billy I walked alongside him.

He looked down at me and said, "No point in us walking together, son. You don't want to be with me, that much is clear."

"What do you mean?"

"I mean I knowed you wanted rid of me from the moment we first met. Couldn't wait to see the back of me, could you? Now you got your wish, 'cause I'm gonna do what you want. Make my way on my own without you. We don't belong together. You don't think of me right, and you don't treat me right."

That hurt me, partly because there was no denying the truth of Billy's words, partly also because I'd gotten to like Billy, and I wanted him to like me. "Okay," I said, "you got me there. I did want rid of you. It warn't that I don't like you, though. I thought I'd have a better chance of surviving on my own."

"My life didn't matter to you, huh?"

"It mattered, just not as much as my own, sorry." I held out my hand.

He stopped and shook it. "Apology accepted," he said. "But I still ain't gonna travel with you. No offense but I ain't got no truck with folk that got no truck with me." He got to walking away again.

Behind him I was, what's that word? Forlorn. "But I respect you, Billy, really I do."

He warn't persuaded. Just carried on walking with his back to me.

"Where you going, Billy?"

"Washington. I'm gonna go fight for the Union army."

"Wait! That's where I'm going. I'm gonna fight for the Union, too. We can go together." He stopped, and I caught up with him again. "We can join the army together."

Scratching his head he said, "Thinking 'bout it, we're not even. You saved my life twice, once crossing the river and a second time with the bear. So I still owe you. Makes sense we stick together for a while longer. That way I might get the chance to save your life again and even up the score."

We walked side by side. "We gonna need a skiff or something to cross the Wabash," I said. "Can't pay for one so we're gonna have to steal one. Gonna have to behave like outlaws for a while."

"Suppose we are outlaws," Billy said, "not that I set out to be one. I'd sooner be law-abidin', but I'm forced to be a runaway slave. That makes me stolen property, and I'm the thief. Yes, sir, just by running away I've stolen another man's property thanks to the law in these parts. And now I'm a murderer, too."

I said, "That makes two of us."

"What do you mean, son?"

"I'm a murderer myself."

His eyes went wide open. "You?"

"Yes me," I said most proudly. "Leastways I'm wanted for murder. Never did it, mind. They pinned it on me. I'm a innocent man. But nobody in my town believes me, so I'm on the run like you. Let's go looking for that skiff."

"First things first, son. Someone gonna happen along and find that dead man I just kilt, then all hell gonna break loose on our heads if we not careful. We oughta get away from here as far as we can before stealing ourselves a skiff to cross the Wabash River with."

I nodded. "Makes sense to me. Do you think we should give him a Christian burial, Billy?" Deep down I knowed the answer, which was we had to leave the dead trapper where he was without any ceremony. A Christian burial or even just stopping by him to say a prayer over his dead body was taking a risk we would be caught and strung up, but I needed someone to tell me what I already knowed. Long and short of it was I knowed we was doing wrong and doing it for a reason, but I wanted someone else to spell it out for me so I could feel justified in doing it.

Billy looked at me like I gone mad. "That man warn't gonna give you no Christian burial, you can count on that, son. No, he don't deserve one hisself."

"That's good enough for me," I said.

"But we should hide the body," he said.

I shook my head. "No need, Billy. Hogs'll sniff him out before you know it. Ain't nothing a hog likes more than a person to eat. Don't much care if the person's dead or alive, they'll eat him, and by tomorrow sunrise he'll be all gone 'cept a few things like his musket and knife."

Billy got this look on his face like he'd had a real useful thought. "You know something?" he said. "Our friend's wearing a right good pair of boots and a fine pair of pants and a mighty fine jacket and shirt. They're wasted on a dead man, specially one who's 'bout to get eaten by a starvin' hog with a taste for people meat. It'd be a crime to leave those clothes where they are. The Lord don't care for waste, leastways that's what my Mama always told me."

Billy took off his rags and undressed the trapper top to toe.

"Hurry, Billy, we gotta get outta here!" I said, glancing around real anxious and sweating because of the delay.

"Doing my best to be quick, son," he said and

standing with his back to me he put on the trapper's clothes, but not before I'd gotten a good look at him butt naked and seen the scars from a whipping running across his back like the railway tracks from hell. He ended up being dressed much like me in a outfit too big for him. Even so it was better'n what he'd been wearing before. He got the Bowie knife strapped round his hip and looked almost like he'd growed up in the woods same as me.

When he was done admiring the look and feel of his new outfit Billy picked up the trapper's musket and bullets and powder. "We oughta take these with us," he said. "If we leave 'em lying 'bout someone's gonna happen across 'em and get a good idea where this feller,"—tapping the trapper with his toe—"met his end, even if the pigs have eaten his remains all up. That'll help 'em find us if they choose to come looking."

"Could be you're right," I said. "Someone will come looking, you can bank on it. Let's head north real steady and get some distance between us and that body then head for Washington."

"You lead, son, I'll follow. You know the way."

Billy was wrong about that. I had no idea how far Washington was or what states we'd have to cross to get there. But at least I knowed the general direction we had to take in the first place. Probably I'd head further north with Billy than I woulda done if I'd been on my own. Further north the better far as I was concerned. You get south in a northern state you likely will come across people who support the Confederacy and don't take kindly to black folk who ain't in chains. Leastways that's what Miss Larsen told me, and I'd got no reason to doubt her on that point. Even up north we could have problems. We'd just have to deal with them when we met with them, I supposed.

Anyways, north it was. I set off walking with Billy at my side. I was fixing to keep us in the woods, but sooner or later we'd have to cross open ground and meet folks. We was a black feller with a white boy, which meant we'd stick out like a tree stump in the middle of a main street. There'd be a lot of explainin' to do without giving away that he was a murderer and a runaway slave and I was a murderer and horse thief. I didn't know how we'd manage that. Also we'd likely have our hands full fending off slave catchers. I'd heard they warn't always particular about whether it was a slave they caught to sell down the river. Sometimes they'd catch a free black man and sell him on account of he was in the wrong place at the wrong time. So even if we convinced ever'body we met that Billy warn't a runaway slave, it didn't mean he was safe from slave catchers. I reckoned that to stay safe we'd have to live off the land as much as we could for as long as we could. Given that neither of us had no money to buy food with, that choice warn't too hard to make.

"Your ma got any more good sayings, Billy?" I asked by way of small talk. It felt like things had changed between us, and I oughta make an effort with that sort of thing. More of an effort than I had before, anyhows.

"Sayings? Yeah, like God don't care for waste and so on. Sure, she had lots of good sayings, son. Can't call any more of 'em to mind right now."

"Your ma must be missin' you, Billy."

"No, I'm missing her."

"What do you mean?"

"My mama's dead. Died before her thirty-fifth birthday. Didn't even live long enough to see out my childhood."

I didn't say anything to that. Warn't nothing I could say. His eyes got this faraway look in them.

"I do miss my wife, though, I miss her desperate."

"Your wife? You left a wife behind when you ran away?"

"Not zackly. We was separated before I ran away."

"What do you mean?"

"When me and my wife got married, we vowed to stay together till death or distance us do part. Well, distance done parted us. I met my wife in Tennessee picking cotton. Master sold me, but he didn't sell my wife. I had to go and leave her behind and leave my children, too. We pleaded with him and begged and shed a Mississippi of tears, but it didn't help none. Master's mind was made up and warn't nothing any of us could do to change it. At first I wouldn't let 'em take me, even when they beat on me, but then they beat on my wife it broke my heart, and I went quietly." Billy's eyes went wet.

I nodded but didn't say nothing at all. Truth was my own eyes were getting wet, and I couldn't have spoken even if I'd wanted to.

He rubbed his eyes. "The day I left her was the last I ever seen her. Tore my heart into pieces. Still feels torn, even now. Ain't seen her for longer than I care to remember. One day I'm gonna go back and find my wife. If this war does what it's meant to, I'll get my chance. And if it doesn't, I'll take my chances. How 'bout you, son? Who did you leave behind when you ran away?"

"My ma and pa," I said, "and I miss 'em turrble."

I warn't making that up about Pa. Even though he'd become useless and treated me worse'n you'd treat a rat you found in your larder I still loved him. Maybe what they say about absence making the heart grow fonder is true after all. I never mentioned Cathy because she was no longer in the picture, but being honest with myself I missed her, too, and Ervan, of course. But no point mentioning Ervan because he was dead. Thinking about all those people I left behind reminded me I'd promised I was going back to clear my name some day and kill the man who kilt Ervan. I made that promise again and told myself never to forget it. Just as soon as I was ready, I'd be going back.

Me and Billy trudged on through the undergrowth.

"It's the same wherever you look," said Billy. "Every which way it's trees and more trees and nuthin' else but trees, and all of 'em look the same."

That's not what I saw. I saw each tree looking real different to its neighbor like a person in its own right looks different to his neighbor, and when I looked north it was a different view from south, west, and east. When I looked at the ground, the trails animals had made stood out like they was somehow lit up. But I didn't try explaining that to Billy. No point. Only a true woodsman sees things that way. So I stopped and put my arm across Billy's chest to stop him.

"What's wrong?" he said.

"Nuthin'. I want you to listen is all."

We stood still for a full minute. "Hear it?" I said.

"What?"

"The sound of the woods, life, it's all around us. Now take a deep breath and smell it. Beautiful, ain't it?"

He breathed in and out and nodded. "Yeah," he said. But I ain't sure he was convinced.

"Listen again," I told him, "and listen real careful this time. That sound you hear is the regular sound of the woods. If it changes it could mean trouble. It could mean someone following us, it could mean a hog stalking us, it could mean all kinds of hell 'bout to fall on our heads. That's why you got to listen out for changes, you hear me?"

He nodded again, looking like he meant it this time.

We carried on through the trees under a canopy of green with brown here and there and a gray sky above it, birds fluttering between branches when we disturbed them, and animals scurrying through plant life at our feet. Can't say I'm confident Billy heard many of those things. He just hadn't been brung up to hear the woods the way I was hearin' them.

"Don't blame you for missing your ma and pa. I miss mine even though they're both dead and gone and I lost 'em years ago. What are your folks like, Joe?"

"Good people," I said. If you're readin' this book it might strike you as odd I was sayin' that to Billy. But my ma and pa were good people deep down even if they didn't always treat me right, and I'd got to missing them real bad. As far as Pa killin' Ervan goes, I couldn't believe he'd done it, even though I'd seen him with Ervan's things. But he mighta done it for all I knowed. I was keeping an open mind on the subject until I could get to know more, and while my mind was open, I still loved my Pa. Hated him, too, mind. It's a thin line as they say, and I had one foot either side of it, respectin' my Pa. I want you to know that.

"My folks been good to me," I said. "Brought me up real well."

Figured it was for the best to not mention Pa's drinking and switching and Ma's leatherin' and all to Billy. No point in tarnishin' Ma's and Pa's names with those tales.

Billy gave me a look that went right into me. "They must be missin' you more than you're missin' them, Joe."

Ma and Pa missing me was something that I hadn't thought of. When I thought about it I knowed Ma would be but as for Pa, there was no tellin'. He would've missed me at one time when I was younger, in the days me and him got on well, but now? I warn't so sure. I thought he might be missing me, though, and my eyes got wet just picturing it. Had to turn away from Billy because I didn't want him seeing the tears running down my face.

He patted me on the back gently as we walked. "It's okay, son. It's natural to be grieving when you're parted from those you love."

"Thank you, Billy."

There was a light rain. Right after the rain let up we went down the side of a ravine. When we got near the bottom I got careless I guess because I slipped. The grass was wet, and my feet went right from under me. Ended up lying on my back next to a stream looking up at the sky through the waving branches of the trees that was always around us in the woods.

Billy came bounding over, his voice fulla concern. "You all right, boy?"

"I think so," I said but as soon as I tried to stand up I found out different. "I've twisted my Goddamned ankle, Billy. I can't walk."

A body can die in the woods when he got a twisted ankle. That's all it takes. An injury like that stops you foraging for food and getting out the way when you hear a pig or bear in search of food. Swear to God those animals know when you're helpless and it attracts them. So it looked like my number was up.

"I need help, Billy."

"I know you do, and I won't leave you." Crouching down he said, "Here, git on my back."

I made a big effort and hopped my way into the right place and got on and he piggy-backed me up the other side of the ravine. He was puffing and blowing by the time we got back to the top of the ravine, but anybody would have been.

"What we gonna do, Billy? You can't keep carrying me."

"Son, you have no idea what I've carried in my time. I've carried things a lot heavier than you are, let me tell you. You don't know it but you weigh nothing at all to me. There ain't nothing to you. Now let yourself offa my back."

I slid off. "What now?"

"Now you get on my shoulders. It's gonna be easier for me to carry you that way on level ground." He crouched down real low. "Now get on."

So I did, and he stood up and set off a-walking. Going real slow Billy kept on with me on his shoulders. To give him credit he kept going with not many breaks until the afternoon became dusk and we turned in, sitting down wrapped in our blankets with our backs propped against a tree and said goodnight. Both of us was hungry but had nuthin' left to eat. We'd a-catch something tomorrow. That's what I told myself when I closed my eyes, anyhow.

Next day hunger woke me up as it so often did. Billy was sleeping, looking real peaceful, but I knowed by now he warn't. I shook him awake. "Gotta get going, Billy. No telling who might be after us and when."

Getting to his feet he stretched, and we set off with him carrying me again.

"I gotta tell you, I'm real grateful for what you're doing for me, Billy. I reckon I coulda died back there or maybe soon after anyways. A body won't last long in these woods if he can't keep moving."

"That's all right, boy." We stopped after a while, and he set me down. "Gonna get us some nuts to eat. We need 'em."

Billy musta carried me on his shoulders for near enough a week, and he never complained none 'bout it. Just put his back into it like it was a job he had to do. At times he'd set me down and get us some nuts or berries to eat so we could both eat.

Eventually I got to be able to walk again, but I hoped to God I wouldn't have to run on that ankle of mine. Felt like it needed more time to heal fully. I'd been walking on my own two skinny legs for but a day when we came to a place where the trees was all gone. Nothing for it but to keep going and hope for the best. Billy could be a free man for all anybody knowed, and we was armed, which meant we could fight if we had to. I hoped that fact might deter some folks from giving us trouble.

Over to the west in the distance was a town. Ahead of us farmland. If we crossed the farmland some of those farmers would get right mad at us just for going over their property. As I saw it though that land was as much mine as theirs. If not for them it'd have trees on it, and I'd be hunting and fishing and generally living in it. But they'd tore the trees all down and called it theirs and took part of mine and Pa's world away from us. I sometimes feared that by the time they was done there'd be no land left for the likes of me and Pa. Anyways, I did my best to see a trail that might take us over the farms without raising too many hackles. As I was looking for a route smoke came up in the distance. A train.

Billy looked at me. "That train might be useful to us son if it's going the right way. If we wait till nightfall we can maybe get a ride on the next train that comes in. If we do we won't need a skiff to cross the Wabash. Train'll take us over it on a bridge."

"I reckon you're right, Billy, that train looks to be headed east. Let's get back in the woods and hide out till it's dark."

Night fell, and I judged it to be late enough for folks to be in bed, so we headed by moonlight to the rail tracks and followed them into the town. Fairfield it was called. Small place with a stopping point for trains. The stopping point was empty.

"What now, son?"

"We wait," I said. "If no train comes through by dawn we go somewhere and keep watch and work out what time the trains come in. Hopefully one is gonna arrive in the dead of night. That's the one we catch."

"It ain't gonna be easy," Billy said. "But then again, nuthin's easy in this life 'ceptin death."

"You got that right."

We sat around next to the tracks waiting patiently half asleep but with the usual one eye open. It was a cold clear night, and I spent a lot of time looking up at the stars. It's one of my favorite things to do in the night when the sky's clear. One of my earliest memories is Pa getting me to look up at into the night sky and enjoy the stars. There was snow on the ground when he did that, and he was carrying me to keep me warm and safe. The memory of what he did came back to me while me and Billy was by the railroad tracks and made me want to be a small boy again and be back in Pa's arms.

At some point I knowed, don't ask me how but I knowed the sun would be up soon. "Time to go, Billy."

"Whatever you say, son."

We walked along the tracks out of town with not a soul in sight, but folks would be up at dawn if they was anything like the folks in my town, and we couldn't afford to be seen, so we walked at a good lick to make sure we got outta sight before anybody stirred. About five miles out of town we turned south crossing over the farmland again, heading back to the safety of the woods. By then dawn was breaking, and I saw a farmer about a quarter mile off giving us the sort of look only a farmer can give. Narrow-eyed, suspicious, and very far from friendly. Me and Pa both seen that look many times. I quickened my pace and Billy did the same.

"Something the matter, son?"

"Yeah, we been spotted."

He glanced around. "See what ya mean. Could be trouble."

"Let's hope not."

We kept right on moving till we got to the trees, and then we still kept moving. No sense in giving the farmer an easy time of working out where we was hiding out. Found ourselves a good spot just inside the tree line from where we could look out toward the railroad tracks. We was both hungry by then. Both of us had knowed a lot of hunger in our lives so it warn't like it was anything new. But no matter how many times you feel it, hunger gets you all the same. You can never get truly used to it. Your belly will drive you mad telling you it needs filling. It'll let off for a while if you ignore it, but then it starts up again even harder till you can't ignore it. Not unless you go a couple of full days and nights and maybe another day without vittles. You do that and your belly will settle down right enough. But me and Billy warn't at that stage. We was still at the stage of being ready to eat an adult mustang if we coulda found one. Best we managed was hickory nuts from a tree and water from a stream.

You know a lot 'bout animals, son, I can see that. Can't you catch us something to eat?"

"I could, Billy, but we gotta look out for that train. 'sides, we'd need to start a fire and cook on it, and that might draw attention to us that we can do without."

Smoke went rolling along the bottom of the valley mid-afternoon. We kept watch, but there was no more. So that was it then. One train a day in broad daylight. I'd been hoping to get one at night, but now we had to get on a train during the day. Either that or keep walking, and from here on in walking might not be as safe as the train. Walking would likely be more dangerous because we'd be exposed to view. If we could but get on that train we'd be hidden from view while it was moving, and we'd get to places quicker.

I looked at Billy. "We gotta get catch us one of those trains."

"Yeah, we gotta do that."

Next day we struck off for Fairfield shortly after noon. It was the only way to make sure we'd be getting to the train on time. Farmer looked at us again, eyes all narrowed, but he didn't do nuthin'. It told me we stuck out, me and Billy. When we were together we looked different from the way other folks looked.

"How we gonna handle this, Billy?" I said as we got nearer Fairfield.

"Handle what?"

"Walking to the place the train stops. Folks gonna be looking at us."

He put his arm 'cross my chest and stopped, forcing me to stop, too, and we turned to face each other. He got this look on his face real determined. "We just gonna walk through that town like we own it," he said. "If we go skulking around they're sure to think we done something that we don't want them to know 'bout. If that happens we'll attract trouble."

Being the naturally sneaky type I said, "I don't know, Billy. We gonna turn heads you and me, and that's gonna land us in trouble. Maybe we should sneak in."

"Sooner land in trouble being bold than being sneaky," said Billy.

Well, I had no argument with that, so I said, "Fine, let's do it."

"Just one thing, Joe."

"What's that, Billy?"

He held up the musket.

"I can shoot this thing. Shooting is just a matter of aiming and pulling the trigger. But I don't know how to load it."

I disagreed with Billy. Shooting is a skill. But I warn't gonna argue. No point. That musket was too heavy for me to carry.

"I'll load it for you, Billy. I know how to do it."

He grinned.

"We make a great team, Joe."

That made me feel real good.

Fairfield was different from the town I came from. Starting with it was bigger and had a longer main street with shops on it, not just a general store. There was a place you could pay to get your hair cut and a shave and a place to buy tobacco and more than one saloon. Lotsa other places to spend your money, too, if you was lucky enough to have any, which we didn't. Also a courthouse with a tin roof. The tin roof made it special. I never saw one of those before. The town was busy, and I could see why. Must have been four or five hundred people lived there judging by the number of houses, which was more people in one place than I'd seen in my life. What's more there was folks just a-wandering, it seemed to me. In my town no one had time to wander. Folks was always busy doing their chores so the streets was empty 'cept for busy people doing chores. Only thing same as my town was the street was made of dirt.

The wind gusted and blew up a power of dust devils. Folks walking toward us screwed up their eyes good and tight. Just as well. I wanted their eyes to stay tight shut and hoped the wind would blow in their faces forever, but it dropped sudden as it began, and after spitting dirt and such out their mouths people could see again, and what they saw right up close to them was a black man dressed like a trapper and a young white boy dressed in a man's clothes rolled up at the legs and sleeves, the pair of them strolling through the middle of Fairfield like they owned the place. I felt more eyes on me than I care to remember. They was making holes in me, then swiveling to make holes in Billy, then swiveling right back at me again.

Out the corner of his mouth Billy said, "Just keep right on walking, son, you ain't got nothing to be af-frighted of." His voice sounded scared though. Mine woulda sounded the same if I'd dared open my mouth.

A man built like a snake all lean and slippery had his eyes on us. Swear to God he came slitherin' as much as walking our way. Mouth on him like an open wound chewing tobacco. He was more'n six feet tall and well-fed in his leanness. Looked like he could take out me and Billy both at once if he got a mind to, and if it was a fair fight of course, which it wouldn't be, I'd see to that. He stopped in front of us turned his head to the side and spat his tobacco into the dirt. Long brown stream of it like piss shot from his thin lips. Made a noise like a stone splashing in the crick when it landed. Then he leered at me.

"Where you going with that contraband, boy?"

"Contraband?" I said. "What d'you mean?"

A frown creased his forehead, and he nodded at Billy. "That's what I mean. That there is contraband."

"I don't know what contraband is, sir, but this here is a free man," I said.

A smile like a gash with teeth split his face. "Is he now? I reckon you're lying, boy, and this here is contraband that needs to be returned to its rightful owner." He made as if to grab hold of Billy.

Even though I warn't looking at them I could tell everyone else on the street was stopping to watch what would happen next. My hand went to the han-dle of my sheath knife. Billy raised the musket he was carrying and pushed the muzzle up against the snake man's belly, or the place his belly woulda been if he'd had one.

"Get outta my way, or I'll blow you to kingdom come," Billy said.

Grinning even wider Snake Man put his hands in the air. "Just joshing with you boys," he said, backing off.

Billy glared, a bead of sweat running down the side of his head from under his curly hair even though it was cold. Sun was high and sky was cornflower blue, but it was one of those chill days you get at the beginning of fall. "We can do without that sorta joshing."

"I'll be on my way then," said Snake Man.

Billy's mouth tightened. Muscles in his cheeks moved. As Snake Man walked away backward Billy kept the muzzle of the musket pointing at him. Snake Man disappeared into one of the town's saloons. Soon as he was gone life returned to normal, and folks got to moving again. They was still watching us, though. Me and Billy carried on up the main street.

"Maybe it was a good thing that happened," Billy said. "Word might get around we're not the types to be messed with."

"Hope you're right, Billy, 'cause if you ain't, you gonna be beaten and sold, and I'm gonna be beaten and maybe even kilt."

We circled to the back of the main street where the railroad tracks was.

"This is too obvious," Billy said. "Folks gonna know we're planning to jump on a train. We gotta walk a little way outta town and get on it while it's moving. Also we should do it from the other side of the tracks so they don't see us getting on. Train will block their view."

"Guess you're right, Billy." We followed the tracks

till we was out of town, hoping no one would think about what we was up to.

"How fast do you reckon it'll be going when it gets to us?" I asked.

"No faster than you can run, I reckon. It didn't look to go too fast when we saw it from way off."

"Not sure I agree. You see a hog from way off it don't look to go too fast. But when it's coming right at you, you get another idea altogether about how fast it goes."

"Well," he said, scratching his head, "what do you propose doing that makes more sense than what we got planned?"

I gave it some thought. "Nothing makes more sense than this. If we try to get on the train when it's nearer town they'll be onto us for sure. We just got to go with your plan."

We sat cross-legged in the dirt next to the tracks. It was on my mind that when the train came I might not be able to get on it if it was going too fast, and Billy might not manage, either. By and by we saw the train in the distance. It stopped in town, smoke billowing from the chimbly on top of the engine and steam a-hissing from the boiler, clouds of it 'round the wheels. People were getting in and out of boxcars carrying stuff on, taking stuff off.

"You ready, boy?" asked Billy, "because soon we gotta make our move."

"I'm ready as I'll ever be."

Four men appeared on the edge of town walking toward us. One not so much walking as slithering. "Billy, we got trouble."

"I know, son, I seen it."

"What we gonna do?"

"I'm gonna shoot at least one of 'em dead, son. Don't know 'bout the other three. I might not have time enough to reload and shoot the other three."

"They're all armed, Billy, and we only got the one musket between us."

Then came a fierce rumbling from the tracks and the train got to moving toward us, slow as a turtle on dry land, but gathering speed. The four men were getting nearer to us. One raised his musket and pointed it at me.

"You! The contraband! Come quietly, or we'll shoot your friend!"

"They're not gonna shoot you, Billy. You're worth a thousand dollars or more. They're gonna shoot me," I said.

Billy lay down in the dirt. "Get down, son, then they can't shoot you so easy." I sprawled right down, and both of us lay there looking at the men. Smoke came from the muzzle of the musket that was pointing at me, and I heard a whine as a bullet kicked up some stones by my head.

Billy aimed his musket at the men. "Gonna kill these bastards if it's the last thing I do," he said, "or at least gonna kill one of 'em, and it's gonna be the skinny one."

The four men danced a crazy kind of jig still getting nearer to us.

"Damn!" said Billy. "You can't aim at a moving target." The train passed them by, and Billy squeezed the trigger. He missed. That was their cue to run. They knowed he only had time for the one shot. Billy and me jumped to our feet. They was getting closer, but so was the train. The engine passed us by. The first boxcar passed us by. Billy threw down the musket. "Ain't no use to us now, just a burden to be carried. Run, son!"

We both ran fast as we could. Train was going real fast now. Second boxcar already gone past us and the caboose warn't too far behind that. It'd seemed a long way off before. Here came the third boxcar. It was open. Billy, in front of me, dived in. I tried to follow, but my bad ankle started hollering at me telling me it'd had enough, and I couldn't jump so good and ended up hanging on to the floor of the boxcar by my arms, feet trailing inches above the tracks. Then I was slipping off. My hands couldn't get no grip on the smooth wooden floor of the boxcar. Speed we was doing told me I'd die or be a cripple when I fell. If I fell under the wheels, I'd likely get my legs cut off at the knee. Never known my heart beat so fast as it did then. Worst of it was that just behind me, the fastest of the four men was reaching out to grab me. So even if I somehow survived falling from the train, I'd end up dead or crippled anyways. No way was those men gonna let me get away without one or the other. Probably one then the other. Billy was sprawled on his belly. He rolled over and saw the pickle I was in and turned, crouched, got hold of my wrists, and hauled me inside the boxcar. At last we was safe, at least for now.

"Looks like I saved your life for a second time, son, maybe even a third depending on how you're reckoning it, so we're quits," he said.

"Does that mean you're going your own way when we get off the train, Billy?"

"No, I reckon we'll stick together till we get to join the army. We're buddies now, ain't we?"

Made me feel right good when he said that. "We sure are."

15.

ONLY SIGHT SADDER 'N A BATTLE LOST IS A BATTLE WON

WE TRAVELED ON FOOT AND RAIL AND HAD OUR fair share of scrapes before we got to Washington in the fall of 1861. I ain't never seen a place so big. Stone buildings high as trees and real fancy to boot. Streets wide as the Wabash River but even so they was crowded. Soldiers and would-be soldiers and folks with no desire to be soldiers everywhere, many of them talking funny. Later I learned the ones talking funny was foreign—German, Irish, Scottish, Swedish, English, you name it—they was all there. It brought home to me that the Union would win this war and win it real quick. There was no way any country on earth would last long against the fellers I saw in uniform and the ones I saw fixing to get in uniform.

"I guess we gotta find us the place where they turn us into soldiers," said Billy. "Hope they give us some soldier food right away, because I'd eat a live rat if I had one I'm so hungry."

That made me smile in spite of the hollow feeling I had in my gut. "Me, too."

Lots of men in blue uniforms was lining up outside of a building across the way.

"Do you reckon that's where we go, Billy?"

Screwing up his eyes he ran them down the line of men. "No, son, I reckon that's a cathouse."

"What's a cathouse? A place where they keep cats?"

"In a manner of speakin'. Son, you ever have a girlfriend?"

"Yeah, I did once."

"Well, a cathouse is where you pay to have a girlfriend for a while."

"That makes no sense to me, Billy."

"It will one day, son."

I ran across the road and tapped the arm of one of the men outside the cathouse. "Where do I go to become a soldier like you?"

He pointed. "That way, boy, head for the Potomac, you can't miss it. Someone there will help you."

"Thank you kindly, sir." I ran back to Billy and told him about going to the Potomac.

"Okay," he said, "let's get a move on. Sooner we do it the sooner we get food in our bellies."

We trekked the streets, and the buildings in Washington gave way to a huge area of grassland dropping down to the Potomac River. That grassland warn't empty like you might imagine. It was fuller if anything than Washington itself, covered all over in log cabins and tents that looked like big white bells, and in and among the cabins and tents was more soldiers in blue than you could shake a stick at. Marching and drilling here, practicing their marksmanship there, and playing musical instruments everywhere else.

"Jesus," Billy said, "have you ever seen so many people?"

"No, I ain't."

"Only thing," he said, "is there ain't a black soul among 'em. I expected to see lotsa black soldiers. Every black man in the country is desperate to fight in this war against the South, why ain't any of 'em here?"

"I don't know, maybe they couldn't get here. You had a lotta trouble getting here."

Soon enough we came to a cabin with a table outside it, a couple of chairs behind the table, and a tough-as-iron sergeant sitting in one of the chairs, a private in the other, both of them writing something in a book. Later I learned the private was the sergeant's adjutant. Adjutants do the paperwork that keeps the army running smoothly. Based on my experience of army life I'd say the paperwork the adjutants do don't always work.

A line of men in ordinary clothes next to the table told me that's where we had to line up to join the army.

"We better get in line," Billy said. "You first, son."

I joined the end of the line of men, and after a long wait got to the front with Billy just behind me. The iron sergeant asked for my details. I gave him my real name and age as I didn't see much point in telling him a made-up name. The people of my town warn't gonna send a lynching mob all the way to Washington to get me, and with all these people about even if they got a message here, it warn't gonna be possible to find me. That's the way I looked at it, anyways.

The sergeant looked me up and down. "Twelve, eh? You're not old enough to join the army, son. You have to be twenty-one."

My face fell.

Then he said, "I'll put your age down as twenty-one, okay?"

"Okay, sir."

He looked at me again. "Joe Wild, eh? You don't

look much like a Joe Wild, but you'll be able to fight so long as you can carry a musket. Reckon you can do that?"

"Yes, sir."

"Then sign here. These are your terms and conditions."

I didn't have time to read all those terms and conditions, but I signed anyways, and that's how I became a soldier. Young as I was, I warn't the youngest boy to join the Union army, but I sure was the skinniest. All that crossing the country from Kentucky to Washington had gotten every ounce of spare meat off of me, and I didn't have any to spare in the first place.

There was one term and condition I did read because it jumped right off the page at me. It read: "thirteen dollars a month." I pointed at it. "Is that right, sir, thirteen dollars a month?"

"It's right, son, you get thirteen dollars a month for being in the army, plus all your meals and a roof over your head some of the time."

My face got a grin on it big as its ever had. Army life sounded real good to me.

Hard-as-iron sergeant gave me a slip of paper. "This here's your chitty." He waved his arm at a cabin. "Go over there and show your chitty to the sergeant. He'll give you your uniform."

"Yes, sir!" I said but I didn't go. Instead I stood to one side and waited for Billy.

The sergeant gave him a look. "What you doing here, boy?"

"I'm here to fight, Sergeant."

"No, you're not. We don't take black soldiers on in the Union army."

"You should," I said. "He's my friend, and he can

fight real good, mister, I seen him fight with my own eyes."

"Sorry," said the sergeant, "he can't be in the Union army whether he can fight a lick or not."

"Well," I said, "I don't want to be in your Goddamned Union army if Billy can't be in it, I'm going." I don't know where that came from.

The sergeant gave me a look that could have kilt a polecat. "It's too late, you can't go, son, you already signed up. Only place you're going from here is the place you collect your uniform or the stockade if you don't shut your mouth right quick."

I had no idea what the stockade was, but I knowed it warn't gonna be a good place, so I buttoned up my mouth and looked at Billy to see what he'd do. Seemed for a while he didn't know whether to be angry or upset. In the end he chose upset and got real sad about the eyes.

"Tell you what," the sergeant said to Billy, making a gesture with his thumb to another part of the camp, "over there is the quartermaster's cabin. You go there, he might have a job for you moving supplies around and digging and that kind of thing. You won't be fighting, but you'll be helping the army."

"Thank you, I'll go," said Billy, looking mighty pissed off. Then Billy turned to me. "This is the end of the line for me and you, son. We might not see each other again."

Don't know why but I got a lump in my throat then, and I felt myself crying. Did my best not to, as soldiers aren't supposed to cry, are they? Mind you I seen plenty soldiers that did since that day.

Billy took hold of me by the shoulders and stared into my eyes. "Don't worry, son. We'll meet up some other time, maybe after this war is done. I'm gonna call myself Freeman by the way, I like the sounds of it. Billy Freeman gonna be my name from now on. Look me up after the war if you get the chance."

I couldn't say anything being so choked up. Billy was another person broke my heart, I never saw that coming, wouldn't have thought it possible but he did. Anyways he slapped my back and rubbed it and then headed off to the quartermaster's cabin, and I watched him disappear, taking a part of my heart with him. It felt like soon there would be nothing left of my heart I'd lost so much of it. First because of Ervan, then Cath, then Ma and Pa, and now Billy. I wondered if you could lose so much of your heart there would be nothing left to live for. I'd heard that was so, certainly felt like it was. Then I reminded myself I was gonna learn to kill and go back to my hometown, clear my name, kill the bastard who shot Ervan, and get back to being with Ma. And if there was any way to do it, I'd get back to being with Pa, too. Me and him would go tracking and hunting and fishing just like we did in the old times. Made me cry all over again just thinking about it. I didn't shed any tears for Cath, though. I'd done enough of that already. She was in my past now.

"Joseph! Joseph!" That was the tough-as-iron sergeant. "Wipe yo' eyes, boy, you're a soldier now, and soldiers don't shed no tears." He pointed. "Go to that cabin and collect your Goddamn uniform like I said."

"Yes, sir!"

The cabin was bigger than any of the houses in my hometown. I joined a line outside the door. Seemed the army was all about lining up. When I got to the front a sergeant and a private soldier was waiting for me. The sergeant wrinkled up his nose. "You need a wash, son, you're dirtier'n any recruit I've seen, and I've seen some stinkers in my time."

My face musta turned bright red 'cause I felt it getting hot. Sergeant handed me something square and small that felt like a candle.

"What's this, Sergeant?"

He laughed. "Ain't you seen anything like it before?"

"No, I ain't."

"It's a bar of soap, boy, you use it to wash with. Go over there. That's a wash cabin. It has water in it. Strip yourself and dip the soap in water and rub yourself all over with the soap then rinse it off with water, that'll take the grime off you. Make sure to use a scrubbing brush. You'll need one, judging by the state of you. Throw those clothes away when you're done, and come back here directly, and make sure you're good and clean or I'll make you do it all over again."

"You mean I have to come back here butt naked?"

"That I do, but don't worry. No one 'round here will be seeing anything they ain't never seen before."

When I'd gotten myself scrubbed clean I stood butt naked in front of the sergeant. He laughed again. "I was just joshing with you 'bout coming back here butt naked," he said, "but maybe it's for the best you did. At least I know you won't be dirtying up your uniform as soon as you get it on. Now where's your chitty?"

I showed him my slip of paper, and he squinted at it and turned to his adjutant. "Ellory, give this young man the smallest size of everything we got."

The private handed me a uniform and boots. "Put 'em on, boy, and get yourself to the quartermaster's store across the way, and take your chitty with you else you'll be in trouble."

"Yes, sir." I got to putting the uniform on.

"Just move out the way so I can see to the next man, son."

Soon enough I was dressed in a uniform blue as the Wabash River on a clear day. Felt right proud I did, even though it drownded me, and I had to roll up the arms and legs to get it to fit anything like it should. I was used to doing that with all my clothes so it warn't any problem doing that, and at least the army boots fit. I was so taken with my new uniform I forgot how hungry I was, at least for a while. Wished I could see myself so I knowed what I looked like.

Then I joined the line of men outside the quarter-master's store and waited, all the while watching out for Billy. No sign of him. Got to the front of the line where yet another sergeant was waiting for me. "You seen a black feller called Billy anywhere?"

"I think I know who you mean, son. I had to send him on his way. Ain't no work for him here."

I choked back my tears when the quartermaster told me Billy had gone. *That's the last I'll ever see of him,* I thought to myself. The quartermaster's adjutant gave me a knapsack and blanket and the other stuff I'd need in the field. As I struggled to put the knapsack on my back, he said, "Get yourself over to the armory with your chitty, and be quick 'bout it!"

"Yes, sir!"

At the armory I went as usual to the back of a line of men and waited. Seemed there was no end to waiting around in the Army of the Potomac. When I got to the front and showed the armorer my chitty, he shook his head. "I ain't never seen anyone as small as you in the army before, not even the eleven-year-old we recruited the other week. You strong enough to carry a musket, boy?"

"Yes, sir!"

"I doubt that," he said. "Maybe you can pick one up, but you gotta be able to march for miles carrying it and then run into battle with it. Don't look to me like your arms are strong enough for that or your back, either, and as for your legs you got legs on you any chicken would be proud of."

"I can manage it, sir, no matter what I look like."

"Kinda keen, ain't you? That's a good sign. But keenness won't help you carry something 'most heavy as you are." Just then his adjutant said, "I got an idea, Sergeant. We could saw the end offa a musket and get it down to this boy's size, then he won't have no problem at all with it."

The sergeant smiled. "Good idea, Private, what you waiting for?"

The private chuckled. "Follow me, son."

I went into the cabin with him. Never seen so many muskets in one place. Death lined up neatly on shelves. The private took one of them, held it to his shoulder, and sighted along it. "Straight and true," he said. "I like to check before we hand 'em out." He put it in a vice, sawed off the end, filed the muzzle smooth, and held the musket to his shoulder again. "Yup, that's perfect," he said handing it to me. "Just what you need to kill Johnny Reb by the score."

"Thank you, sir."

"Now you gotta go join your unit."

"What is my unit?" I showed him the piece of

paper the recruiting sergeant had given me.

"You're lucky, son."

"Why's that, sir?"

"Because you're gonna serve in the best God-damn division of the Union army that's why." Shading his eyes with his hand he looked way into the distance. "See the end of that line of men?"

"Yes, sir."

"Go over there and join it. When you get to the front show your chitty to the sergeant. He'll assign you to your unit."

More waiting. What else? Finally I was shown my new home, a canvas house called a Sibley tent shaped like a big bell. Fifteen men already called that Sibley home. I made it sixteen. Big as it was, it was crowded and kinda smelly. The sergeant introduced me with the words, "We got us a new man, this here is Private Joseph Wild. Take care of him willya?"

The men that lived in that Sibley was all sitting around outside it doing some cooking. Smelled right good it did, but stewing bobcat woulda smelled good to me that day, I was so hungry. The men stood to attention and saluted, and one of them stepped forward. "Don't worry, Sergeant, we'll take good care of Private Wild."

Sergeant didn't look convinced. "Make sure you do." Then he left.

The man who'd stepped forward was only just a man, he hadn't got no whiskers to speak of, barely more'n me. Might have only been six or seven years older than me. He had fair hair and a look I liked, square-jawed and smiling. "Come and join us Joe, we're 'bout to eat."

"Thank you, sir, I'm real hungry."

He held out his hand. "Don't call me sir. My name's Daniel Butler, but you can call me Dan. I'll introduce you to the rest of 'em in a minute. We're all New Englanders here. You don't sound like one of us, you sound like a Reb! Where you from?"

I felt my cheeks burning. "I'm not a Reb, I'm from south Illinois. We talk that way down there, and we support the Union as far as I know."

He laughed. "No need to get sore at me, Joe, I was just joshing with you." Later I learned you have to take a lot of joshing in the army, 'specially if you're younger than the rest, and even more 'specially if you sound different, too.

Dan made a good stew with salt pork and vegetables cooked in a pot over a campfire, and after we'd eaten it one of the men boiled up some coffee. I ate and drank everything that came my way. First time my belly had been properly full in weeks. With my belly stuffed like a turkey ready for Thanksgiving, I lay on my back near enough the fire to get some benefit from it. The evening was cold, but in my uniform with my blanket around me and the campfire blazing I was warm enough to sleep, and man! I needed to sleep. I'd been on the go since dawn, and months of worrying and running around and not sleeping much had caught up with me in a big way. Shutting my eyes, I drifted off, thinking I could get used to army life. Then a bugle sounded so loud it hurt my ear and the toe of a boot prodded me in the side.

"Wake up, Joe, and pick up your things, we got some drilling to do."

Opening my eyes I saw Dan, got to my feet, and followed him to a big open area where all the privates from a lot of units was lined up. We spent the entire

Goddamned afternoon a-drilling and a-marching and a-pointing muskets and a-charging with bayonets fixed on our muskets. By the time we'd done I was exhausted. I went back to the Sibley barely able to walk.

Dan made more of his stew, and I found the strength to eat it and got to know more of the fellers in my unit. Main ones I remember besides Dan was Sergeant Donnelly on account of he was huge and had a head like a bag of nails, and James Torbet, known to one and all as Stretcher.

Stretcher introduced hisself to me first chance he got. "Don't you worry 'bout nothing, Joe," he said. "I'll keep you safe when Johnny Reb shows his face. I'm the best shot in the Union army, in fact I'm the best shot in the entire Goddamned Union."

Dan caught my eye and grinned when Stretcher said that. Did it in such a way that Stretcher didn't notice, just carried on talking. "When we fix bayonets and charge the enemy, stay by my side, Joe, I'll stick those Rebs like pigs, done it before at Manassas. Musta stuck a score of 'em if'n I stuck one." Dan caught my eye and grinned again, and again Stretcher didn't notice him doing it, just carried on with his tale about killing more Rebs than there could have been in the entire Confederacy.

Harris Kemble sticks in my mind also, a short stocky feller with brown sideburns like overgrown weeds, he was always blinking like he just seen daylight for the first time in his life. Musta blinked twenty times a minute.

After we ate, the fellers sat around playing cards and singing and such to while away the time and talked about a lot of stuff and complained about a lot of stuff, mainly about the fact they was in a Sibley and lots of soldiers was quartered in log cabins. Army was trying to replace all the Sibleys on the banks of the Potomac with log cabins but hadn't gotten 'round to it yet.

"Typical army," said Dan. "I don't want to spend a winter in this thing, but it looks like I just might have to."

Swear to God whatever they griped about, army life was a good life as long as you warn't in the front line getting shot at. You got your belly filled regular for one thing, first time my belly got filled that regular was in the army, plus, you didn't get leathered all the time, plus, you got more money than you could spend. But most of those boys managed to spend it somehow, mainly in the cathouses. If there was one cathouse in Washington there was five hundred of 'em and each and every one was busy night and day with army men lining up outside the doors and going in soon as someone else came out. The ladies who worked there musta had some stamina, because those soldiers couldn't get enough of the cathouses. Dan swore by them. Swore he couldn't think straight if he didn't go often enough, which was pretty damned often, it seemed to me. He tried to get me to go with him more'n once, but they seemed scary places, the women hanging around them ushering the men in looked like they'd eat you soon as look at you, and that was enough to put me off. Stretcher reckoned he been in every cathouse in Washington and sometimes they paid him he was so good at being a boyfriend to those ladies that worked there. Fellers 'round the campfire all looked at each other when he said that and one or two of them shook their heads looking kinda sorrowful, but none of them said nothing.

One day was much like another in the army on the bank of the Potomac in those days. You got up at the crack of dawn to the sound of the bugle and went on parade and drilled, then you ate, then you drilled some more and marched and trained till midday. Then you ate, then you drilled and marched and trained till dusk, then you ate again. If you had any strength left after that, which usually I didn't, you stayed up talking with your friends and sometimes singing or playing music. Some of those fellers could chew the rag for hours and never know more than a billy goat what they was saying even while they was sayin' it. But they was good fellows who looked after me, 'specially Dan. One thing struck me was they warn't just in it for the money, they wanted to fight for the cause, that cause being the Union, and they were keen to strike a blow against the Rebel traitors.

Day after day we drilled all day long, come rain or shine. The fellers who stayed up talking at night probably talked about the same things day after day and sang the same songs day after day and those that had musical instruments played the same music day after day. The routine was comforting because you knowed what was coming, and still you enjoyed it, believe it or not.

Army life suits some folks, and it certainly suited me. The ones who didn't take to it got homesick, and some of them cried. Even grown men cried because they ain't seen their loved ones in a while, and some of 'em deserted. Many deserters was rounded up, and they enjoyed if you could call it that, a spell in the stockade. The intention of the stockade was to make deserters and other miscreants rethink what the sergeant called their priorities. A month in the stockade was enough to make most men rethink their priorities. Believe me when I tell you there ain't many more miserable places on the earth than the inside of an army stockade.

Only drawback to army life so far as I could tell was when it rained you got soaked to the bone before breakfast, and you stayed that way all day long if the rain didn't let up. It rained for a week once, and we soldiers dripped for a week all day every day. Wrung our clothes out before we turned in and put them on wet next day, and they got even wetter before we'd even lined up for the first drill of the morning.

A month after I signed up our unit was sent to the range for target practice. I woulda expected Stretcher to be desperate to go to show off his marksmanship, being as he was a expert shot and all, but he warn't keen.

"Ain't nothing the instructors can tell me 'bout shooting," he said. "I know more'n them 'bout it. No point in me practicing my shooting. I don't need it, I'm good enough already, and 'sides, I'm feeling ill. Got a touch of the fevers so it's best I don't have any truck with the range. I'm gonna lie in bed all day to get over my sickness."

When Sergeant Donnelly found Stretcher lying in bed, Sergeant's head changed color. It turned red so it looked like a red bag of nails with the nails shifting around angrily in it. "What you think you doing, Private Stretcher?" Even the sergeant called him Stretcher.

"I got the fever, Sergeant, I need rest."

The sergeant grabbed Stretcher and pulled him to his feet like he weighed no more'n a small bag of feathers. "Get to the range with the rest of the men, or I swear to God you'll get all the rest you need and then some in the stockade!"

Stretcher did his best to salute while the sergeant shook him like a rat in a dog's mouth. "Yes, sir!" he said in a shaky voice.

Down at the range I shot a whole lot better'n Stretcher did. Turned out he was the worst shot in our unit bar none. Even Harris was a better shot than Stretcher, and you would've thought all that blinking woulda made Harris the worst. But Stretcher took the biscuit for bad marksmanship. Way he shot you woulda thought he'd never handled a musket in his life. After his spell on the range Stretcher didn't talk much about his marksmanship no more. I reckon I woulda been the best shot in our unit if my musket had been a regular length. Short barrel made it harder to aim. Even so I warn't bad.

Most popular man in the army was General George McClellan. He was the top man, the feller who was training us up for battle. We all felt he was looking out for us, don't ask me why. I saw him once. He was a handsome looking man with dark hair and a well-trimmed moustache. Always had one arm stuck inside his army jacket for some reason. But then, a lotta the generals I seen done that. No idea why. You can't use your arm if it's stuck inside of your jacket, so what's the sense in it? It makes no sense to me. But the smartest men in the army—the generals— all seemed to think it was a good idea. Maybe they warn't so smart as we privates all took them to be.

Disease swept through the camp that winter. Fevers, army cough, dysentery, and lotsa other illnesses. Most of my regiment came down with sickness of some kind but not me. I'd spent too much of my childhood wading through anthills to get sick easy. Worst case of fevers was Private Clayton Brister, a good soldier with a golden heart. He did my guard duty for me once when I was too tired to do it myself before I'd gotten used to the army way of doing things. The army way is to do things when you're too tired to do them, and if you're not too tired the army makes damn sure you get too tired. Felt like my spell of guard duty woulda kilt me when Clayton did it for me, so I had a lot to thank him for. Anyways he came down with a fever and was shivering in his bed. Couldn't stir hisself enough even to get to his feet. Sweat shining on his forehead made it look it was made of polished wood.

Dan took one look at him and said, "We gotta take you to the hospital, Clayton."

Clayton warn't having none of it. "I'm not going there. I seen too many men go in that place and not come out again." So we all had to leave him be.

Sergeant Donnelly went to see Clayton with a mind to call him a slacker and get him out of bed, but he took one look at Clayton's forehead and walked out the Sibley where Clayton lay. Spoke to the men. "If he gets no better in a day, one of you make sure he gets to the camp hospital."

Me and Dan spoke up together, "Yes, sir!"

Stretcher knelt by Clayton's side saying he knowed all there was to know about doctoring, and he'd learned it at some fancy medical school. Only reason he warn't a doctor now was the war had got in the way, but soon as it ended he'd be setting hisself up to cure people of all their ills, and he gave Clayton some fancy medicine he'd got. "That'll make you better real quick," he said and out he went. We left

Clayton to it, but I looked in on him after a while. He didn't look no better to me. Forehead gleamed even brighter than before. As I stared at him his lips curled back like a dog's does when it's angry, and he smiled with the strangest kind of smile you ever did see, skin all pulling tight in his cheeks. Didn't look like he was happy even so. I knelt next to him and put my arm under his shoulders trying to get him to sit up to give him some water, but I couldn't because he'd gone stiff like a corpse although he warn't a corpse. Not yet, anyways. Skin on his cheeks pulled tighter, and he grinned the fiercest grin I ever seen in my life. Lips pulled so far back you could see all of his gums, never minding his teeth. Then his back arched till the only parts of him touching the ground was his heels and his head. Head bent back so far it was his forehead on the ground. I don't believe in the devil and never have done, but if you told me right then Satan had taken over Clayton Brister I woulda believed you. I ran out that Sibley so fast my feet barely touched the floor.

"Fellers!" I said. "You gotta come in. Somethings happening to Clayton!"

We all went in, and he was lying still and quiet like a baby, not grinning no more, no longer arched up in the middle. Just looked like he was sleeping quietly, all peaceful like he should be.

Dan crouched next to Clayton, looked at him, then at me, and stuck out his square jaw. "What do you mean Joe? What's the problem? Clayton looks all right to me."

"I can't explain it, Dan," I said.

Then Clayton a-shuddered and a-shivered and his eyes opened wide and his lips peeled back again like the skin of a rabbit when you skin it, and he grinned like the devil from ear to ear.

Dan jumped up, eyes big as clocks. "Lord have mercy on us all," he said, crossing hisself. Stretcher, who was in there with us, went all pale and said, "Amen to that," and right about then, Clayton's back arched, and he got on his heels and forehead, and we all ran out the Sibley fast as we could, some of us shrieking. "The Devil got him!" Dan said. No one else said nothing. Too affrighted to speak I reckon. I knowed I was.

Next time we dared go in the Sibley Clayton was dead. We dug an extra deep grave for him and gave him a good coffin made of thick wood instead of the wafer-thin stuff the army specialized in for coffins on the rare occasion it used them. Nailed the lid on good and tight. Put rocks on top of it for good measure before covering it up with earth.

"Swear to God, if we not careful this one gonna rise up from his grave," Dan said as we shoveled the earth in on top of Clayton. Dan warn't the only one afeared Clayton might rise from his grave. I afeared it, too. Listened out for Clayton every night for long enough after we buried him in case he came out of his grave to get me.

When the burial was over we all went back to the Sibley. Men got to drinking to remember Clayton or forget about him, I'm not sure which. Dan offered me some whiskey.

"Thank you kindly, Dan, but I can't."

"Why not, Joe?"

"Sergeant just told me I'm on sentry duty tonight, and I don't want to be caught drunk on duty and get sent to the stockade."

Stretcher came right up to me saying, "I know

Clayton was a good friend of yours, Joe. You must be torn up 'bout him dying like that. You need a drink much as anyone does at a time like this. Tell you what, I'll do your sentry duty for ya, so you can have a drink."

"That's real good of you, Stretcher." All the men called him by his nickname to his face by then. "I'll take you up on that offer. Like you said I need a drink real bad."

"Think nothing of it, Joe."

I did a powerful lot of drinking for a while after that. I warn't one for whiskey, not really, but I knocked back a peck of it that day. None of us who saw him die will ever forget Clayton, that's for sure.

General McLellan kept us camping next to the Potomac all winter and into the following spring. I woulda been happy to stay by the Potomac, enjoying that life forever, but all good things come to an end. In March 1862 he had us shipped by way of the Atlantic to Fort Monroe in Virginia. There was a hundred and twenty thousand of us crammed into more ships than you can imagine and it took two weeks to get us all on shore. Made me feel mighty glad I was in the Union army. Warn't nothing gonna stop us with so many men and guns and ammunition and horses and whatnot we got going for us. Rebs'd be lucky if they had half our number. What's more, all the men I was with was keen to fight. It's a feeling that's infectious. I found myself wanting to get into battle just because I was with other men who felt the same way.

That American army I was part of warn't so much American as an army of all nations, 'cept black Americans, of course. We got Irish, German, English, Polish, Dutch, Canadians, Italians, Jews, and even Mexicans,

even though it warn't long since we fought a war
against the Mexicans, whupped them, and stole their
land offa them. Irish and Germans had their own regiments. English, Polish, and such generally mixed
among the rest of us. I heard tell there was some Indians mixed in, too, but I only ever saw one of 'em, and
I didn't see him until the very end of the war.

From Fort Monroe we moved northwest so as we
could take Richmond. I reckoned I could walk to Richmond in two or three days, but we got held up at a
place called Yorktown. Word came down from the top
that a hundred thousand Rebs was holding Yorktown
against us. That news surprised me as I didn't know
there was so many Reb soldiers in the area. Made me
wonder if the war was gonna be won easy after all,
especially when I saw the gun barrels sticking out
from the fortifications the Rebs had put up. I ain't
never seen so many cannons. Huge they was, too.
Big enough to blast a house down with a single shot.
Made me shiver just looking at them.

General McClellan decided we warn't gonna attack because the odds against us was too great. Instead we laid siege to the place and waited for our
own big guns to come up to blast them Rebs to hell.
Our big guns arrived a month later, but we never got
to fire so much as a single shot with them. Rebs had
left Yorktown the day before. Place was empty. We
walked into the town nice and easy with our arms
swinging like folks taking a Sunday stroll. General
McClellan put the word out that we'd won a great
victory, and we'd won it without firing a shot, which
warn't entirely true, as some of us had taken potshots
at Johnny Reb during the siege, and he'd returned
the compliment. But you can excuse the general his

bit of poetic license. He warn't that far wrong when he said a shot hadn't been fired.

When we got into Yorktown we found out that those big cannons the Rebs had was mainly what you call Quaker Guns, tree-trunks painted black so's they looked like cannons. Great for building a fire with, but not so good if you want to shoot a body of men. You could tell there had never been no hundred thousand men there, just a small bunch of men marching around and around all over the place back and forth to make it look like there was a horde of them. Probably no more'n twenty thousand had been facing us in Yorktown at most. We coulda stormed the place and overrun them any time we wanted dead easy if'n we'd just been given the order to fix bayonets and charge.

Top and bottom of it was General McClellan had been fooled, and so had the rest of us. We privates laughed at the way the Rebs had pulled the wool over our eyes. Felt a bit silly, too. But not half so silly as the general felt, I'll bet. Didn't stop him trumpeting about his great victory though.

Warn't long before we got to marching on Richmond again. It was a fair slow march because the general was still worried we was facing a huge Rebel army. Folks called him "The Virginia Creeper" on account of he was so slow getting his men into battle.

We'd been over a month on the peninsula near where Richmond was, and we hadn't none of us been in what you'd call a real battle yet. Then we got our first taste of one. Got ourselves bloodied, so to speak. And we had a stroke of luck. We wounded the Reb general commanding the Reb forces against us. Johnston he was called. Turned out to be a stroke of bad luck though, because General Robert E. Lee took over from Johnston, and Bobby Lee whipped us from pillar to post. First time he sent his men at us I was in the line next to Stretcher. When the Rebs charged us Sergeant Donnelly told us to level our muskets and take aim, "But don't shoot till I give the order!" We all stood steady with our muskets leveled, all 'cept Stretcher who turned tail and made as if he was going to run. Sergeant Donnelly punched him in the belly, grabbed him, faced him toward the enemy again, and kicked him up his rear. Stretcher didn't dare turn away from the enemy after that. He was more afeared of the sergeant than he was of Johnny Reb. We all was. That's how the army works. You got to be more afeared of your own side than you are of the enemy to make sure you charge in the right direction.

"Ain't you gonna stick those Rebs like pigs, Stretcher?" Dan said.

Stretcher gave Dan a look like he had poison in his eyes. "No, I'm gonna shoot 'em. They're not close enough to stick like pigs yet."

We spent the next seven days retreating from Bobby Lee and his men down the peninsula to Fort Monroe as fast as we possibly could. Upshot was we ended up being taken back to the Potomac on the same ships that had brought us to the peninsula.

On the Potomac we had another long spell of drilling and such every day. I was happy enough doing that, and the men was all happy, too, being as they could get along to the cathouses to spend their army pay on what they enjoyed the most. But it didn't last. The good life came to an end when General McClellan took us down to Antietam on account of Bobby Lee was on the march again.

I went up to the front with my unit, keeping close as I could to Dan and Stretcher. We gave each other strength, and we needed to. We had a bloody time in Antietam.

As we was getting ready to attack, Dan turned to me. "Why did you join up, Joe? I ain't never asked you that." Guess talking was his way of dealing with the fear we all was getting as the time to fight got nearer.

When your life is on the line ain't no point in lying so I told him, "Because everybody thought I kilt a man, and I decided to make myself scarce, and joining the army seemed a good way of doing it."

His eyebrows shot up. "Well, I'll be! You don't look like a killer, Joe." Later when I was defending the sunken road at Antietam I fired my musket so much and so often the barrel got too hot to touch and my jaw ached from tearing cartridges open with my teeth. Put me in mind of the occasion I'd been out a-shooting with Mr. Purdy. But I didn't have time to dwell on that. Just tore another cartridge open and shot another Reb who got through our hail of fire almost to our line. I brung him down with a bullet in the belly. Tore out his guts.

Dan winked at me. "Changed my mind 'bout you not looking like a killer, Joe. You started looking like one now."

All around us men on both sides was falling like bowling pins. Others who didn't fall were throwing up because of the heat. Still others had blood running outta their noses and ears from the blast made by their own weapons. My ears got singed with powder burns, and so did my hair. Dan's face was black with powder burns, and mine must've been the same but I had no way of telling.

We fought all day long. Only reason we stopped fighting was it got too dark to fight. Around our camp-fire after the shooting had stopped we was drinking coffee when Dan turned to me. "Think your folks are missing you, Joe?"

"Maybe. Are yours missing you, Dan?"

He shook his head. "I don't have no folks, I'm a orphan. The Army of the Potomac is the closest thing to a family I got. Closest thing to a family I ever had. I ain't never experienced comradeship before like I got now. Don't know what I'm gonna do when this war ends. Bad as the war is, it'll break my heart to leave the army."

"Maybe you'll be able to stay on in the army after the fighting is over."

"Maybe, I hope so. Army's all I got."

Antietam was nothing like the Peninsula. The Peninsula had been a cakewalk. Antietam was all hell. We'd attack Johnny Reb then he'd come right back at us, tide of men and bullets surging first one way and then t'other, hail of shot so thick it was a miracle so much as a single man survived it. Hell, if a rabbit survived on that battlefield it was a miracle.

You ain't seen so many dead bodies as I saw in a single day of action there, enough bodies to fill every graveyard in the land it seemed, lying around all twisted. Worst of it was some of them warn't dead yet, but you knowed there was nothing you could do for them, and they'd be another number soon. Army was real big on numbers. We had a count-up after every engagement to find out how many men we'd lost. But we privates didn't need a count-up. We could see plain enough for ourselves that there warn't half so many of us after any given battle as there had been before it.

We was told we won a great victory at Antietam. I didn't see how it could be called a victory with that many bodies in blue lying around, but we sent Bobby Lee and his boys packing, so it musta been a victory of sorts. Bobby Lee left a lotta men in gray lying around in the field, as many as our blue boys it looked like.

After Antietam President Abraham Lincoln decided the war was all about freeing up slaves from the South. Up till then he and I had both thought it was about keeping the Union intact, but suddenly he'd changed his mind on that it seemed. Anyways, I warn't about to argue with the president. He was an Illinois boy like me, and I had nothing against freeing up the slaves. In fact I was all for it, having seen the way they was treated, and a lot of the older men in our unit agreed. They reckoned freeing the slaves was all to the good because it gave us a cause, something virtuous to fight for.

Next we saw action at Fredericksburg and Chancellorsville, battles that made me feel I'd been wrong about whose side God was on. I came out of them with no hope the Union was ever gonna win the war. We was always being told we had more men than the Rebs, but whenever we lined up against them their lines seemed long as ours, and they whupped us more often than not. But I was glad of my choice. I guess deep down I believed in the cause of freeing the slaves and maybe the cause of the Union, too.

The first battle that made me think we might have a chance of beating the Rebs was Gettysburg, where we whupped the Rebs good and proper for a change. I went to fight at Briscoe and Mine Run after

Gettysburg and kept fighting on and off till December of 1863. Somewhere along the line I swapped my musket for a rifle, and somehow I managed to not get myself kilt. Thinking about it, that was my biggest achievement during the war. A lotta good men I knowed, better men than I am if I'm to be honest, didn't make it.

Army hunkered down for the winter of 1863 at Brandy Station in Virginia. When it did I felt I'd had enough. The feeling had been growing in me for some time. Don't get me wrong, I loved army life, but when you see so much blood being spilled you need a rest from it. You need to get among trees and enjoy nature and track animals and fish for your supper and light fires and just plain get wild like you're supposed to be.

I asked Sergeant Donnelly for leave but he wouldn't give me any.

"You're needed here, son," he said.

Truth was, he was worried I might not come back, and that's why he warn't letting me go. Army was in a bad state by that time. Our regiment had started with a thousand men and only three hundred of the original thousand was left. Numbers had been made back up to a thousand by men who'd been paid a bounty to join. But the army needed to hang on to its original soldiers. They was like seasoned wood and kept the thing strong.

"Don't worry, Sergeant, if you give me leave I'll be back," I said.

Sergeant shook his head. "Can't let you go, Private Wild."

I left anyways, in the dead of night, and no one saw me. But first I went to the colonel's cabin, which was well-guarded, but I got past the guards like a fox gets into a henhouse. To cover myself so as I wouldn't be punished for desertion I snuck into the cabin and left a note on the colonel's table. Near as I can remember it said:

> Dear Colonel Livermore:
> My name is Private Joseph Wild, and I'm the youngest soldier in your regiment. I can't take the army no more, not for a while anyhows, so I'm going. But I'm not deserting, sir. I'm just taking me a rest. I'll be back before you know it.
> Yours truly, Private Joseph Wild

When I sneaked out the colonel's cabin none of the sentries was any the wiser for what I'd done. Not one of 'em so much as even noticed me. Creeping among the rest of the cabins to the camp perimeter I snuck past the sentries posted all 'round who was keeping a lookout for deserters and enemies. Might sound like a hard thing to do, but it warn't all that hard for a boy brought up in the backwoods who'd tracked an animal or two and learned to keep quiet when he was on the move.

16

LOST IN THE WILDERNESS

BY THEN I WAS FOURTEEN YEARS OLD AND ARMY food had made me bigger and stronger. Didn't have to roll up the arms and legs of my uniform so far to make it fit. Carried a full-size rifle, too, and it was a modern one that shot a Minie bullet shaped like a window in a fancy sorta church, one of them what you call gothic windows with a point at the top. That bullet is accurate, and it'll break your bones wherever it hits you. It gets you in the arm, you need your arm sawed off, it gets you in the leg, you need your leg sawed off, it gets you in the gut you're dead, even if you don't die right away, because your guts is gonna spill out, and there's no way any doctor on earth can fix that.

Made my way to Washington and stayed overnight in a good hotel, leaving my uniform with the man at the desk. Paid him some money to look after it for me and bought a buckskin jacket, buckskin pants, new boots, gloves, a fur coat, and so on in a shop. Cost me a fortune, but I had a fortune to spend being as I hadn't spent much of my army pay. Warn't nothing to spend it on if you didn't gamble or go to cathouses. Dressed in my new outfit I went to Wisconsin. It was winter and cold as you like up there. Place suited me through and through because it was wooded country with trees as big as a man could wish for and as many as he could want.

I paid an old couple to let me bunk down in their

log cabin. It put me in mind of life with Ma and Pa. That made me feel good and bad all at the same time. Went out real early one morning into the woods when snow was thick on the ground and perfect for tracking. I found some rabbit prints and followed them till they disappeared, then I sat still on my haunches watchin'. Warn't long before I saw the rabbit, or rather I saw the eyes of a rabbit. Eyes are the first thing you see of a rabbit in the snow. You only see the rest if you look real hard. Rabbit looked around, and its ears twitched, then it moved a yard, and then it was in the jaws of a bobcat. Turned out I warn't the only one who'd been watching that rabbit. Bobcat had been there all along waiting for his next meal. It didn't bother me none as I hadn't been fixing to eat that rabbit. Couple I was staying with had plenty of salt pork and other vittles and had agreed to feed me. Only reason I was there was to be in the woods and see the wildlife.

Came across tracks in the snow that was made by hooves and followed them to a big herd of elk. Must've been two hundred of them sheltering among the trees. That sight made my heart swell up.

I did that kind of thing every day for two months before I felt like I was ready to do more killing for the benefit of the Union and the abolitionists. Then I made my way back to Washington, where I stayed in my hotel and enjoyed the city for a week and got me a girlfriend who was what you might call real experienced. Lost my cherry to her. Wouldn't tell me anything much about herself. Said she had a job in a shop. When I pressed her, she said, "You wouldn't want to know, Joe." I got the picture and never asked again. But it kind of put me offa her, and we drifted apart, much as you can drift apart in a week, that is. War woulda come between us anyways, so it warn't like either of us lost anything. I'll never forget her though, because she was my first one. They say you always remember the first, and it's true.

At the end of the week I picked up my uniform and got the train back to Brandy Station. General Grant had just been made head of the entire Union army. Me and General Grant arrived at Brandy Station on the same day at the same time on the same train. I liked to think that us two boys from Illinois was teaming up to win the war on behalf of the Union.

It was a cold rainy morning when we both got off the train. I doubt General Grant even noticed me. I noticed him all right. He warn't showy or anything, but he carried hisself with a air of confidence and authority.

My unit was lined up on the Parade Ground, wet and miserable with Sergeant Donnelly drilling them. The way Donnelly barked his orders it's a wonder he had any voice left.

I got in front of him, stood to attention, and saluted. "Private Wild reporting for duty, sir!"

That bag of nails Sergeant Donnelly had for a head turned red like it always did when he was rattled. Nails shifted around in his mouth area. "You went over my head, Private Wild."

"What do you mean, Sergeant?"

"You asked Colonel Livermore permission to go on leave. Colonel Livermore told me about it. Said when you came back to the unit I warn't to discipline you for being insubordinate." He wagged one of his thick fingers in my face. "But let me tell you this, Private Wild, you ever go behind my back to the colonel or anyone else ever again I'll hang you up by your thumbs till you cry out for mercy, have you got that?"

A drop of rain ran down my nose and fell off the end. I ignored it. "Yes, sir!"

"Good. Now get in line. You got drilling to do, and plenty of it."

During the drilling I thought about what Colonel Livermore had done for me. I'd said in my note to him I was going on leave. I hadn't asked him, I'd told him. Colonel had read my note and told Sergeant Donnelly I'd asked for his permission. The colonel had done me a big favor. He'd made it sound like I'd followed the rules to keep me out of trouble. He was a good man. I owed him one.

When the drilling was over we retired to the cabin where we was quartered for a rest and some food. It was warm and comfy, much better'n a Sibley! Warm because it had a fireplace with a fire burning in it, and comfy because it had enough room for everything we got. We ate bread, beef, beans, and rice that day. Upshot was we was well housed and well fed, because of which I was looking forward to spending more time at Brandy Station. Rest of my unit warn't, though, they was bored stiff. Give you Dan as a example.

"Can't wait to get back to fighting Johnny Reb," he said, sitting in front of the fire. "Had enough of this waiting around in camp. Seems like we're just killing time but we're not. Time's killing us." Harris nodded and did some blinking with it.

There was a great expectation in us all because General Ulysses S. Grant had taken command. We'd all heard he'd won every battle he'd fought. He'd taken Vicksburg from the Rebs and done a whole lotta other stuff, so we were looking forward to being led by him, all but a handful such as Stretcher who said, "You think Grant's good? Well, he ain't fought Bobby Lee yet. Bobby Lee'll whup him, you'll see. We ain't got no general in the north good enough to take on Bobby Lee."

An Irish feller, a little guy from Cork with black hair and the bluest eyes you ever seen, heard Stretcher and said, "Grant could lick Bobby Lee any day of any given week."

"No, he couldn't," Stretcher said. "Bobby Lee is too good for him."

"No, he ain't."

"He is, too."

"He ain't, and you're a traitor saying Bobby Lee is better'n our man U. S. Grant."

Stretcher looked the Irish feller up and down like he was making sure he was the bigger of them, which he was by a long mark. If it had been a height contest Stretcher woulda won it dead easy. He must've had six inches on the man from Cork and then some. When he saw he was looking down on the top of the Irish feller's head from a great height even though he warn't standing on anything 'cept his own two feet and the soles of his boots, Stretcher got this confident look on his mug and said, all threatenin', "You calling me a traitor you good-for-nothing Irish sonofabitch?"

"Yes, I am you lanky Yankee idiot."

"Well, then I'm gonna lick you hollow same as Bobby Lee gonna lick Grant hollow," said Stretcher.

The Irish feller took off his jacket and rolled up his sleeves. "You're nothing but a useless streak of piss, and I'm gonna lick you same as Grant is gonna lick Bobby Lee."

Stretcher gave me and the other fellas in our unit

a wink that said this Irish feller don't know what he's letting hisself in for and took off his own jacket and rolled up the sleeves of his shirt. Then Stretcher struck up a pose with his fists in the air circling them like a bareknuckle prize fighter. "I'm warning you I'm the best fist fighter in the whole of New England, and I'm gonna lick you so bad you gonna wish you'd never left the Emerald Isle for these shores!" Waved his fists around like he was going knock the Irish feller's brains clean out of his head. "Beat more men with my fists than you've had hot din—"

Irish feller's left fist crashed into Stretcher's gut, and Stretcher bent at the middle like a giant was folding him in half. Before he was fully folded the Irishman's right fist crashed into Stretcher's mouth, and Stretcher fell on his back gasping like a fish landed on the dry bank of a river on a hot summer day. Irishman stood over him. "Stand up! I ain't finished with you yet."

Stretcher could barely move 'cept for his chest, which was heaving as if he was gonna throw up. He summoned up all his strength and just about managed to raise his head and say, "I can't stand up. I'm done."

Irishman put his jacket back on saying, "I knowed it'd be easy, but I never expected it to be that easy. I ain't even broke a sweat." Walked off with this satisfied look on his face.

The Irish won most of the fistfights in the Army of the Potomac. You woulda thought Stretcher woulda known that by 1864. He'd been in the army long enough to notice things of that sort, almost three years by my reckoning. Anyways he laid there for a while with blood coming outta his mouth. I helped him to his feet, and he wiped the blood from his swole-up lips, and said, "That Irishman cheated. He got me when I warn't looking, I woulda licked him easy as my grandma's apple pie if he'd fought fair and square." I didn't say anything, nor did any of the other fellers in our unit who'd been watching. We just let him make his excuses and keep what was left of his dignity as best he could.

I didn't get to enjoy the good life at Brandy Station. Day after Stretcher fought the Irishman bugles a-sounded, drums was beaten with a military beat, and trumpets added their noise to the general racket. While this was going on the Army of the Potomac was lined up regiment by regiment, battery by battery, and we all knowed something important was happening. The drums and so on fell silent, and we was read out our orders to march south. Not stretching the truth to say every man-jack on that parade ground cheered till he couldn't cheer no more. Even I did, and I had wanted the good life to carry on in our log cabin. But we all, even me it turned out, wanted this war over and done with and thought General Grant was the one man who could get it over and done with for us. Well, he was, in more ways than one.

We left the parade ground and got ready to march in the morning. Made fires that lit up the camp and sent smoke wafting to the sky. We was burning the stuff we wouldn't need for the march and packing what we would need for the journey in our knapsacks. Veterans like me packed light. Didn't carry anything 'cept food, water, ammunition, tobacco, a rubber blanket, two woollen blankets, spare underwear, and spare shoes. Raw recruits carried more stuff on their backs and in their arms than you could fit on a wagon.

Dan gave me a crafty look when he saw what they was doing. "Bet you they'll be dropping a lot of that stuff before long," he said. "When they do, make sure you pick some of it up. Only the food, mind you. No sense burdenin' yourself with anything else, or you gonna be regretting it, and letting go of it down the line."

The army of 1864 was different from the one I joined in 1861. Black men had been allowed to join, so we had regiments of black men with us, and also about half our men was bounty men who were fighting for money, not for the cause. They'd signed up because they got paid a four-hundred-dollar bounty for agreeing to fight Johnny Reb. That was on top of their thirteen dollars a month army pay. Even so I swear to God every man in the Army of the Potomac was up for fighting Johnny Reb tooth and nail and hammer, too, if it took that. We all had it in our heads make a spoon or spoil the horn.

On May 4, 1864, we struck camp well before dawn. I warn't counting, but there was more'n a hundred thousand of us set off marching in near darkness. Infantry, cavalry, artillery, and wagons with supplies, and flags a-flying everywhere you looked. A excited feeling was running through every one of us. Military bands was playing military tunes and that added to the general air of excitement. All of us felt we was gonna finish off Johnny Reb or die trying. Our unit was under General Hancock, who was under General Meade, who was under General Grant. We'd all have sooner just been under General Grant, but we had to take what little we was given in the army and be grateful for that.

Sun came up in a good clear sky, and everyone

marched with an easy swinging step. Me and Dan and Stretcher and Harris was together next to each other, buddies going into battle. All along the line ahead of us and behind us flags was a-flappin' in the breeze, and that line of men was long; it stretched for miles. Could have been five miles long, could have been ten or fifteen or anywhere in between. It was a hell of a long line is what I'm saying, and following at the back of it was a convoy of canvas-covered wagons that also stretched for miles. Musta been a thousand wagons or more fulla supplies for us. Guns, too, cannons and mortars to shoot the enemy with. You wouldn't have thought nothing could stop us and that we could have stormed the gates of hell with our army if we wanted, it was so big and mighty. Hell was zackly where we was going if we did but know it. It was a hell that went by the name of the Wilderness.

The Wilderness is a mess of trees like you never seen. Trees close together with brush tangled among them so you can barely walk between them, and foliage so thick you can't see more than a few feet ahead in places. Hidden ravines to fall down, streams to fall into, and clearings to get shot to bits in. Dark hellish nightmare it is. Normally I like the woods but not these, they warn't natural. They grew after the old natural woods been cleared for smelting. Maybe I coulda got to like them but for the fact the Rebs knowed the Wilderness better'n we did. Rebs knowed every trail, clearing, and stream in the Wilderness. Gave them the advantage in what you'd call the perfect killing ground. Soldier has a fight in there he might never see his enemy till he gets a bayonet in his gut.

We went there by way of the Rapidan River. Every

one of us knowed we oughta get through the Wilderness right quick. Last thing we wanted was to get caught in it and fight Johnny Reb on his own terms so to speak, but we got delayed crossing the Rapidan at Ely Ford. Soldiers ahead of us couldn't cross quick enough so all the soldiers following on behind them had to bunch up and wait for them to cross. While waiting some of us was sent to a pontoon bridge our engineers had put up, and we crossed the Rapidan on that without getting our boots wet, which was something.

On the other side of the Rapidan we walked through a lush valley while the day got hotter and hotter with the sort of cloying Southern heat that makes you sweat even when you're not exertin' yourself. I ain't exaggeratin' none when I tell you that valley felt like it had no air in it whatsoever. At the end of the valley, we walked a long uphill slope with sweat dripping offa us, uniforms clinging to our skin, and our knapsacks making our arms feel they was coming outta their sockets at the shoulder. Our mouths were as dry as Death Valley, and the skeeters were biting us every chance they got.

Ahead of us soldiers who'd overburdened their selves had thrown away some of their belongings.

"I got me a loaf of bread," said Dan stooping to pick something up.

Stretcher looked like he was ready to cry. "I saw it first!" he said.

"Don't worry, I'll share it with you," said Dan putting it away in his knapsack. I got some rice that way, and Stretcher felt better about things when he picked up a few plugs of tobacco.

Top of the hill we came to what we all dreaded,

the Wilderness. Some of us been there under Hooker in 1863 and knowed what to expect, namely all hell. We marched quick along the road hoping to get through the trees that make the Wilderness what it is before Johnny Reb made his move. Got to the old Chancellorsville Courthouse without incident and camped in a field nearby. All the men was murmuring they didn't want to fight in the Wilderness. After we'd eaten, me and Dan and Stretcher and Harris walked over the old battlefield we'd fought on in 1863 remembering what we'd been through.

It warn't hard to remember. There was enough reminders, by which I mean bodies sticking up outta the soil. Most of them was buried but because they'd been buried in a hurry, they hadn't been put deep enough under the dirt, so wherever you looked you'd see a leg sticking from a mound of earth or an arm. Poke about with your foot and you'd soon enough see a ribcage or a hand.

Dan found a whole body all twisted up. "This could be what's lying in store for one of us," he said.

"I hope not," I said. The body's legs was here and its arms there. Rags of a uniform hanging off of them. Skull grinning like you just told it the best joke ever. Put me in mind of Clayton on his deathbed. Harris took one look and turned right pale and walked away.

"Gotta take a leak," Dan said and went to a tree.

Funny how a tree helps a fella take a leak. Ain't no reason to stand against a tree to do it. You could just as easy do it without a tree in front of you.

The twisted-up body must've reminded Stretcher of Clayton, too, because while Dan and Harris was out of earshot Stretcher looked at me like a dog that's been whupped and said, "It's all my fault Clayton's dead, I kilt him."

"What?"

"I kilt Clayton. I didn't mean to. I given him strychnine to make him better, and I given him too much of it." At first I thought Stretcher was telling one of his stretchers, but looking at his face I knowed he warn't. "What's a body to do when he feels bad as I do, Joe? I joined the army to kill Rebs, not kill men on my own side."

I took Stretcher in my arms and hugged him. We must've been a funny sight being as he towered over me even though I'd grown some. Slapped him gently on the back. "Like you said, you didn't mean to kill him, Stretcher, so you ain't done nothing wrong, it was a accident."

Tears welled up in his sad eyes and rolled down his cheeks. "Thank you, Joe."

Dan came back from the tree fastening up his pants. Looked at us like we gone mad. "What you two doing? You in love or something?"

I let Stretcher go, and he wiped his eyes and did his best not to look upset no more. "I was just out of sorts. Joe helped me feel better, is all."

Dan looked from me to Stretcher and from Stretcher back to me. "Next time you feeling out of sorts go to a cathouse."

We all laughed and went back to camp and sat around our campfire chewing the rag. We were interrupted by the sound of firing coming from the woods. "Hear that?" Dan said. "I bet it's a Reb skirmish line. That means we'll be fighting them in the Wilderness tomorrow."

Group of us sitting round the fire nodded but didn't say anything. Guess we didn't want to think about it, far less talk about it. Turned in at midnight and didn't sleep none too easy. Nobody did.

Bugle call sounded good and early, but I didn't need any bugle call to wake me up. My eyes was already open, and I was wondering what the day would bring and whether I'd survive it. Got up and roasted some pork and had it with beans, and followed that with coffee and two pieces of hard tack. Hard tack was so hard I nearly broke my damn teeth on it, but still I got it down. If this was to be my last breakfast I wanted it to be a good big one. By the looks of things everyone else felt the same way I did. All the men were cooking up the best storm they could. Sergeant rounded us up and marched us on the turnpike leading toward the Wilderness forest. Me and Dan and Stretcher and Harris was in the middle of a long column of men. I was glad we warn't at the front of it. Men there'd bear the brunt of whatever lay ahead. There again, we could get taken by surprise and hit in the side, in which case it don't matter which part of the line you're in, you're bearing the brunt good and hard.

We turned left from the turnpike onto an old dirt road slanting into the densely packed trees. Picket firing we'd heard during the night was still going on, louder and brisker than before. Then I heard a noise that chilled me to my young bones. Best I can describe it is to say it was like the sound a rabbit makes when you kill it with your bare hands, a sort of death shriek, 'cept it lasted longer than the noise a dying rabbit makes and was a sight louder. It fairly made a body's hair raise on end. It was the Rebel Yell. The Rebs didn't plan it. That yell just came out of their mouths in the heat of battle like the roar of a lion or the hiss of a snake.

We now knowed for certain that somewhere nearby the Rebs was on the attack. How long would we wait before it was us they was attacking? Sergeant's nails moved 'round in his head, and he spoke up. "A-whooping can't hurt you none men. We're gonna give 'em hell. By the time this day is over there won't be any more whooping from those Rebs. Sobbing is all we gonna hear from 'em after we're done with 'em."

We carried on down the track a long ways till orders came down the line. Sergeant held his arm up. "Stand firm! Nobody move!"

We was all loaded up and ready to go. Now we had to not go, just stand still waiting for more orders while in the distance we could hear a battle going on.

Dan raised his eyebrows. "What they trying to do to us, Joe, keeping us standing here like this?"

I shrugged.

Stretcher answered him. "The Rebs is trying to kill us good and dead like that feller we saw last night."

"That warn't what I meant," said Dan. "What I meant was what's our own side trying to do to us? The waiting around is worse'n the fighting. Makes your brains get all scrambled up." I knowed what he meant. My own brains was feeling pretty scrambled.

All around us was tree cover thick as you like and hardly any daylight getting through and the sound of guns firing and men yelling somewhere, but we didn't know where.

"Someone has to be in reserve," I said.

Dan shook his head. "Wish it warn't us in reserve. I want to get it over and done with."

Stretcher looked like he was gonna faint. "I don't. I'd as soon wait as go first into battle." Sounded like

Stretcher was telling the truth. Not often that happened.

Warn't long before we saw men coming back from the front. First they came one at a time, then in twos and threes, some of them limping, some of them crawling, and all bleeding from one place or another. We wanted to help but warn't allowed, because we had to be ready to go to the front when the order came. You could tell right away some of the wounded men warn't gonna make it. One feller with half his face missing, for instance. He was a walking goner, and he warn't the only one by a long chalk. Soon it seemed there was a stream of wounded heading for the hospital behind the lines.

"Is it big enough to take 'em all?" Dan wondered.

"Is what big enough? The hospital?" asked Stretcher.

I shrugged. A shrug seemed the only answer to some of the questions we got to face that day.

Don't know how long we stood waiting for the order to attack, could have been hours, but eventually the order came, and we went forward toward the noise of the guns. Bullets soon began passing over our heads, cutting branches off trees. Some of the branches fell on us, and it warn't long before we saw a pall of blue smoke. That was the smoke of the battle either side of the Orange Plank Road. In it was a ragged line of our men taking cover behind trees and firing for all they was worth, while on the ground was scores of the wounded too badly hurt to move, just lying there a-moaning and a-groaning.

Sergeant Donnely's voice cut through the din. "Join the line men, take cover and fire!"

Me and Dan and Harris and even Stretcher

charged and got ourselves behind neighboring trees. Gritted my teeth, leveled my musket, and fired into the gray wall of Reb soldiers I could see through a rift in the smoke.

We swept the road with a hurricane of lead. Anybody who tried to cross it woulda met with certain death. Warn't so much as a skeeter coulda crossed that road and lived. There was 'nough bullets in the air to down every flying insect there ever was in the world in a second. What we was doing was butchery pure and simple. A slugging match in dense brushwood where men but a few yards apart fired through the smoke at each other for hours on end. Dead and wounded fell thick and fast, and more came up from behind to replace them and get kilt and wounded in their turn. Neither side gave any ground nor any quarter. Only reason we gave up the killing was it got too dark to kill. Like two prize fighters needing a breather between rounds both sides settled down to rest for the night, and we found we was among the dead from the battle the previous year. Old decaying bodies were all around us and lotsa fresh bodies of our own recent making, also.

In the darkness I was kept awake by the cries of the sufferers, the rumble of ambulances, and neighing of mules and horses, while all around was the glare of campfires shining in the darkness and in the eyes of the dead and the wounded. This good old earth ain't never seen anything closer to hell than a battlefield. Bush had caught fire in places, and men too wounded to move were burnt alive where they lay. We heard their crying all night long. Some of them got kilt by their own ammunition going off in the heat.

Orders came through we was to attack Orange

Plank Road at dawn, and we made the attack at 5:00 A.M., me and Dan and Stretcher and Harris and the rest of our unit all trying to keep together. A lot of our fellers hadn't made it, having fallen on the first day. Unit was so much smaller now than it had been only twenty-four hours before. How many we lost I don't know. Count-up hadn't been done yet, but you didn't need to count to know we'd lost a lot. Anyways those of us who were left charged and pushed back the Rebs and got them running scared.

Somehow I was separated from my unit and found myself in a small clearing full of dead and dying men. Bodies groaning in pain were all around me, and musket fire was whipping through the trees. I jumped in a ditch hoping it'd save me from stopping a bullet and found myself face to face with a man in gray. Took me completely unawares. He was barefoot and his gray uniform warn't a uniform so much as old clothes turned to rags from too much wearing and washing. He leveled his musket at me. It was an old musket like Pa's, but that was enough to blow a big hole in a body at this range. Plus, it had an evil-looking bayonet attached to it. Can't have been more than a foot between me and the point of that bayonet. Before I had time to think, he put it to my belly. I dropped my rifle and put my hands up above my head hoping the Reb would show me clemency. His face didn't look right. It looked hard, the sorta hardness that told you he'd seen things in his life a body never should see. That was how my face musta looked to him, being as I'd seen some of those things myself these three years past, and I knowed right then clemency was out the window. That's how it felt, anyways.

Something else I need to mention about his face.

It was black. Made me wonder if I should beg for my life or tell him I was fighting for his freedom and I deserved something off of him for helping such a noble cause.

It wouldn't have been true, of course. I was fighting for my survival when the Rebs came at me. The cause was no more than a speck in the distance compared to my survival when I was in the heat of battle.

The black Reb pressed the bayonet gently against my belly that is such belly as I had, which warn't much. The Union army made none of us fat. I chose that moment to piss my pants. First time I done that in my life. Didn't even do it when a bear ran at me once. Anyways, I couldn't have chosen a better time. When better to piss your pants than when you're close enough to death to shake hands with it? Felt the warm piss running down my leg. Don't know if Johnny Black Reb noticed. But he eyed me up and down while I waited for him to pull the trigger and blow me to kingdom come or spill my guts with his bayonet.

Then he said, "Turn around," so I turned and he pushed the bayonet gently against my back. Shivers ran up and down my backbone, and I guessed he'd decided he couldn't shoot me or stab me while he was looking at my face, but if all he was staring at was the back of my head he wouldn't have a problem with putting a bullet or a blade in me. If I'd had any piss left I would've pissed my pants a second time while I stood waiting to be blown to smithereens or carved up like a turkey at Thanksgiving.

His musket went off. Noise of it close up was deafening, but then again, all gunfire is deafening. I waited to fall dead from the hole he'd blown in me, but I didn't. Then up ahead I saw a wounded Reb lieutenant falling backward, a pistol in his hand and a hole in his belly. The black Reb had shot dead the lieutenant and saved my life.

He said, "There are Rebs on their way, and as you see if they find you they'll kill you soon as look at you. Pick up your rifle."

Lowering my hands I looked at him over my right shoulder all curious. Nearly looked over my left shoulder before I remembered it was bad luck. Plenty of folk I know have looked over their left shoulder and had the most awful luck, so I warn't gonna risk that. Not when I stood to get a hole in me big enough to stick your hand in.

"Pick up your rifle and no funny business now, you hear me?"

"Don't worry, funny business is right off the menu." Bending low I picked my rifle up real careful so as not to spook him. I seen wild horses less skittish than he seemed, so I warn't taking any chances.

"Start walking back to your own lines," he said. "When we're nearly there we'll change places. You can make it look like you caught yourself a prisoner. That way your friends won't shoot me. And when we're safely behind the line I'm gonna swap sides and fight for the Union, I've had enough of helping my master fight a war so as he can keep me at his beck and call."

I set off walking steady back the way I'd come. Ahead of us was deafening gunfire and a blue haze was drifting through the trees. Soon enough we came to a scene like the one we'd just left. Fallen men on the forest floor, most of them dead and a few of them living but on the verge of death. Clothes torn, some of the tears caused by bullets, some by the wounded wanting to know where the bullet that felled them had gone in. Everybody knowed that if you'd gotten hit in the gut your number was up. With a gut wound you was gonna die no matter what help you got, if you got any at all. So everybody who'd been hit and not kilt tore off his clothes to see whether his guts was intact. Seeing as the guts are the biggest target, if you get a bullet in you that's the place you'll most likely find it. What I'm saying is most of those boys who was still alive was disappointed when they tore open their jackets because they found they had big holes near their belly buttons with blood oozing out of them like sap coming out of a maple tree.

Some of the dying was our men and some was Rebs, and even above the din the guns was making you could hear their moanings and groanings. One of the Rebs was lying sideways on an anthill. He was still alive but too crippled to get off it. Officer by the looks of him. Fancy braid on his jacket. Ants was crawling all over him having a field day feasting on his flesh and blood. Must've been the best meal they'd enjoyed since the war began. The fallen Reb gave me a look that said, "Help me." Musta been too weak to call out. I didn't dare do anything with a bay-onet at my back, so I shook my head. The black Reb prodded me and said, "Stop," and hurried to the man on the anthill.

"Bottom rail on top now, masser," he said. Said the word *masser* like me and Pa would say it only worse even than us if that's possible. But the rest of his words he spoke them mighty fine the way Miss Larsen would talk if she was a man. Then the black Reb turned to me. "Masser here taught me how to be a good Christian, but he never practised what he preached, and I've got the scars to prove it." Dying Reb looked up at him with the most affrighted eyes I ever seen, and I seen some affrighted eyes in that war. Black Reb dropped his musket and grabbed his former master by his open jacket, pulled him off the anthill, and brushed the ants offa him.

"I don't know whether you'll live or die, masser," he said, "but I've given you a chance to live. It's more'n you ever gave me. All I got from you was a living death."

The dying Reb found the strength to open his mouth and speak. "Wait," he said. "I ain't gonna live. I got shot in the bowel, ain't you seen it?"

Black Reb bent down and saw the blood flowing from a hole near the dying Reb's waistband. "So you have, masser, sorry I can't help you."

"Yes, you can help me," said the dying Reb, "in the name of Jesus please shoot me."

Black Reb picked up his musket. "Don't know if I can do that, masser. I ought to kill you for what you done to me and to so many others, but it don't seem right shooting you when you got no chance to fight back."

The dying Reb grabbed hold of the bayonet even though it cut his hands and pulled it till the point was pressed against his forehead. "Pull the trigger," he said. I could tell he used the last of his strength saying those words.

"It's not loaded," the black Reb said, "but I'll oblige." He loaded up his musket real calm and put the bayonet against the dying Reb's forehead. There was a sound like a roll of Illinois thunder, and the dying Reb became a dead Reb. Top of his head blown clean off. Black Reb looked at me. "Ain't no time to hold a service for him, we gotta go."

Right then was when I knowed the black Reb warn't a soldier in the Rebel army. He was a runaway slave who probably kilt at least one Reb to get hold of that musket. Now he was worried the Rebs would shoot him for being a black man with a musket in his hand, and the Union troops would shoot him for being a Reb with a musket in his hand. Same as me, the Union troopers would take those gray rags of his to be a Reb uniform, or what was left of a Reb uniform. So the poor bastard couldn't win. Whichever way he turned he was likely to get shot. No wonder he was skittish. I was his ticket out of there. Some ticket. I hoped I could help him, but I knowed there was every chance one of us would catch a bullet making our way back to the Union lines, as likely from the front of us as from the back of us.

We headed toward the Union line, bullets smacking into the branches over our heads.

"We've been seen by your Yankee friends, change places," he said.

We changed places, and I held my rifle to his back like I'd taken him prisoner, and somehow we both avoided getting shot, to this day I don't know how, and I brought him in as my prisoner though in truth I was his prisoner.

That was the last I saw of the black Reb, though I heard tell he joined the Union army like he said he would and fought in a black corps against the Rebs. Also I heard he got through the war without dying. I hope that's true. I owe him one after all, because he coulda shot me but he let me live. Maybe he was doing hisself a favor by sparing my life, but all the same

I'm grateful. Good job he got the drop on me and not the other way around. I say that because looking back on it if I'd been the one holding the musket I'd have blown his head clean off first chance I got. I was jumpier in that ditch than a lone cat in a town full of wild starving dogs.

I found Dan and Harris and Stretcher, and with the rest of our unit we charged the Reb line yet again and pushed them back till we came out the trees into a field. Then their artillery, which was at the other end of the field waiting for us, blasted our line to bits and a corps of Texans charged and drove us all the way back to Brock Road. We'd got barricades ready and took cover and shot from behind them. Brush-wood caught fire and the wind got up driving the fire our way, which burnt our barricades. Blinding smoke made my eyes water, and I warn't alone in that. None of us could see a damn thing, so we had to fall back yet again, and that night the wounded who couldn't move had to lie where they was and still more of them got burnt alive. We heard the wailing of the burning men all night long. Pleading for help they was, some of them begging for someone to come and shoot them, but no one did. After all we'd been through, we was too worried about our own hides to risk carrying out a mercy killing in the middle of a bush fire.

The battle was over. A lot of men been kilt, more of us Yankees than Rebs. We took a real mauling in the Wilderness. After every other battle we had where we'd taken a mauling we'd turned tail and fled. Turned tail and fled under McClellan more times than I care to recall. Turned tail and fled under Hooker, too.

Orders came through we was going on a night march, and we set off for the courthouse, the four of us buddies still together near the front of the line, me, Dan, Stretcher, and Harris. We all were wondering whether we was gonna turn tail and flee under Grant like we done under Generals McClellan and Hooker. Marched a ways until the courthouse was just ahead.

Harris, with his sideburns bushier than ever, blinked at me." If we turn left at the courthouse we're beaten," he said, "'cause it means we're giving up, and marching north, and going home. But if we turn right we're going south to carry on fighting the Rebs."

"Let's hope we're turning right," Dan said, "because I want to get this thing over and done with once and for all." Then General U. S. Grant and his staff rode past us. Order came down the line: "Give way to the right!" That's when we all knowed we was gonna go south to carry on fighting. Right away a cheer went up from all the men. We cheered for all we was worth, because General Grant had become our hero. He was letting us fight on. He warn't giving up just because we lost a battle.

It was a twelve-mile march to the next battle-ground, which was Spotsylvania. During the first day's fighting in Spotsylvania we sent a lotta men to heaven and probably more still to the other place. Rebs sent a lot of our men to those places, too.

End of the day we was resting around with our campfire lighting up the darkness when a sergeant walked up to me. "Private Joe Wild?"

"That's me."

"I got orders from Colonel Livermore, he wants to see you right away. Come with me." The sergeant led me back through the lines past the reserves to the colonel's tent. It warn't like the dog tents we privates had in the field—when we got a tent that is.

The colonel's tent was shaped like a house and big enough to stand up in. The sergeant stepped to the side, opened the flap at the front, waved me in, and shut it. He stayed outside.

The colonel was sitting at a table, cigar in his mouth, uniform all clean, black leather boots shining bright. Black leather eyepatch over his left eye. Right eye a piercing dark blue. Black hair parted at the side. Moustache you could sweep a floor with. Average height and build but he cast a long shadow.

"Take a seat, Private Wild," he said waving an arm to show me where to sit down. Rain pounded the tent so hard I only just heard him.

"Don't mind if I do, Colonel."

He took the cigar from his mouth. "We got a situation, Joe, and I need your help. The Rebs have this big defensive position called the Mule Shoe. We need a volunteer to go into the Mule Shoe to get some information 'bout it for us."

"You talking 'bout spying, Colonel?"

He jabbed the air with his cigar. "The word for it is reconnaissance, Joe."

"Don't know 'bout that, Colonel. If the Rebs catch me behind their lines looking at things they don't want me looking at, they gonna hang me for being a spy surer than eggs is eggs."

The colonel leaned forward with his one blue eye all a-glitter. "Question is, are you gonna do it for me, Joe?"

"I don't think I want to volunteer for that job, Colonel. It's a suicide mission. I'm already lucky to be alive. Don't want to push what's left of my luck taking any more risks than I have to. Sun don't shine on the same dog's butt all week."

The colonel leaned back in his chair and took a thoughtful pull on that cigar of his. "All right, Joe, I respect your views."

"Is that all, Colonel?"

"That's all, Joe, you can go now."

I stood up and saluted and went back to my unit.

That night while I was chewing the rag with Dan and Stretcher and Harris we heard a Rebel band across the way playing "Nearer My God to Thee." When the band finished, one of our Union bands played "The Dead March."

"Gotta take a leak," Stretcher said, going behind a tree.

Reb band played "The Bonnie Blue Flag" while he was gone. Then our band played "The Star-Spangled Banner." Rebs finished the concert with "Home Sweet Home," and I reckoned by then we all wished we was home, even me, and a few of the fellers wept. My own eyes got wet, I confess. But all of us knowed we had work to do before we could leave this place.

Harris was blinking more than usual because of the tears working their way outta his eyes, and he rubbed them and looked around the trees. "What's happened to Stretcher?"

"Looked around myself. I don't know," I said. With the fatigue I was feeling from the day's fighting I didn't feel like going out to find Stretcher. "He'll be back," I said, "he always is." Then we did our best to sleep.

Next day came rain so torrential it looked like Noah was gonna be needing his ark again. No let up to it. Raindrops big as nails followed by raindrops big as bullets and everywhere it got muddier than the bottom of the Mississippi. Orders came we gonna attack. I got ready. Before we moved out a sergeant grabbed me by the arm.

"I got orders here from the colonel," he said. "You gotta come with me to meet him right away."

"Again?" I said.

"Yes, again." He led me to the colonel's tent. Colonel was sitting at his table just like before. Looked me up and down with his blue right eye. Felt like he was using it to drill a hole right through me. He seemed pleased to see me the same way a wolf is pleased to see a baby deer. Waved his cigar at me. "Take a seat, Private Wild."

Glancing to the side I saw Stretcher. He was tied to a chair with two burly adjutants standing either side of him. I didn't take the seat I was offered. Instead I stood in front of the table and looked Colonel Livermore in his one eye. "What's going on Colonel?"

Colonel's eye glittered as if I'd said something funny. Taking a lazy pull on his cigar he blew a cloud into the air. "Your friend Stretcher here was caught running away last night. He's a coward and a deserter."

Stretcher shouted, desperation in his voice. "I promise you, Joe, I ain't a deserter. I was bushwhacked by the colonel's adjutants last night when I went behind a tree for a leak. They dragged me here and tied me up."

Truth was near as damnit a stranger to Stretcher's mouth, but I knowed him well enough to know this was one of the few times he warn't telling one of his stretchers.

The colonel waved his cigar at Stretcher. "Shut him up!" One of the adjutants tied a gag around Stretcher's head so it covered his mouth good and tight, but it didn't shut him up zackly. You could hear him muttering and cussing through it. "That's better," the colonel said. "Now we can talk." He waved his cigar at the empty chair in front of the table. "Sit down like I said, Joe."

I sat down. Didn't want to, but what else could I do?

The colonel leaned back in his chair all relaxed and smiling. Lines creased his face at the sides of his eyes. "Suppose you're wondering why I brought you here, Joe."

"Yes, sir, I am."

"Have you ever wondered why I didn't have you shot for desertion when you came back to Brandy Station after running away?"

"I thought it was because you understood I hadn't deserted, sir. You was doing me a favor, I thought, giving me the leave I needed after all the fighting I been doing for the Union."

"That's not the reason. I woulda had you shot on sight soon as you showed your face to set a example for the rest of the men, but for one thing."

"What's that one thing, sir?"

"I knowed you could be useful to me. I kept you alive for that reason and that reason only."

"In what way can I be useful to you, Colonel Livermore?"

Putting his cigar in his mouth he knitted his eyebrows together and had a long thoughtful draw of his cigar. Took the cigar out again and blew out another cloud of blue smoke. "It's like this, Joe. When you left that note for me in my cabin at Brandy Station you had to get past all my sentries to do it. You went in and outta that cabin like a ghost. You got some special skills, and I want you to use 'em to help me."

"And if I don't?"

"If you don't then your friend Stretcher here gets shot for desertion and cowardice, no wait, I got a better idea than that, he gets hung."

Stretcher's eyes grew into dinner plates, and he made a whole lotta new noises from under his gag.

Colonel heard him and smiled. "Hanging the way we do it in the Union army takes a sight longer than shooting," he said. "Gives a man time to properly appreciate what's happening to him while he's dying and to reflect on how painful and unfair such a death is. Ever heard a man gurgle at the end of a rope, Joe? Ever seen a man jerk and shudder as his life gets taken from him real slow?"

"That I have, sir. I seen deserters hanged in my time. Only ever seen it done to deserters who went over to the Rebs and fought for them and then deserted back to the Union again. Stretcher never done that. He never deserted at all in any way, and he's not a coward. Tells a few stretchers, mind. That's the only thing he done wrong that I ever seen, and it ain't inconvenienced the army ever so I don't see why you're talking 'bout shooting him or hanging him."

"What he's done or not done is besides the point, Joe. Point is he'll be hung whether he's a deserter or not if you don't do as I ask. Have you got that?"

"I got it, Colonel Livermore. What you wanting me to do?"

"That's my boy. It's like this. We're fixing on some new tactics which ain't never been used before, and we're gonna use them to push those Rebs right outta the Mule Shoe all the way back to Richmond."

"I seen the Mule Shoe, Colonel. Rebs are well dug-in there, and it's gonna take an awful lot of Union lives to get those Rebs outta their trenches. Don't see how I can help any to make it easier."

Colonel tapped a load of ash from his cigar to the floor. "This is how you gonna help, son. General Hancock put me in charge of getting what we call intelligence for the operation. It's my job to find out the strength of the Rebs facing us, or it was my job. Now it's yours. You gonna sneak behind enemy lines and get yourself inside of that Mule Shoe. Then you gonna have a good look 'round at what's going on and report dreckly back to me. I want to know how many Rebs there are in the Mule Shoe, how well they're armed, and what reserves they got. Should be easy for you to pass yourself off as a Reb. You sound like one of 'em. So talk to 'em. I want to know what they're thinking and what the state of their morale is and how good their weapons are. In a nutshell I want to know what we'll find when we attack and what resistance we'll encounter. And remember, report back to me dreckly when you got the information I need. If you don't, your friend Stretcher here will find hisself getting stretched at the end of a long rope. You got that?"

"Yes, sir, Colonel."

"Then what you waiting for?"

"Waiting for three things, Colonel. First, I gotta hear you gonna let Stretcher go if I do what you want."

"You have my word."

"Second, I need some Reb clothes to help me look like a Reb."

"Then take some offa a dead Reb, there's enough of 'em lying 'bout."

"Okay, the third thing I need is some written orders from you, otherwise when I come back to our lines from the Reb side I'm liable to get my head blown off if I'm seen by one of our skirmishers."

"Very wise, Joe." The colonel put his cigar in his mouth scribbled something on a piece of paper and handed it to me. "There you go." I shoved it in my pocket and turned to leave. The colonel's voice drew me to a halt. "Oh, and Joe?"

I turned my head lookin' at him over my shoulder. My right shoulder of course. "Yes, Colonel?"

"I want you back by eight tonight with your report. If you're not back by then chances are Stretcher won't be looking too healthy when you see him next as he'll be swinging from a tree, and that kind of activity don't do much for a person's health."

Stretcher heard the colonel and kicked up such a fuss the chair he was tied to wobbled, and spit came from under his gag.

I walked up to him and patted his shoulder. "Don't worry, Stretcher, I'm gonna do what the colonel says, and I'll be back with my report before you know it." Then I turned to the colonel and saluted even though the bastard didn't deserve it. "I'll hand in my report before eight tonight, Colonel."

"Make sure you do, I'm countin' on you, Joe, in fact the whole Union army's countin' on you—and most of all our mutual friend Stretcher is countin' on you."

Stretcher nodded so hard I thought his head was gonna drop off. I gave him a salute and walked quickly out, picking my way between the trees.

17

SAVING PRIVATE STRETCHER

I MADE MY WAY TO ORANGE PLANK ROAD AND saw more corpses there than any undertaker seen in his entire life of undertakin', some of them in blue, others in gray. Hard to tell which was which till you got close up to them because of all the mud sticking to them. Ones wearing butternut was in rags mostly. Rebs didn't have decent uniforms by that stage of the war. Lots of them didn't even have shoes and went into battle barefoot. I searched among them for a Reb corpse about my size. Took me a while but I found one. Had a musket on him, which was handy. I undressed him and put his clothes in my knapsack, which I had to do to carry out my mission, but it didn't sit well with me. Felt kind of disrespectful. When I was done undressing him, I arranged the Reb so he was neatly lined up with his arms crossed on his chest. I closed his eyelids with my fingers and weighted them shut with pebbles. Did it to make amends for taking his things. Couldn't help but notice that none of the corpses lying around had anything worth taking on them. The battlefield ghouls had gotten to them before me.

Colonel Livermore wanted me to do a mission that would get me kilt if the Rebs cottoned on I warn't one of them. They'd shoot me for being a spy, or more likely hang me if they had time. Everybody hates spies, and hanging is one of the things that passes for entertainment in the army. Some of the boys like nothing better'n to watch a good hanging. They like to see a deserter or better still a spy with his hands tied behind his back, his face purple as a ripe plum, and his legs a-kicking and his body all a-twitching while he swings in the wind at the end of a rope. I didn't fancy that fate.

I knowed I wouldn't get behind enemy lines if I circled west so I circled east, keeping a healthy distance from where the Rebs was dug in. I was all bent over, moving stealthily bush to bush, tree to tree, keeping careful watch just like I was in the woods back home tracking a animal. Reb line was four miles long. Mule Shoe was where their line stuck out in a big sorta point. As I rounded the point at a healthy distance I heard a power of a commotion at the back of me. Our men was attacking the west side of the Mule Shoe. By the noise they was making I could tell it warn't a big attack. Had no idea how it might be going.

I got close enough to the Rebs to see the defenses they'd put up. First line of defense they had was an abatis. That is, they'd cut down trees and laid them on the ground with the branches sticking forward sharpened into points. Behind the trees was a glacis. Glacis was a strip of land about forty yards wide they'd cleared. No cover on it for attackers to hide behind. Rear of the glacis was their trench with cover for their sharpshooters.

Anyone storming their line had to get through the abatis. All the while he was doing that he was at the mercy of their sharpshooters. If he got through the abatis he had to cross the glacis. While he was crossing it he'd be peppered with bullets. If he somehow survived that, he'd get to the trenches where he'd fight Johnny Reb hand-to-hand.

Circling to the east of the Reb line I wondered how I was ever going to get through their defenses without being seen. In broad daylight on the glacis with nothing to hide behind I'd be a big fat sitting duck waddling to my doom. Wouldn't last more'n the length of time it took one of them to draw a bead on me. Only way it might be possible to get among the Rebs would be if I waited till dark. It might just be possible to cross that glacis safely under cover of darkness if I first covered myself in mud. But if I waited that long Stretcher would hang. It warn't gonna be dusk till nearly 9:00 p.m. Far too late for me and Stretcher. That was a full hour later than the time I had to report back to Colonel Livermore. Only way Stretcher was gonna have a chance was if I got my spying done during the day. I had to get inside the Mule Shoe in broad daylight. That would be suicide, but it was the only chance I had of saving Stretcher.

I kept moving east hidden among the trees with rain lashing down on me. Found the end of an unfinished railroad track hidden among the undergrowth. Must've been built before the trees grew, when the place was being used for making iron or whatever. That track led right to the Reb line. I hid my uniform and rifle and knapsack at the end of the track and put on my Reb outfit. It had more ventilation than I cared for and gave me a butt-hanging-out-of-my-pants sorta look, which I reckoned would help me blend in all the better. Found a patch of mud and rolled around in it and scooped up mud in my hands, smearing it all over my face. Then I rolled on the ground among the leaves and other stuff that'd dropped from the trees. Warn't long before I looked like I coulda been a piece of foliage. The mud was clingy, so the rain didn't wash it off right away.

Carrying my Reb musket I got into the track and snuck along it in a crouch to the other end and crawled out of it into the undergrowth. When I did the Reb abatis was just ahead of me real close. Skirmishers behind it would put a hole in me if they saw me. I crawled and crawled through the scrub covering the ground. Good job I done a lot of crawling in my time.

Their line was broken where a stream ran through it. They'd covered the stream over with their abatis as best they could, and any attacker trying to get through there would've been kilt for sure. But I warn't attacking. I was creeping slowly, close to the ground. They warn't expecting that. They was looking out for Union soldiers standing in line coming at them. I was like a lizard, belly to the ground by the steam. Slithered over the muddy bank and slid into the water. Man, it was cold. And the rain was a-lashing down on me from above. But I'd swum in cold rivers all my life, so it was nothing new to me. I crawled as best I could along that stream making sure not much more than the top of my head was sticking up outta the water.

It was hard going as I had to go uphill against the current with slippery rocks under me none of them too comfortable to put a foot on. I got to the abatis without being seen. Pointed branches stuck out at me. I held my breath and plunged my head underwater and kept moving as long as I could. Then raised my head just high enough to take another breath. Found I was still under the abatis. Snuck under it and got to the glacis. Up ahead warn't a trench. The land here didn't allow it. Instead the Rebs had built a high wall made of earth. The stream ran under it through a tunnel made of wood.

I held my breath, ducked my head under water, and forced myself forward against the current till I was at the bottom of the earth wall. No one looking over the wall was likely to see me here. I took another breath and went in the tunnel. No telling how long it would be. Water in a torrent was forcing me back, but I fought my way through it with lungs fit to burst. Felt like I was gonna drown. Everything was dark, and I couldn't see a damn thing. I couldn't breathe and my eyes was a-popping from my head. Never been so affrighted in my life. No choice other than to hope I was through the tunnel and stick my head up enough to draw breath. If I warn't through the tunnel I'd surely drown.

Hallelujah, I was inside the earth wall. Took a sneaky glance at was what going on. No one looking my way. The air was gray with mist and rain and men in gray with gray faces was standing in line behind the earth wall looking over it. Among them was field guns raised up so as to shoot down from the top of the wall. Other men sitting in groups behind the wall smoking and doing their best to keep up their spirits. All of them kind of raggedy. In and among them was scores of crates of bullets and kegs of powder. A long ways behind us was another earth wall, what you'd call a back-up wall. The smell of latrines was wafting through the air, kind of sweet and sickly with it. That smell is never far away in the army.

Throwing my musket by the side of the stream, I pulled myself out of it. One of the Rebs shouted. "Who the hell are you?" He had bayonets for eyes and long dark hair sticking to his head with the rain and a beard like a billy goat. His uniform was in rags. It had chevrons on the sleeves telling me he was a sergeant.

Getting to my feet I saluted him. "Private Wild, sir."

He got close so his face was only inches from my own. Those bayonet eyes dug right into me. "What the hell you doing here, Private Wild?"

"I slipped, sir. Musta fallen in the stream, banged my head, and knocked myself out. Don't remember what happened next, but I musta got washed downstream and when I came to I was in the water here so I clumb out. Good job I did because I coulda gotten myself drownded."

"Who's your commanding officer?"

Scratched my head. "Can't remember, sir, I took a hell of a knock to the head. It'll come back to me."

The suspicious look left his face and something more like pity took over. "You feeling all right, Private?"

"I think so, sir."

"Likely you could do with a smoke to make you feel better, couldn't you?"

"Yes, sir, I surely could."

He turned his head. "Charlie, give Private Wild here a plug of tobacco."

One of the men sitting down came over through the drizzle and gave me a plug. "You gotta pipe, Private?"

"No, Charlie, I lost it."

"You can borrow mine." He packed his pipe with tobacco for me and lit it from the fire. Him and his friends had all hell on keeping that fire burning in the rain, but they was managing somehow. "Have a good toke on that, Private Wild. It's gen-nuh-wine Virginny tobacco. Best there is. It'll make you feel a whole lot better."

"Thank you kindly, Charlie."

"What's your first name anyhows?"

"I'm called Joe."

He held out his arm and we shook hands. "I'm Charlie, as you know. We might be able to rustle up some coffee for you, Joe. We're short on it here same as everywhere else, but we got a bit we can spare for a man been taking a unplanned swim." He laughed and a couple of his friends laughed, too. "Get some coffee in the pot, Phil!"

Half an hour later me and Charlie and Phil and a couple of others was drinking coffee, and I was still smoking Charlie's pipe, and we'd become the best of buddies.

"Hope the Yankees don't attack before the rain stops," I said. "I need to dry out. My powder's so wet I won't be able to shoot my musket."

Charlie nodded. "We're all pretty much in the same boat, Joe. Ain't one of us managed to keep his powder dry."

"Yankees probably managed it," Phil said. "Their cartridges are better'n ours."

"Well, if they attack we'll fight 'em with whatever we can," Charlie said. "We'll use our muskets as clubs if we have to. Ain't no way a damn Yankee gonna get the better of me."

"Or me," Phil said. The others murmured so as to make it known they was agreeing with that sentiment.

"Looks like we have a lotta men here," I said, looking all around. "More'n enough to see off the damn Yankees. We got cannon, too. We'll blast 'em before they even get to us."

Charlie nodded. "We got twenty-two cannon

trained their way. More'n enough to blow those Yankees all to hell."

I felt I'd got enough of what Colonel Livermore called "intelligence" by then and took a pull on the pipe wonderin' how I was gonna get the intelligence back to him. First, I'd have to get out of the Mule Shoe, and that warn't gonna be easy. I got to my feet and looked around, taking in the view. Reb soldiers as far as the eye could see, thousands of them, and thousands more behind the other earth wall. No way could I leave without them seeing me.

The sergeant walked up to me his eyes looking like bayonets again. "You remember who your commanding officer is yet, son?"

I rubbed my head like it was still hurtin' me. "No, sir."

"Stand to attention, soldier!"

I stood to attention.

"I'm gonna feel your head and feel for myself just how bad that injury of yours is. If it's anything as bad as you sayin' it is, you gonna have a lump big as a duck's egg under your hair." The sergeant towered over me. He put one of his calloused paws on the side of my head and rubbed it through my hair. "I can't feel nothing," he said. "Where is it?"

I turned and ran, and he got a hold of my sleeve. It was so tattered it ripped, and I was free. His voice bellowed at the back of me. "Stop that man, he's a spy!" Rebs got to their feet ahead of me looking my way. Dozens of Rebs leveled their muskets and took shots at me. Only one of their muskets went off. Rest of them, the powder musta been too wet to work. The bullet from the one that went off made a splash by my head as I dived in the stream and swam for my life toward the tunnel.

When they saw their guns hadn't stopped me the Rebs rushed at me, but by then I was disappearing into the tunnel and out I came the other side. A few shots rang out, and water splashed by my head. Glancing back I saw what looked like a hundred men with their muskets leveled. Only a handful had gone off. One brave soul jumped off the earth wall onto the glacis and ran at me through the mud. I swam for it. He closed in on me musket in hand, ready to crack my skull with the butt. Grabbing a round stone off the bottom of the stream I turned, stood up, and when he was only a few feet from me I rushed him. Managed to push the butt of his musket to the side and smash him in the face with my stone. Sounded like his eye socket got smashed up, and he fell back holding his eye.

A roar went up from the men looking over the earth wall. Seemed like pretty much all of them vaulted it to try their hands at catching me. Odds of at least a thousand to one again me. I ran to the abatis, dived in the stream again, and worked my way under the branches. On the other side I ran for it, zig-zagging to make it harder for them to hit me, bullets whipping into the foliage by my head. A thousand men mighta been shooting. Not more'n a dozen muskets went off. The rain saved my life that day.

I went to the end of the rail track and was changing back into my Yankee uniform when two men grabbed me. A third, a sergeant, watched them. They was Yankee skirmishers.

"What you doing, fellas? I'm one of you," I said.

A sergeant stood with his hands on his hips. "You don't sound like one of us. You sound like a Reb. Plus, you was wearing a Reb uniform and now you're wearing blue. Looks like you're a spy, and you're gonna hang."

"Let me go! I got proof in my knapsack I'm no spy."

"You got a gun in there?"

"No, Sergeant, I haven't."

The sergeant picked up the knapsack and rummaged inside. Finding no gun he passed the knapsack to me. I fished around and grabbed the orders Colonel Livermore had given me. "I got orders from Colonel Livermore, see?" I handed the note to him. It was all soggy from the downpour.

Sergeant opened it real careful, narrowing his eyes at it, then held it up for me to see. "You ain't got no orders. All you got here is a mess of smudged ink. Now you gonna hang like the spying vermin you are. Tie his hands behind his back, boys, and make sure you do a good job of it. And one of you pick up that Reb uniform he was wearing so we got proof he's a spy."

They tied my wrists tight as a tourniquet. Hurt like hell. Then they marched me back to the Union line. All the way there they was kicking me, slapping me, and punching me. I was black and blue by the time we got to the line. The sergeant stopped in front of a captain.

"What you got there, Sergeant?"

"We caught us a spy, Captain. He came from the direction of the Reb line wearing a Reb uniform. We caught him changing into the uniform of the Army of the Potomac. Stopped him from doing any damage."

"Keep him tied up," the captain said. "We'll hang him soon as we can."

"Wait, Captain! I'm not a Reb spy! I was spying for

the Union. Ask Colonel Livermore, he ordered me to do it. He'll vouch for me. I got a report to give him. If I don't get it to him and he finds out you're the one who stopped me, you and the sergeant here both gonna be busted down to privates before you know it and likely put in the stockade for good measure."

"He's lyin', Captain. He ain't got no orders."

"I gave 'em my orders in writing, Captain, but they didn't believe me."

The captain turned to the sergeant. "Let me see what he gave you, Sergeant." The sergeant pulled my raggedy sheet of paper from his pocket. "This is probably what his Reb spymaster gave him, Captain."

The captain squinted at it. "Could be, or it could be from Colonel Livermore. Best to check with the colonel before we do anything. Better safe than sorry, I always say. Give him to me, I'll deal with this from now on, Sergeant."

The sergeant saluted. "Yes, sir!"

The captain grabbed my arm and pulled me along with him. "What's your name, Private?"

"Joe Wild, sir!"

"Well, Joe Wild, we gonna see Colonel Livermore now. He better vouch for you because if he don't I'm gonna personally cut off your pecker with my knife real slow and ram it down your throat, and you gonna choke half to death on it before I even start givin' orders for you to be strung up, that clear?"

"Yes, sir, Captain."

We stopped outside Colonel Livermore's tent. Two private soldiers who were standing guard outside the tent saluted the captain.

"At ease, men. I got a visitor for Colonel Livermore by the name of private Joe Wild."

One of the guards went in the tent. Came out a second later. "Show him in please, Captain."

The captain pushed me in so hard I fell on my face. Roar of laughter told me the Colonel warn't too upset about that.

"This man says you given him orders to spy on the Rebs, is that true, Colonel?"

"It's true, Captain. Thanks for bringing him in. You can go now."

The captain saluted and left.

With my hands bound behind my back I struggled to my feet. "You gonna untie me now, or what, Colonel?"

"First you gonna give me your report, Joe. Then I'll decide whether it's worth untying you and whether it's worth sparing your miserable friend's life." Stretcher was still tied fast to his chair making cussing noises. Colonel looked daggers at him. "You watch your mouth, Stretcher. Open it too far and I'll have you hung no matter how good Joe's reportin' is."

Stretcher went all quiet after that.

"I thought we was all on the same side, Colonel," I said. "You acting like me and Stretcher are Rebs or something."

The colonel opened a fancy wooden box and took a cigar from it. Used the cigar to point at a chair in fronta his table. "Take a seat, Joe."

I sat best I could with my arms inconvenienced the way they was. Colonel lit his cigar up. "War means sacrifice, Joe. Costs a lot of lives. Sometimes you have to take a few in the interest of saving a lot more. It don't always matter what side you take your few from so long as you get the job done. You get me?"

"I get you, Colonel." Of course I didn't agree with

him, but I warn't about to tell him that. I knowed by then the colonel was vicious as a diamondback and twice as deadly.

"Now give me your report."

I took a breath. Out the corner of my eye I saw Stretcher takin' a breath, too. Guess he needed one being as it was clear to both of us his life depended on what I said next. "Well, Colonel, I got good news and bad news. Which do you want first?"

The colonel took a good long pull on his cigar and blew out a big cloud of blue smoke that hung in the air. Wind gusted and rain rattled the sides of the tent. "Tradition dictates I ask for the bad news first, Joe."

"The bad news is the Rebs is well armed. They got more'n enough bullets and gunpowder to shoot every soldier in the Army of the Potomac. They got twenty-two cannon lined up to cut our men down and a power of case-shot to put in the cannons. The shape of that Mule Shoe means their cannon and muskets can enfilade us if we get close to their earthworks. And our artillery ain't no good against earthworks. There's thousands of men camped in that Mule Shoe and thousands in reserve behind it eager to take their place. Their morale is real good. Those men gonna fight tooth and nail if we attack 'em Colonel. They ain't gonna give up, no sir."

The colonel gave me what you'd call a piercing look with his one dark-blue eye. "What's the good news, Joe?"

"Good news is their powder is wet so if we attack while it's still raining they ain't hardly gonna be able to shoot us. Not more than ten Reb muskets in a hundred is worth a damn in the Mule Shoe right now, not if you wanna kill anything with it."

The colonel pulled on his cigar and nodded slowly. "You done good, Joe. I'm gonna pass the information you given me to General Hancock. Him and General Grant got plans. What you told me is gonna be a big help with those plans." He took another suck of his cigar. "With those plans and your information we're gonna push those Rebs right back to where they came from. If we've a mind to, we might even push 'em back to the Atlantic Ocean and drown 'em all in it." Leaning back in his chair he got a contented look on his face. Looked like he was imagining what we was gonna do to the Rebs once we'd pushed 'em into the icy waves of the Atlantic.

"Colonel?"

"Yes, Joe?"

"How 'bout freeing me and Private Stretcher now?"

The colonel laughed. "I guess you've earned your freedom and his, too. Private Longhorn!"

One of the guards came in the tent. "Yes, Colonel?"

"Set these boys free."

"Right you are, Colonel." He pulled a knife from his belt and cut the ropes that was tying us. I had to shake my hands around for a minute or two to get the blood flowing through them.

"Private Longhorn, get these boys a rifle each and ammunition and whatever else they need and send 'em back to their unit."

Back at our unit me and Stretcher joined Dan and Harris and the rest, and we all filled our bellies with beef, hard tack, and coffee then slept as best we could in the driving rain. I thought about the attack we would no doubt be making next day.

I woke up the next day, which was May 11, 1864, to

be told we warn't gonna go into battle, which was a relief. Meant we could drink coffee and get fully rested ready for when we was called on to storm the Reb earthworks at the Mule Shoe, which we all knowed we'd have to do sooner or later.

May 11 was spent getting ready to attack. General Hancock got the entire second corps into position, all twenty thousand of us. It was done in strict secrecy. We marched to our start points on a dank wet night to attack at dawn. Plan was to storm the Mule Shoe without stopping to fire as we went. Just run at it fast as we could. Take Johnny Reb by surprise to make the most of his damp powder. Ours warn't so damp as his because we had rifles and they had muskets. The rifle cartridges we had was better at keeping the water out than their musket cartridges. We was told not to load up our rifles or put caps on them till we got to the Reb trenches. That way we wouldn't be able to fire our rifles till we got there. We'd be forced to do as we'd been ordered and run the whole way without stopping.

The rain was torrential all night long.

The sky began to lighten.

I was affrighted but fired up, too. I just wanted to get it over with and looked at Dan. He looked at me, and we both nodded. No need to speak. He knowed how I felt, and I knowed how he felt. Soldiers always get tense before a battle knowing this might be their last engagement.

Order came out to get moving. As one the whole line of us at the front charged, and what a line it was. Maybe five thousand men in that line. No hollering. No screaming because we aimed to take Johnny Reb by surprise. First line of us got to the abatis. Groups of us pulled trees away to make gaps in it like we'd been told. Then we stormed through to the glacis. This was where we normally came up against a hail of shot cutting scores of us down, but hardly any shots got fired. Didn't see none of us cut down. Worst thing we was up against so far was the driving rain in our faces. At least that didn't hurt none. We got across the glacis. Where there was earthworks behind it we scrambled over them, and where there was trenches behind it we dived into them.

Then we was fighting hand-to-hand in torrential rain using our rifles as clubs. Our officers and theirs slashed each other with swords making terrible wounds, and some shot each other with pistols in the face point-blank. Blood was spurting in fountains from officers' necks, legs, and arms. There was men going down everywhere you looked, mainly Rebs. Rebs taken by surprise fell back, and we all chased them with the battle fever raging in us. We'd kilt, and we wanted more killing, so we charged through the forest hollerin' and whooping like we all gone mad, a-slaughtering every fleeing Reb we saw. Swept every living thing from in front of us for fully a third of a mile. Warn't so much as a fly survived our onslaught. The whole world to hell and gone. Then at last the battle sickness left us, and we took Rebs prisoner instead of just killing them, rounding the survivors up like cattle.

The Rebs brought in their reserves and counter-attacked, and we fell back, fighting in the tip of the Mule Shoe in what became known as the Bloody Angle. Back and forth the fighting went, I ain't never seen so many men kilt in such a small space. One time when we took over the Reb trenches there was a line of trench no more than twelve feet wide by fifteen feet long that musta had a hundred and fifty bodies at least heaped up in it, not all of them dead. In some places the dead had fallen on the wounded, and the wounded couldn't get out. The living ones lay there a-moaning and a-pleading for help, trapped under a ton of dead flesh. But there was nothing any of us could do for them. We was too busy killing each other to un-bury the living from their makeshift grave of corpses.

Finally our attack was called off. The Mule Shoe was ours. Our field hospitals was full to bursting. I'm sure the Rebs' field hospitals was full to bursting, too. Surgeons working all day and all night sawing off arms and legs. Butchery on the battlefield then butchery in the hospitals when the battle's over. No end to the butchery. One place I always kept well clear of was the field hospital. Hearing the misery coming from inside it was bad enough without having to look at it.

On May 21, 1864, General Grant decided it was too wet to fight there anymore, and it warn't getting us anywhere. He was fixing to outflank Bobby Lee and moved us east and south instead of fighting on in Spotsylvania.

I ain't going to tell you much more about my time in the army. It's all pretty much of the same after that. More battles and more bloodletting. Only a handful of things stand out. Here's what they was.

I shot a lotta dogs. Anytime we saw a dog we put a bullet in it. If it was a bloodhound we put two bullets in it. That's because we knowed they was used for tracking runaway slaves. It warn't fair on the dogs of course. It warn't their fault what jobs they was given. But we shot 'em anyways. That's war for you.

When we besieged Petersburg General Burnside had his men tunnel under the Reb earthworks and fill the tunnel with explosive and blow them up. You ain't never seen such a explosion as that one. Earth and rocks and men and guns flying in the air on a column of smoke, then raining back down again. Made a hell of a racket. The blast was a huge success, killing a whole lotta Rebs. Then things went wrong. Our Yankee soldiers went into the crater left by the explosion intending to get out the other side and break into Petersburg while the Rebs' brains was still scrambled by the explosion. But our officers took their time getting the men into the crater and no one had thought about how anyone was gonna climb out of the crater. Fact is, they couldn't climb out once they were in. And with all the time that had been wasted the Rebs had time to recover and bring in reserves and get their muskets loaded so they were putting down a wall of lead into the crater where our men were trapped. Most of our men in the bottom of it was black soldiers, a whole division of them. The Rebs didn't spare a single one, but they took some of the white ones prisoner. The black soldiers was surprised they was singled out for slaughter because they expected to be treated the same as white ones. But the Rebs thought the black soldiers was traitors to the rebel cause, as if any black man on earth was ever gonna support that cause.

It should have been gut-wrenching watching those soldiers of ours being shot like the proverbial fish in a barrel but it warn't. By then my eyes was dead like those of a lotta soldiers. I'd seen so much carnage it no longer got to me. After it was over I bumped into the few survivors. A couple of white soldiers and three black soldiers, all but one of them badly wounded. Men who hadn't been in the battle was helping the wounded get to the hospital.

The one man who warn't wounded grinned at me. "Joe Wild, as I live and breathe," he said.

I felt my own grin coming on. "If it ain't Billy Freeman!"

"Sorry I can't stop to talk, Joe. I gotta go with my unit or what's left of it to the field hospital. Remember to look me up after this war is over."

"I will, Billy." As he walked away I shouted, "Hey, Billy, where will I find you?"

"I'm gonna go south to get my wife and kids, Joe. Then we're all gonna lit out west as a family, Californy way. A man can be free in the west, even a black man."

"Hope you're right, Billy!"

General Lee surrendered his army to Grant at Appomattox Courthouse on April 9, 1865. A Seneca Indian it was drew up the surrender terms. I caught a glimpse of him once. He put me in mind of Pa for some reason.

I was one of the men saluting Bobby Lee's Rebs as they rode home after the surrender. Other Reb armies fought on but not for long. They all knowed the game was up after Bobby Lee gave up the ghost. On May 23 and 24, 1865, there was a grand review of the armies in Washington. Soldiers from all the Union armies paraded through the streets for two days. But none of the soldiers from my unit was there in Washington. We was in West Virginia cleaning up the place from a menace that called itself guerrilla soldiers. We called them bandits. Treated them like bandits, too. Shot to kill without mercy even when we got them defenseless. It's no more'n they deserved.

The Army of the Potomac was disbanded on June 28, 1865. We soldiers felt sad but relieved at the same time.

When Dan got the news his shoulders slumped. "Don't know what I'm gonna do now, Joe, or where I'm gonna go. What are you planning on doing?"

"I'm going back to my home town, Dan. Gotta clear my name of that murder I told you 'bout. If I can I'm gonna bring the real murderer to justice."

"You reckon you might need any help with that, Joe?"

"I reckon I might."

"Then I'm coming with you."

"That's good news, Dan." His shoulders went to their normal position, and he got back to standing up straight. We all said goodbye to each other, those of us that were parting company. Harris hugged me and did even more blinking than was usual for him. Stretcher told me how he had lotsa great looking women waiting for him back home, and he could have his pick of the lot of them, but he'd probably not pick one and just enjoy them all whenever he pleased hisself. He warn't to know it, but that warn't one of his stretchers. Fact is so many men had been kilt during the war that a lot of the womenfolk was wondering where they was gonna get their selfs a man. Wouldn't surprise me if Stretcher did get his pick of the women in his town, or of some of them anyways, just because he was likely one of the few young men in his town left standing.

Me and Dan set off on horseback from where we'd been stationed in West Virginia to Washington. On the way we got bushwhacked by Rebs who didn't think the war was over. They fired a volley of shots at us, but we had good horses, and we managed to escape. Left the Reb bushwhackers and their mounts far behind.

"That was a close shave," I said.

He gave me a sad sorta smile. "Too close," he said. Then I saw he had his hand across his belly and a red stain was spreading out from under it into his clothes. Next thing I knowed he'd fallen from his horse.

I dismounted and crouched next to him. "Don't leave me, Dan," I said, "I want you by my side when I go home."

"I want to be there, but I can't, I'm sorry." Those was his last words to me. I put him back on his horse and took him to Washington where I had him buried. Gave him the best send-off I could. Then I caught a train heading west.

By that time I was sixteen and a lot stronger than I had been at age twelve. Had some army muscle on me. Got it by hauling things around on battlefields, drilling with my rifle, and marching with a full knapsack. I was bigger, too. No longer needed to roll up my sleeves and pants to make my army clothes fit. And I was an expert shot with pistol and rifle. Had money saved up because I'd hardly spent any of my army pay. The whiskers 'round my jaw told everyone I was no longer a boy. The look in my eye after four years of killing told them I was a killer.

It was time for me to go home.

Time for me to do what I'd vowed to do all those years ago.

Clear my name and avenge Ervan's death.

18.

I FIND ERVAN'S KILLER

I GOT TO SOUTHERN ILLINOIS BY TRAIN AND stagecoach and bought a horse in Fairfield. Rode toward my hometown, but before I got there, when I was still two miles out of town, I headed down the track leading to Ma and Pa's cabin. It was mid-afternoon, hottest part of the day. The windows didn't have no coverings over them, a sure sign it was summer. Ma was in the vegetable garden turning over the soil. She seemed skinnier than I remembered her. Older, too. She'd aged ten years in the last four. No sign of Pa. I stopped at the gate, dismounted, and tied up my horse. Ma raised her head and looked at me, all narrow eyed. I pushed back my hat so she could see my face properly. Her mouth opened, and she put her hand over it. Then she said, "Joe! Come here, Joe!"

Running over to her I picked Ma up in my arms and we hugged. It was hard to believe she'd affrighted me so much and leathered me so much only a few years before. That was in the past. Putting her down I said, "Where's Pa?"

"He's inside. Go and see him, he's been pining after you, Joe."

Pining? That was hard for me to swallow. I went in the cabin and saw Pa slumped in a chair and looked around for the whiskey but there warn't none. He raised his head. "Who are you? What you doing in my house?" Then he stood up. "Get out before I throw you out!"

I took off my hat. "Pa, it's me, Joe, your son."

He looked like he'd seen one of them miracles in the bible. The feeding of the five thousand with two fishes and five loafs maybe or the raising of Lazarus from the dead. He stood in front of me, and it came to me I warn't looking up into his eyes, I was staring down at them. That's when I realised how much I'd grown the last four years.

Pa put his hands on my shoulders. He had to reach up to do it. "Joe, it's so good to see you, I thought I'd lost you." Then he put his arms round me and sobbed, and I'm damned if I didn't start crying myself. Don't know what came over us both.

Next thing I knowed Pa had let go of me and slapped me on the cheek so hard my head rang. Waving his finger in my face he said, "Now don't you dare do a thing like run off again, son." First time he ever called me "son." He always called me "boy" before, or worse. "You're not too big to get a switching offa me."

I felt myself getting angry. Then I saw the funny side of this little man looking up at me a-threatening me with his switch. Couldn't stop myself from laughing. "All right, Pa," I said in between laughs. "I won't do it again."

"You better not."

"Where's the whiskey, Pa?"

"Me and your Ma given up drinking it. Neither of us touched a drop since the day you left. Townsfolk been saying all kinds of things 'bout you. We don't believe a word of it. Don't see much of any of 'em now, to tell you the truth. Me and Ma keep ourselves to ourselves." He made it sound like they'd changed, but they'd always kept themselves to themselves. I admit though that doing without whiskey was a change.

"What made you and Ma stop drinking?"

"We both reckoned we coulda done better for you if'n we hadn't been drunks, son. That's what made us stop." He sniffed the air. "You've been drinking. You oughta do the same as us and stop, boy, before it's too late."

"I will, Pa."

That's when I saw Ervan's railroad cap outta the corner of my eye and remembered why I was back in town. It was hanging on a nail by the door. Looked shabbier than when I'd first seen it on Pa four years before. I walked over and picked it up, held it in front of his face.

"Where did you get this, Pa?" I was afeared of what the answer might be and what it might mean for the two of us, but I had to ask.

Pa snatched it from me. "What business is it of yours?"

"It belonged to Ervan Foster, and he was my friend."

"Well, now you know where I got it then."

"What do you mean?"

"I got it offa Ervan."

My hands started trembling. "What you talking 'bout, Pa?"

He laughed. "You think I kilt him, don't you?"

"Just tell me how you got it."

"I was walking past his cabin one evening, and he called me in. He knowed who I was, and he gave me some of his whiskey. We got drunk together, and he gave his cap to me. Gave me his boots, too. Said he 'preciated me, and that I'd brought up a fine son who was a good friend to him, one of the few friends he had, and he hoped we could be friends, too. I said we surely could."

I didn't ask if Pa was telling the truth. I knowed him well enough to know he was.

Left me with my puzzle to solve. Who kilt Ervan? And how would I prove it warn't me?

I spent the night in my old shed at the back of Ma and Pa's cabin. It felt good to be back in spite of all the insects and a family of mice that'd taken up residence since I'd left.

Next day I waited till afternoon and headed into town. I was wearing my broad-brimmed hat, a long coat, jeans, and boots. My dark hair came down below my ears from under my hat. There was three days of stubble on my face. Around my waist was a thick leather belt with a couple of six-guns stuck in it. Rifle strapped to my horse. Pockets bulging with ammunition. I looked around. Church was being rebuilt. Saloon looked like it'd had work done. Mr. Purdy's place had grown some. There was a new building down the main street that hadn't been there when I'd left. No idea what it was. I'd find out in good time. In the meantime I was putting two and two together. There was new money in town. Serious money. Where had it come from? Had someone found hisself a pile of gold? Gold that rightfully belonged to Ervan?

I snuck in Pastor Graham's house and waited for him in a chair with my rifle across my lap. Warn't till he'd shut the door behind him that he noticed me.

"Who the hell are you?"

I pushed my hat back on my head. "Calm down, Pastor, unless you want a bullet in your guts."

"Joe," he said, "you shouldn't have come back."

"Well, I did come back, and I'm not going till I'm good and ready. You can let folk know 'bout my plans, Pastor. You can tell 'em I came to find the person who kilt Ervan Foster and when I do he's a dead man. Tell 'em also I ain't gonna be run outta town. There's gonna be a lot of dead bodies piled up if anyone's foolish enough to try it. You got that?"

Bead of sweat ran down the side of his head. He nodded.

"Where did the money come from to make your church all so big and so fine, Pastor? This town was poor last time I looked."

"Corman Purdy gave it to me. Said it had to be spent on building a new church, one the town could be proud of. When it's finished it'll have his name on the cornerstone, and everyone will know he paid for it."

I stood up. "I'll be going, Pastor."

He didn't say anything. Just stood there breathing like he'd run a fair distance at a good lick.

My next port of call was Corman Purdy's place. Took me only a minute to get there. That bear of a man was outside his stables admirin' a horse. "Mr. Purdy," I said.

He looked at me and it's fair to say it warn't a friendly look. "Where you been all these years, Joe?"

"I been in Antietam, Gettysburg, the Wilderness, the Bloody Angle, Cold Harbor, Petersburg, Appomattox, and a few other places with the Army of the Potomac."

He nodded. "Thought it had to be something like that. What do you want, Joe?"

"I want to talk."

"What 'bout?"

"Where did you get the money from to build the church?"

"That ain't none of your business."

I'd had a cold rage in me ever since being run out of town. It'd festered inside me for years, eating me up whenever I cared think about it. That rage was getting hotter, because I was with the man responsible for running me out.

"I'm making it my business." Didn't so much say those words as snarled them.

"Don't push your luck, Joe."

"You better tell me where you got that money Mr. Purdy."

His big bear's face turned red, and he came toward me with his fists all a-clenched.

Taking both my six-guns from my belt I leveled them at him. It pulled him up short.

"Think you're a man now, Joe? Then why don't you fight like one?"

"I am a man, Mr. Purdy, but I ain't a stupid man. Tell me where you got the money, or I'll blow twelve holes right through you."

He nodded and got this thoughtful look on his face. "Remember that time I told you how war gives a man opportunity, Joe? I saw what the opportunity was when the war started, right after the first battle of Antietam. It was wooden arms and legs. Got some carpentry boys making 'em for me in my new factory at the end of the road. They can't turn 'em out quick enough. Wooden arms and legs has made me a fortune. Half the survivors of the Civil War need one or the other and some need both."

"Yeah," I said, "and where did you get the seed

money from for that arm and leg factory of yours, Mr. Purdy?"

"From my horses. I made good money horse trading over the years."

Backing away I kept my guns on him. "You better be telling the truth, Mr. Purdy, or I'll be back."

"I think the army scrambled your brains, boy, but I'm not gonna have you run outta town again, not unless you cause trouble. I'm gonna give you some leeway on account of the fighting you done this last four years. Reckon you deserve that much. But be careful now. I ain't got infinite patience, so don't outstay your welcome."

"I'll stay as long as I like, Mr. Purdy, long enough to find the man that kilt Ervan Foster and put him in the ground. And any man gets in my way is as good as dead hisself."

I went 'round the back of his stable where I'd hidden my horse and got on it. Rode over to the saloon and tethered my horse on the rails outside. Climbed off and walked slowly to the swing doors and went through, my boots a-clopping on the floorboards. Place smelled of new wood and paint. The way it was dim inside put me in mind of dusk at the end of a long summer day. Bartender was polishing a glass. I knowed at once he was a stranger. As I might have said before, you couldn't start a face in town I didn't know. Group of men at a table drinking whiskey. Long hair and beards. Sly faces. Darting eyes like rats in a hole. Guns in their belts. Drifters by the looks of them. You got a lot of drifters after the war, varmints every one of them, outlaws who'd do you down as soon as look at you. They'd go to a settlement, do some mischief, then move on to another place to harm the folks there with more mischief.

I waited a few yards away from them and stood my rifle on the floor butt down, barrel propped against the front of the bar. "Bartender," I said, "whiskey, please."

He put a glass in fronta me, uncorked a bottle, and half-filled the glass.

I took a sip of my whiskey.

One of the men turned to me. He was balder than a coot with a brown beard dangling halfway down his chest. Got this face on him I'd seen on men in the army when they was starting fights. Wiped the whiskey from his whiskers with the back of his hand and his slobbering lips parted. "Hey fella, you staring at me?"

I studied him out the corner of my eye. All he could see of my face was my profile as I stood at the bar. "What's it to you?"

He bristled. "I asked you a question."

"I gave you a answer." I took another sip of my whiskey, set the glass on the bar top, and said without turning my head his way, "You'd be advised to keep yourself to yourself."

He bristled some more. "Sounds like you asking for trouble."

"No, I'm asking to be left alone, and I'm advising you to do that." I felt him glaring at me.

"And what if I don't take your advice?"

"I'm a man you don't want to mess with."

"Yeah? We'll see 'bout that." The barman disappeared. The man put down his glass and headed my way.

I took a six-gun from my belt with my right hand, cocked it, and pointed it his way. Then I turned my head to look at him and stared him down with my dead eyes. "I've kilt so many men I've lost count," I said. "One more won't make no difference at all to me."

Putting up his hands he said, "I didn't mean nothing, feller, honest I didn't." He backed off quicker'n a dog backs off from a porcupine after its gotten a mess of needles stuck up its snout.

"You might want to spread the word I'm not a man to be messed with," I said. Keeping my gun trained on him I leant against the bar all casual.

Him and his buddies drank their whiskies and got the hell out. Heard their horses disappearing down the street.

Barman came out of his room at the back. "What did you do that for? They was good paying customers."

"Did they pay you?"

"No, they was waiting till after they'd drunk their whiskey same as you."

I put a dollar on the bar. "They looked like the type that warn't gonna pay to me. By the way this place looks bigger and better than I remember it."

"Owner came into some money," he said.

"Looks like the whole damn town came into some money, bartender, even Pastor Graham."

"Well, I wouldn't know 'bout that." He picked up the glasses the varmints had left behind.

I picked up my rifle and gave him a stare. "Got a message for your boss."

"What's that?"

"Tell him Joe Wild is back, and he ain't gonna be run out of town by anyone, any time. You got that?"

The bartender turned kinda pale. "I got that."

I went back outside and got on my horse, twitched my knee, and got my horse walking steady out of town. Kept the brim of my hat lowered so no one could see my face. I'd allow the townsfolk to see what I looked like when I was good and ready, and when I knowed I had the drop on them. Soldiering had taught me something, especially under General Grant.

As I rode down the street I saw a young woman who took my breath away, and I couldn't help but stare. It took me a while but finally I realised who she was. Cath Purdy. She looked a whole lot different from when I last saw her. Had the figure of a woman, carried herself real well, and was dressed all in finery she musta bought in a big city.

She stared at me just as hard as I was staring at her then put her hand over her mouth for a moment. Lowering her hand she said, "Joe? Joe? Is it really you?"

I pulled up my horse with a twitch of the knee. You don't need to do more'n that with a well-trained horse. "Yes, it's me, Cath."

"You look . . . different," she said.

"I been away a long time."

"Can we talk, Joe?"

Torn is how I felt. We'd had something four years ago, but it was gone and would never come back. "That we can, Cath, but not now. I got things to do right now."

"Tomorrow then?"

"Could be."

"Well, goodbye, Joe. Do come and see me tomorrow."

I put my hand to the brim of my hat. It was my way of saying goodbye. I felt Cath's eyes on my back every inch of the way as I left.

On my way outta town I took a detour to Ervan's cabin. Door was hanging offa the hinges. Windows was all broken. Wind was gusting through. When I went inside there was dust everywhere and anything worth a damn had been stripped from it. Place was to hell and gone. All that was left of that man's life was a layer of dirt on a few sticks of old decaying furniture. Not much to show for a life. Made me hurt inside. I looked out one of the broken windows and saw a rider coming toward me dressed all in black. Max Purdy. I went out to meet him. He got off his horse and tied it up real easy just like I remembered him doing when I was a boy.

"What you doing here, Max?"

"Came here to think 'bout Ervan Foster. What are you here for, Joe?"

"I'm here to think 'bout Ervan, too, he was a good friend of mine. You seen your pa today, Max?"

"No, I been outta town all day. Why do you ask?"

"No reason. How was your war, Max?"

"I didn't fight in the war. Pa paid someone to fight for me."

That figured, I thought. When the guv'ment started drafting people into the army, rich folks paid for poor folks to be drafted in their place and in place of their sons. It didn't surprise me one bit that Mr. Purdy was one of them. He knowed how to make his money buy him and his family advantages the rest of us didn't have.

"What you got in your waistcoat, Max?"

"A pocket watch."

"Can I see it?"

"If you want." He undid the chain and handed the

pocket watch to me. It was silver. Looked just like the one I remembered Ervan Foster having. I turned it over. There was a message on the back that had been scratched out so you couldn't read it no more.

"Where did you get this, Max?"

"Won it in a card game."

"You're lying. You got this offa Ervan the day you kilt him." The blood drained from Max's face, and I knowed I was right.

The killing rage burned hot inside of me. Drew out one of my six-guns and hit him on the side of the head with it. Knocked his hat clean off, and he fell sprawling in the dust, blood oozing from a gash on his temple. Pointing the gun at him I cocked it. "I didn't kill you right off because I want you to suffer, Max. You don't deserve to die quick. You're gonna die real slow, and every second you're dying you're gonna be thinking 'bout Ervan and what you did to him, and 'bout how you don't deserve to live no more because of what you've done."

Max held up a hand. "Wait, it's not what you think. I didn't kill him."

Cocked my gun and got ready to put a bullet in his leg. "No point lying to me, Max. You might as well admit it, because I'm gonna kill you anyways whether you admit it or not. If you tell the truth, I might be minded to show some mercy and kill you quick. If you don't, I'll shoot a dozen holes in your arms and legs and your belly, too, and leave you to bleed out without giving you the benefit of a kill shot."

"I'll tell you the truth!"

"I'm listening."

"The truth is, me and Ervan . . . me and Ervan . . . me and Ervan . . . we . . . we . . . we was . . ."

"You was what, zackly?"

"Me and Ervan loved each other."

My eyes opened up real wide, and my jaw mighta dropped at that point.

"You heard me right," he said. "We were lovers."

"Go on."

"I told him I was gonna join the army and fight for the Union. He said he couldn't live without me. Said he'd kill hisself if I didn't change my mind. I thought he was bluffing, but he warn't. Then I went to his cabin all in secret like it had to be between me and him, and I found him dead. Broke my heart. I took the watch because I'd given it to him, and I wanted something to remember him by."

Miss Larsen taught us the world is round and it spins. I don't know whether she taught us right, but when Max told me that my world spinned so fast I nearly fell over.

"Why did you let the townsfolk run me outta town when you knowed I hadn't kilt him?"

"You know my pa. I couldn't let Pa know the truth about his son, it woulda kilt him. He woulda died of shame. Whatever else I do in life, I can't let my pa down. He's never once let me down."

"What happened to Ervan's gold and all his things?"

"I got in touch with his son, and his son came and took what he could."

"If you was so keen to be in the army why didn't you go, Max?"

"My pa wouldn't let me. Said he could see by my eyes I'd changed, and I had a death wish. And I couldn't go against my pa. That's the one thing in life I've never been able to do. When they tried to draft me in the army Pa paid to keep me out. He said too many people was dying in that war, and he didn't want his son to be one of them. And truth be told I was still broken by what had happened to Ervan, and Pa was right. I did have a death wish, and I was figuring to get myself kilt in that war. I'm over it now."

The rage left me. I lowered my gun, uncocked it, stuck it back in my belt, and helped Max get to his feet. "I won't tell anyone 'bout this, Max, and I ain't gonna judge you, I promise. I seen things like this in the army, and I know it goes on. Please do your best to keep your pa and the townsfolk offa my back. I don't want them running me out of town again for something I never did."

"I will, Joe. I'll put in a good word for you and help you as best I can."

That night while I was with Ma and Pa, Pa's face got an odd look on it like there was wheels a-turning in his head and he said, "How 'bout going tracking in the woods together, son? And doing some fishing, too? Just like when you was a boy?"

I felt myself getting happier than I could remember in a long time. "That'd be good, Pa."

Next evening we was both sitting deep in the woods cross-legged on either side of a campfire we'd built. Pa looked at me across the flames. "Got something to say to you, son. Something I should've told you a long time ago."

"What's that, Pa?"

He took his time before he told me what he was figuring to get off his chest. "I'm your Pa, but I'm not the Pa you started out with."

"What do you mean?"

"Your pa was a man who beat your ma real bad.

You was too little to know what he was doing. One day he beat on her so bad I had to stop him. Well, I stopped him all right. I put him in the ground. No one but me and your Ma knows I did it. After I done it we moved on so we wouldn't have to face any tricky questions. Your pa beat your ma so bad that last time that she couldn't have any more children after you. And Lord, she tried. Your brother was the closest she came, if you remember."

"I remember, and I'm sorry to hear that."

"Worst of it was that when I looked at you when you was growing up, after your brother died, your face put me in mind of . . . in mind of . . ."

"You don't have to say it, Pa."

"Point is, Joe, I was unfair to you for a long time. I hope we can get past that."

I went to Pa's side of the fire and put my arm around his shoulders. "We've already got past it, Pa. Ain't nobody's fault, and ain't no point in worrying 'bout it." Then I felt something in my face like an ache. Felt it in my heart also. Next thing I knowed tears was running down my cheeks. His, too. We was both a-sobbing, me and Pa together. And when we was done sobbing we hugged each other.

We never spoke about those things again.

19.

HARDEST WORK I EVER DONE

IF I'D KNOWED BEFORE I STARTED WHAT HARD work writing this book would be, I would never have started it. It's thanks to Miss Larsen I got it finished. She told me I had to keep going every time I wanted to quit. I want to thank her for keeping me going, and also for making the writing better. She says I don't need to thank her. All she did was change a few spellings and add a few commas and some of them things she calls apostrophes here and there. She said she warn't gonna change anything more than that because it's important for me to tell my story in my own words, and it's important for folks to hear it that way. "Authentic," she calls it.

Miss Larsen don't mind none that I'm telling folks about the canings she gave me. According to her they didn't do me no lasting harm—in fact they did me a power of good. She says if not for the canings I wouldn't be able to write, and you wouldn't be reading my story. I don't know about that. I think I'd have figured out how to read and write someday even without Miss Larsen's cane on my behind helping me learn. You can make up your own mind which of us is right.

I'm not fixing on letting anyone 'cept Miss Larsen see this story of mine, not while I'm still alive. It'd cause too much destruction in the Purdy family if I did. Miss Larsen is sworn to secrecy about that episode with Max and Ervan, and about what Mr. Purdy later told me. She won't tell a soul about it. Chances are if you're reading this, me and the Purdys are long since dead and gone. Anyways, whoever you are, I hope you're getting something from my story.

20.

MR. PURDY'S SECRET

I GOT A BIG SURPRISE THE OTHER DAY WHEN MR. Purdy showed up at Ma and Pa's place. Took off his hat and held it in his hands real respectful at the door. Never thought the day would come when I'd see that happen. He nodded hello to my folks and said, "Can I talk to you in private please, Joe?"

When I'd gotten over the shock I said, "Sure Mr. Purdy, no problem," and joined him outside.

"Sorry I thought you was behind Ervan's killing, Joe," he said. "I called it like I saw it, I always do. But I called it wrong, and you suffered because of it." Holding out his hand he said, "Can we be friends again like in the old days?"

I grabbed his hand most eagerly in both my own. "Sure, we can, Mr. Purdy. It's all water under the bridge as they say."

"Thank you, Joe. And ain't it 'bout time you called me Corman? You're all growed up now."

"Don't think I'm quite ready to do that, Mr. Purdy. In fact you'll always be Mr. Purdy to me." He got this thoughtful sorta smile. "It was Miss Larsen told me, 'You got it all wrong, Corman,' when I saw her yesterday. Wouldn't tell me how she knowed I was wrong, but I trust her, and I believe her. She told me something else, too."

"What's that, Mr. Purdy?"

"She said you're writing a book. It's all about

283

telling the truth, and it's a big secret, and I'm not to tell anyone 'bout it."

"Please don't, Mr. Purdy. I wouldn't want anyone knowing 'bout my book till I'm good and ready to tell 'em."

"I understand, Joe. I got something I want you to put in that book of yours."

"What's that?"

"It's a truth for you. Miss Larsen said you got a lot of truths in it already, but there's room for one more."

Cocking my ear, I said, "Fire away, Mr. Purdy."

"I growed up on a farm in Kentucky," he said. "I'm a former slave."

"But you're white, Mr. Purdy."

"A few slaves were. Do I need to explain why?"

I thought about it. "No, I don't s'pose you do."

"I had what you might call a benevolent master. He kept me well fed and treated me kindly, or kindly as far as it went for a slave, which warn't far. And he let me buy my freedom from him. I had to earn the money mind, and that warn't easy. Luckily for me I knowed how to make money right from being little. It's a gift from God, you might say."

"You want me to put 'bout you being a former slave in my book, Mr. Purdy?"

"Yes I do. And I want you to put something else in it, too. It don't matter how kindly you're treated when you're a slave, a slave is a slave is a slave, and he knows it, and he can never be happy. He hungers for his freedom every hour of every day of every week of every month of every year, and it ain't right. You got that?"

"I have, Mr. Purdy."

"Make sure to put it in your book. And another

thing. If I'd a been younger when war broke out I woulda fought in it and fought my heart out against the Confederacy. My son Max was hell-bent on doing just that, but something happened, I don't know what. It looked to me like he lost the will to live all of a sudden, and I knowed if I let him go to fight in that war, he was gonna do everything in his power to get hisself kilt. A father can't let his son do that, so I stopped him. Anyways, that's it, Joe. Put it all in your book for me." He got his hat back on. "I'll see you around, Joe."

"You sure will, Mr. Purdy."

21.

AIN'T NO BETTER WAY TO LIVE

THE WORLD SEEMS DIFFERENT NOW FROM THE way it was before I went to war. Partly because it *is* different. The fighting changed things, and it ain't finished changing them yet. If I was a betting man, I'd bet on it causing turmoil a hundred years, maybe two hundred years down the line.

The world is also different because my eyes have been opened right up. I seen things going on in my town and even in my own family I had no inkling of when I was a boy and could have had no inkling of. Couldn't wait to grow up when I was twelve. Now if you gave me the chance to go back, I'd jump at it.

So I'm gonna take off soon. Just light out into the wilderness. I never feel so good as when I'm living among nature.

There's supposed to be some big old woods in California. Billy Freeman's headed that way. I got some catching up to do with him. I might just head out west.

ABOUT THE AUTHOR

Andrew Komarnyckyj has been a lawyer, odd-job man, PR Consultant, hospital porter, and dishwasher among other occupations. As an author, he has published under the pen names Jack D McLean and A K Reynolds. When not writing or reading he loves conversation, listening to anecdotes, craft beers, and hiking in mountains. Komarnyckyj lives in the town of Huddersfield in the U.K.

CPSIA information can be obtained
at www.ICGtesting.com
Printed in the USA
JSHW021950300622
27466JS00006B/8